Manhattan Transfer

Also by Leslie Waller

Fiction
Tango Havana
Deadly Sins
Mafia Wars
Amazing Faith
Embassy
Gameplan
Blood and Dreams
The Brave and the Free
Trocadero
The Swiss Account
The Coast of Fear
Number One
The American
A Change in the Wind
New Sound
The Family
Overdrive
Will the Real Toulouse-Lautrec Please Stand Up?
K
The Banker
Phoenix Island
The Bed She Made
Show Me the Way
Three Day Pass

Non-Fiction
Half Life
Hide in Plain Sight
The Mob: The Story of Organized Crime in America
The Swiss Bank Connection

As Patrick Mann
Falcon Crest
Steal Big
Close Encounters of the Third Kind
Dog Day Afternoon
The Vacancy

Manhattan Transfer
Leslie Waller

HEINEMANN : LONDON

First published in Great Britain 1994
by William Heinemann Ltd
an imprint of Reed Consumer Books Ltd
Michelin House, 81 Fulham Road, London SW3 6RB
and Auckland, Melbourne, Singapore and Toronto

Copyright © Leslie Waller 1994
The author has asserted his moral rights

A CIP catalogue record for this title
is available from the British Library
ISBN 0 434 00095 7

Phototypeset by Intype, London
Printed and bound in Great Britain
by Mackays of Chatham PLC

One – 1969

Only the brave, or the heavily drugged, walk alone in lower Manhattan past two in the morning.

Detective Sergeant Michael Rossi moved swiftly along Mulberry Street on his way home. Abruptly, nothing felt right. He stopped, the way a cat does, dead in his tracks, no sound, no sway, just an absence of motion.

There is a night-feel to every corner, especially the ones you know as well as Rossi knew his own turf. In a big city's enclaves some streets feel closed down, sealed off, memorial-enclaves of injustice, as paralysed as the lives lived behind these shuttered streets.

Other cells of a big city-hive exude a different smell. They seem, even deserted at two in the morning, to ooze success or, at lowest level, a fair chance of winning. A cab unloads a well-dressed fare. A doorman offers entrance. Horizons appear, if not endless then at least come-on bright.

Rossi had made his own life bright. You could argue that Mulberry Street was one of the places injustice roosted and laid its eggs. But Rossi had overcome all that by sheer intelligence and effort. His life . . . ?

Achievement. Respect. A kid off the streets had become that rarest of treasures, an honest, smart cop. This despite the meanness of a system that grilled everyone a spattered shade of excremental brown.

Honest. Smart. Rossi glanced at his watch. At home his eight-year-old son slept. It wasn't right, leaving little Pat in charge of his three-year-old sister. But their lives were tied to circumstances as deeply as anyone else's down here. Rossi usually had a relative he could count on. But this night aunts and cousins were too busy to help.

It happened, even in an extended family that included the Rossis and the Callahans, even with a plethora of teenagers ready to earn babysitting money. So Rossi was hurrying home. He resented this sudden halt. But up ahead lay trouble.

Catlike, his eyes narrowed. He stared hard at the corner liquor store, blazing with light at this impossible hour. Fulvio's had been the neighbourhood booze shop since before Prohibition. At 2:15 a.m. it shone like a medical specimen under operating-table lights, quivering, piebald, liverish pustule flinching from the lance.

Rossi's parents had told him: when booze was illegal in the 1920s resourceful Old Man Fulvio sold grapes, barrels for fermenting your own wine. Making booze wasn't illegal, just possessing it. Like the income tax, Prohibition was a self-destructive scheme for turning Americans into crooks.

Fulvio even sold iron chains. To clean a barrel smudged with last year's must, you dropped in a chain and some water and rolled it around for a day. The abrasion got the oak inside as clean as a chopping block.

Tonight, in 1969, Old Man Fulvio with his leather apron was long dead. His son, in shirtsleeves, waistcoat and a ballpoint pen, was now Old Man Fulvio. He closed at nine p.m. sharp. Too many late-hour hold-ups. So what was he doing tonight, past two a.m., with every light in the place shining so hard it hurt Rossi's eyes?

The street had eyes, too. It kept them shut, as if the theatricality of the scene made it wince. Manhattan was such a braggarts' showcase, so overloaded with self-important exhibitionists hogging everyone else's oxygen, that a show-off display wasn't unusual. But at two a.m.?

He edged up to the right-hand window. Inside, just his head showing, Old Man Fulvio stared wildly at someone or something hidden from Rossi. Fulvio's eyes bulged with fear, sockets twitching. His mouth shook. The wattle under his chin swayed as if in a gale. His ballpoint pen jittered wildly behind his ear.

Detective Sergeant Michael Rossi was on home ground, the Italo-American ghetto known as Mulberry Bend. Any local dip, heist guy, pimp, pusher or auto thief he'd bagged a dozen times. Any maf button man he'd regularly thrown in the slams whether he needed it or not.

Unless they were so high on scag or snow that they'd lost any brain they'd ever had, no local crook would hold up Fulvio's in such a stagey way. Lit like a Hollywood set? At an hour when no street traffic diverted attention? When the street itself slept, twitching in its ugly nightmares?

Maf muscle it couldn't be. The maf didn't heist liquor stores, it *owned* liquor stores. So it had to be some new druggie on the block whose chemically enhanced head didn't realise this turf belonged to Detective Sergeant Michael Rossi.

Rossi withdrew his small Colt Cobra from its battered shoulder holster. His pale green irises seemed to produce their own light from within. His slightly almond-shaped eyes mimicked those of a cat hunting.

Slowly, slowly he edged sideways towards the open doorway. No liquor store anywhere in Manhattan kept an open door like an invitation: Hey, hit me!

Any ordinary cop would have withdrawn and radioed for back-up. Later, talking with his son, Pat, Rossi would curse himself for making such a rookie's mistake. But how could he have guessed it wasn't a hold-up at all?

No adolescent junkie. No wild-man thief. A stake-out, an ambush. And not for just anybody.

Not, let's say, for any ordinary cop, the kind who boosted Fulvio for a fifth of Seven Crown whiskey on the cuff. Rossi was not an ordinary cop. He paid for his booze. And now, padding on light paws, Rossi stalked carefully inside the store. The Cobra, held two feet ahead of him, quested hungrily from side to side like a seeing-eye snake.

He had only a sketchy idea of what he was looking for, some injustice being perpetrated. Manhattan was Ground Zero for it, not just bilked widows, impregnated secretaries and rolled tourists. Not just minorities pounded down the shithouse drain like activated charcoal. Not just voters betrayed, employees conned, consumers rooked. What the hell, that was the norm all over the earth, wasn't it?

No, a personal injustice, like taking a life.

Rossi was not a tall man but he looked tall because he carried himself almost on tiptoe, an acrobat cat ready to back-flip in and out of danger. Since the floor hadn't creaked, he took a second careful, weighing step.

The weapon of choice turned out to be an ancient .22 calibre Colt Woodsman, the kind of smartass piece a real sureshot takeout artist uses. The first slug hit Rossi half way down his spine, aimed with low piercing thrust but surgical expertise.

As the pain slammed him flat on his belly, Rossi half-knew what the shot had accomplished. He was getting his BA at night school, the brightest cat in town, and his medical knowhow on the streets. He'd seen enough maf hits to know the spinal column and its nerve endings like he knew Mulberry Bend.

Lower down a slug would paralyse hips and legs. Higher up it would affect his arms. The spot where the .22 slug, small as a pencil eraser and squashed flat on impact, had lodged, would take care of all four limbs. To make sure, a pair of blood-brown morocco wing-tip brogues approached. Rossi knew the shoes from a dozen line-ups.

The owner of the shoes remarked, in a hoarse, familiar tone: 'Eh, Rossi. Vinnie wants you should take it easy f'um now on, 'kay?'

With that he fired a second .22 slug just north of the first. He operated with the sureness of a surgeon who produces quadriplegic cripples every day of his life. Being of small calibre, the slug penetrated half an inch before smashed vertebrae stopped it.

The sole of the morocco shoe wiped itself fastidiously across Rossi's lips. 'Tha's what Vinnie wants, Rossi. Me, I want you should eat catshit.'

'You're talkin' to a dead man,' his back-up guy complained.

But Detective Sergeant Michael Rossi heard. He even heard

them shoot Old Man Fulvio in the mouth. Another neat wound, almost bloodless.

He heard the old man's body hit the floor beside him. His ballpoint pen hopped halfway across the floor. Rossi heard the *colpo di grazia* that made sure a witness was truly dead.

On this shut-down street another life had given up the battle with injustice. He expected his own takeout any second. He already knew he could thank Tommy Uschetti's delicate work on the .22.

The two takeout men stood silently for a moment as if in mourning. What the hell, every drinker knew Fulvio, a real neighbourhood service person. Clearing his throat, the back-up killer whispered: 'Sh'I tain off the lights?'

'Why?' the .22 artist demanded in a blustering voice. 'Give Con Ed a t'rill. Leddem burn all night. Le's amscray.'

The floor underneath Rossi shook slightly, then more gently as the two men left. After a moment the floor was motionless. And so was Rossi, motionless as a dead man.

Dead? Some stranger paid by the city to foster little Pat and three-year-old Eileen? The ultimate injustice? No such luck.

Motionless, yes. But the street hadn't quite claimed him yet. Motionless . . . but only for the rest of his life.

Two

By 1983, Patrick Michael Rossi had graduated college. He felt far too old to be sitting around the house waiting for a particular envelope to drop through the mail slot.

'The neighbours are complaining,' Eileen kidded him at breakfast. 'How does it look, they ask me, a skinny hunk like Pat with a degree from that Hahvid and all he does is sit around reading magazines.'

'Here's a dime, baby sister. Go see a movie.'

'One thin dime?' their father groused from the living room. 'You're all heart, Paddy. Start earning, me boy. Why'n'cha out there robbing Korean fruit stores? Or setting fire to derelicts? You stuck-up or something?'

Pat finished chewing his last bite of toast. He had always had this habit, even as a boy, of seeming to finish chewing even if there was nothing in his mouth. This was particularly true when something in the offing might be a surprise.

This house had always held an aura of surprise, rarely a pleasant one. Pat supposed it had begun the night Lieutenant Groark, his father's closest cop friend, had knocked on the door at four a.m. and awakened three-year-old Eileen and eight-year-old Pat.

'It's bad news I got fer you two kids,' Groark had grumbled, managing like any experienced cop to make it seem as if they themselves were the guilty parties.

'It's yer Da. Them bast–! Them dirty, rotten–!' The big man had broken down in tears.

It had taken him a long time to get himself under control and tell them the news. The words failed to sink in. But, after a silent, gruesome trip to the hospital, the sack of bones on the bed, shot full of nembutal, convinced them, even though it was no more their father than the Man in the Moon.

Pat Rossi had already had enough surprises to last him a while. On their way home he noticed a small grey Ford following them. 'Uncle Tim,' he told Lt Groark, 'we picked up a tail.'

Groark swivelled his massive frame around. 'Hit the brakes, Kelly!' He reached for his .38 and leaped from the car. 'Heist 'em, punk!'

The grey Ford emitted a feral howl and slammed past Groark, cracking his knee apart as it disappeared in the night. 'Oh, the bastard,' Groark hollered, hugging his knee. 'Kelly, I owney got his first three numbers, 446. Radio an all-points, fast!'

Pat chewed on that for a moment. Then he turned to his three-year-old sister. 'You have the eyes, Eileen. Tell them.'

'4461,' she sang out in a high soprano, 'AR 17.'

With even sharper eyes, but a contralto now that she was nearly eighteen years old, his sister surveyed her brother at close range. He could read her thoughts as if set in neon.

A guy like Pat, she'd think, would've long ago got married. His wife, not his sister, would make his breakfast. Send him out on some easy job carrying nothing heavier than a ballpoint pen. Somewhere within the power structure of either the Wops or the Micks, since he can claim both.

The mind-reading wasn't a trick. It came from being raised so closely together. Not knowing who kept such constant watch on them, produced an eerie mental state. They learned tricks with their eyes and faces that silently communicated volumes no eavesdropper or watcher could decipher.

They often tried to tease an answer out of their father as to who kept such close watch. Who and why. He was good at evading an answer and, when that no longer worked, grew even better at pleading ignorance. But, finally, he'd had to resort to a lie. It marked the true end of childhood.

Pat remembered it with painful clarity. Although members

of the Rossi and Callahan clans took turns taking care of Michael Rossi, he and Eileen did their homework under their father's supervision. After Eileen went to bed, the last hour of Pat's time was given over to Manhattan news, the killings, scams, elections, scandals.

'Tell your teacher it's "Current Events," ' his father would explain. 'Got any questions?'

Pat was thirteen years old. He knew that his father, lying on his couch, worried about the dogged surveillance of their comings and goings during the years since the Fulvio hold-up. If there was ever a time to pin him down . . .

'One question.' Pat felt his throat start to close up. He went on fast: 'Who's got our house staked out? Who's always watching us?'

'It's the cops,' his father spat out, just as fast. 'Guys from my own precinct,' he added to flesh out the lie. 'They're watching over us.'

'Does that mean they're our friends?'

Pat's father's green eyes narrowed. 'Paddy, like everybody else, a cop goes bad either for money or power.'

Pat still had a gangly choirboy look to him. He blinked, owl-like, and chewed on the fact that his sister was surely eavesdropping and knew as well as he that their father had finally told them a lie.

Didn't he realise what kind of life it was for them, living like germs under a microscope? Not knowing why? Always assuming the worst, that they were next on the list of those who had nearly destroyed their father?

On the edge of losing his temper, Pat chewed back his anger, as he always did. What kind of complaint was that, to whine to a man turned into a motionless sack of regrets?

He clawed his mind forward from that memory into the present and smiled at Eileen now, almost eighteen years old. Her chin moved sideways towards the other room. Her lips moved silently, commanding him to see to their father. As if he didn't know, without being a lip reader, that neither of them had ever left their father alone more than ten minutes since the night Tommy Uschetti turned him into a sandbag.

In the end, the question of who had kept such a cruel arc light focused on their childhood as they grew up became one of those issues that answers itself. It was their enemy. Who? Anyone still afraid of what the quadriplegic knew. But still somehow constrained to let him live. Why?

Why not destroy the aura, finish off all three Rossis? Well, that was no mystery. The reaction of the cops to a massacre would be to retaliate in kind. Even a corrupt precinct with a crooked captain knew enough to retaliate with terror and blood, lest complicity begin to smell too ripe.

Pat's face warped into a sideways grin of no mirth whatsoever. It hardly mattered, in this scheme of things, that his life and Eileen's had been twisted into every sort of distortion, their psyches filled with every kind of fear, their conversation all camouflage-Irish blarney and banter.

Who else had survived such a childhood? What job were they fit for?

Pat stood up slowly, his expressive brunette's face, with its narrow nose and widest eyes of startling green, turning itself deadpan. How else could you face the man sitting in the other room, the smartest cop in Manhattan with exactly two moving members, the thumb and forefinger of his left hand? How else could you hide the pity you felt? And how his father hated pity.

'What's the latest, Pop?'

He stood in front of his father, looking far taller than the old man had ever been. Former Detective Sergeant Michael Rossi was wedged upright by large upholstery pillows like an old tom cat before a fireplace.

Eileen had fixed the *Times* on his lap. She would crease the multi-sectioned newspaper vertically down the centre of each page. Slowly, Pop's thumb and forefinger would turn the first half, second half, new page, first half, secon . . .

'What d'y'want,' he asked his son, 'hot spit from the *Times*'s fiction writers? Or video chewing gum the TV serves up?'

'Tell me what Mike Rossi thinks is happening.' Pat sat down at the far corner of his father's sofa.

'I think . . .' His father paused for effect. 'I think the

financially disadvantaged are experiencing a diminution in fiscal parameters, coupled with a marked contraction in socially transmissable abstinence.'

The air vibrated with the new pause. 'Whilst, as your Ma used t'say, whilst d'rich git richer.' He laughed. 'The Callahans were tremendous social observers.'

'I asked for news.' Pat gave his father a pained look.

Two fingers reached for the TV remote control. Livid images flashed past as he zapped his way to '... called yet another failure in the search for anti-AIDS drug treatments. However, Onslaught Pharmaceuticals common shares stood firm against a selling haemorrhage on Wall Street while – '

The screen went blank. 'Whilst more suckers are born every minute,' Rossi hooted at the defenceless TV. 'Grow up, America! Stop finding new ways to suicide!'

'Calm down, Pop.'

'Stop shouting, you Rossis!' Eileen yelled from the kitchen.

'How did I raise such a pair of loudmouths?' Rossi wanted to know.

'Can't fight heredity,' his son remarked.

At that moment the mail dropped through the front door slot of their narrow red-brick old law tenement. Pat scooped up the big manila envelope. He shook it at his father.

'Feel that paper. It's like cardboard.'

'Frontier Foundation, Boston. Massachusetts?' Rossi's pale green eyes lit up. 'You think...?'

Eileen stood in the kitchen doorway, drying her hands. 'Open it, Pat. Put us out of our misery.'

Pat made a face, tasting a bitter surprise. 'You know, this has to be a turndown. My college grades weren't that great for the Foundation to feel it got its money's-worth out of me.'

'Okay,' his sister agreed. 'I get the picture. They backed a dud. But maybe they don't know what a hopeless terminal klutz you are? Open it.'

Her eyes, the palest of the three shades of green, were startling under her black hair and brunette colouring. Such feral eyes seemed to light up great interior caverns even when simply being mischievous.

Pat slid his thumb under the envelope's seal and cracked it open. The ease with which this happened made him wonder if someone had tampered – as often happened – with the envelope. A letter and a brochure slid out. He cleared his throat and read aloud:

'Frontier Foundation takes great pleasure in announcing that your application for a two-year post-graduate fellowship has been approved. In coordination with Harvard University. your entrance application for the Law School is being processed. Meanwhile, the accompanying brochure undertakes to explain in some detail the workings of . . .'

'Please sit down before you fall down, Paddy, me boy,' his father shouted. 'You fooled 'em again, kiddo! Those dodos think you're brilliant.'

Eileen's searchlight eyes felt like lances to her brother. 'Didn't that envelope flap feel odd?'

He gave her a fierce shut-up frown. 'Odd?'

'Re-glued.'

'What a joy it is to have a sharp-eyed baby sister.'

Eileen's pale, carved-ivory face took on a mulish look. 'Who gives these Frontier fellowships, a board of sex-starved old ladies? Did they ask for a photo of you in a bikini?'

'Totally nude.'

'What other reason would they have? Come on, Pat,' she teased him, 'you're nothing but a pretty face.'

'I only got beautiful kids,' their father reminded them. 'Some day some guy is going to swoop down on Eileen and make her something grand. A senator's wife. A President's First Lady.'

'Mrs Pontiff the Twelfth,' Eileen agreed. 'He'll get off the Second Avenue bus at a limited stop, kiss the ground and knock on our front door. Hey! Pope! I can take your temperature and blood pressure, I can run a urine test and fold your newspaper neatly and make sure the battery in your remote-control is fresh. I can wash you and dress you and rub your back and . . . I can cook, too, along with the rest. Sweep me off my feet!'

The two men fell silent. After a while Eileen gave a small

laugh, devoid of humour. She plopped down hard on Pat's lap. 'Some day, my prince will come,' she sang, 'let's pray he's not so dumb.'

'She wants it all,' her father cracked. 'He should love her *and* be smart?'

'This gift-horse lover,' Pat said, 'is he going to face some sort of inquisition? Because – '

'Of course he is. Nobody's too good for our Eileen,' Eileen reminded him. 'With a petite pearl of such price, you simply can't be too careful. So the nuns made abundantly clear about us vessels of holiness.'

'Holy terrors, you mean,' their father remarked. 'I say, "never look a gift-horse in the mouth." '

Eileen frowned. 'Why is that?'

Her father's almost immobile face got a small vertical wrinkle between his grassy eyes. 'Because you might see more than you were ready for.' He managed to get his thumb into the scant pad of incurving flesh above her hip and tickled hard.

The three of them collapsed sideways in a tangle of giggling. When Aunt Clorinda arrived to help with the weekly cleaning there was no sign of the tension, the dread that this house had.

'You three comics,' she hooted. 'A real barrel of monkeys, you three.'

Three

There may well be a Climax Cafe in every American city whose collective memory goes back to before the First World War. Certainly this one in Cambridge, Massachusetts, just across the river from Boston, had a collective memory that could regress to colonial days under British redcoats.

It was September, start of the term, and yet there already existed new students from nearby Harvard and MIT swearing that the sawdust underfoot at the Climax must surely contain particles granulated from George Washington's discarded wooden molars. Since the Climax rarely replaced sawdust once a month, if then, the chances of there being a bit of George about were greater than merely mathematical.

Pat Rossi sat at the window end of a long wooden refectory table. He nursed a half pint of beer while he reviewed his lecture notes of the day. A scholar as mediocre as he felt himself to be had to be a demon note-taker to make the grade here in the Law School.

The window behind him, not recently washed, allowed a faintly yellowish glare of autumn sun to highlight Pat's aquiline face. It turned his green eyes chartreuse.

Soon the Climax would be crowded. Its particular aroma, part tobacco, part beer, part sawdust, part acrid pickle chunks in open jars, hadn't yet been stirred to active life. But right now...

Pat stretched his long legs out along the wooden bench and scribbled words and phrases saved from today's lectures.

'Mind if I...?'

The young man was Pat's height, well over six foot, but blond and 'sandy'-looking like the shirt models drawn by

James Montgomery Flagg in the 1920s. In fact there was, Pat saw, a strong 1920s look about his high-collar shirt, cuffs snugged to his wrists below elastic arm garters on his biceps.

Arm garters? Pat indicated the bench he wasn't monopolising and the man sat down, putting an empty pint stein and a large pitcher of beer on the table before him. His straw-yellow hair, parted in the middle, lay slicked down over pale fuzz where sideburns had been shaved.

'Don't I know you?' he asked Pat. He put his hand across the table. 'Jack Pierce.' His voice had the usual Ivy League lockjaw, uttered without lip movement. But in his case there seemed to be a lot more life behind the semi-strangulation.

'Pat Rossi.' They shook hands. 'I think we were both in the Evidence lecture they brought old Holland up from New York for.'

'Some lawyer. He looked like one of those old-time German butchers who makes his own bratwurst.'

'With a very sharp shiv. Holland's a famous cross-examiner,' Pat explained. 'I imagine next week he'll start to demonstrate technique.'

'Carving up witnesses?'

They both laughed and Pierce lifted the pitcher. 'Refill?' Without waiting, he filled Pat's glass and then his own. 'I couldn't help noticing how gung-ho you are about taking notes.'

They touched glasses and sipped the icy beer. 'Without notes I'm lost,' Pat admitted. 'I'm hoping the professors here have egos like the rest of Harvard. They test you on what they've told you, not on the assigned reading.'

The blond young man shrugged. 'Beyond me.'

The jukebox was wheezing an olden goldie, 'Great Ballsa Fire'. The young man fell silent, sipping beer, and Pat continued expanding his notes. 'I wonder . . . ?' Pierce stopped and lifted the pitcher to refill his almost empty stein. 'Top you up?'

Pat put down his pen. He paused, as if chewing something that had first to be swallowed before he spoke. Then he went on: 'I'm on a fierce budget. All us Frontier Fellowship people are. They pay us just enough to survive. So I'm not able to reciprocate.'

'What? By buying me a beer?' Pierce's broad face cracked into a wide grin. 'Man, you've got something better than money.'

Pat watched Pierce's glance lower to the notepad in front of them. 'Great Ballsa Fire' ground to a halt. Pat turned the pad around so that the other man could read it, and shoved the notebook towards him. 'Rate of exchange? A half pint a page?'

Someone fed coins into the jukebox. From deep inside the Climax a rachitic loudspeaker produced a jaunty thread of melody that neither of the young men could name. It had a certain remembered bounce, a tune from their childhood.

'Holland on Evidence,' Pierce announced firmly as he unscrewed a fountain pen and flipped open a small spiral-bound notebook, 'is worth anything up to and including sharing a pitcher. Uh, you're giving me the wholesale price, right?'

'The professional discount, one shyster to another.'

Pierce's grin grew even wider. 'You and I are going to get along, my friend.' He topped up Pat's glass. Neither of them mentioned that at their current rate of ingestion, roughly three to one, Pat was getting the short end of the deal.

As Pierce scribbled, Pat produced a thin between-the-teeth whistle version of the jukebox tune. Pierce hummed.

The window behind Pat began to grow dimmer. A tall red-headed young woman switched on three overhead lights hanging with their conical metal shades from the ceiling, mementoes of a pool table that no longer was. This hardly improved visibility. Pierce's fountain pen made faint rasping noises.

'Rossi,' he said, 'this is my lucky day. Are you here every p.m.? Say yes.'

'Usually.'

'Will you marry me?'

'Only if the kids are raised Catholics.'

Pierce drove his fingers through his centre-parted hair without disturbing its set. 'Glad that's settled.' Resuming his hum, he finished off the notes rather quickly. *'This could be...'* he sang and finished with a hum.

'That's the song,' Pat yelped. 'What the hell's it called? *This could be...'*

The tall redhead stopped at their table. She seemed to tower over them, waiting for one or the other to take note of her presence. When neither did she said:

'Holland on Evidence? Didn't I see you two there?'

Pat glanced up. His eyes widened in the permanent dusky fug, part malt, part hops, part roach-killer, that combined to produce the Climax's charm. He saw that she was pretty in a strong-jawed way and, beneath her XXL knitted fisherman's sweater, she had quite intimidating breasts.

Female power, he mused, resides in the mammaries. They're a symbol of a lot more than mothering. As long as the rest of the body is as sleek as this one, there is nothing a big-breasted woman can't demand from a man, and get.

'And those are your notes?' she went on. Her hair was an orange-red mass of loose curls that stuck out horizontally in every direction but down. 'The ones you,' she turned her glance on Pierce, 'have been swiping.'

'Guilty, Judge.'

When Jack Pierce looked at her, Pat noticed, the undertone was quite clear. He had often wished he could get that God-I-want-to-fuck-you look in his eye. As a short cut it saved days, weeks of courtship. Except that when he tried it, Pat knew, it only made him look woebegone, not rampant, worshipful, not masterful.

And here was Pierce, projecting it without a flaw. 'Are you coming on to me or the notes?' he asked in a tone of such mock politesse that it came fully equipped with its own answer.

'You must be his agent. I'm Didi.'

'Oh, excuse me. This is Pat Rossi. I'm Jack Pierce.'

'Beth?' she turned away to address another tall girl sitting a few yards away. 'They do have the notes.'

Beth was more willowy, Pat noted, no breasts to speak of but a very bright, driven face. 'Pat Rossi notes,' Pierce announced, getting to his feet as if for a public announcement, 'are available for one pitcher of premium ale.'

'Highway robbery,' the redhead proclaimed.

Her large eyes, mascaraed enough to make them stand out from her delicately freckled face, shot sideways to Pat, then back to Pierce. In high-heeled black boots, she stood eye-to-eye with him. Finally her glance rested on Pat for a long moment. Longer. He felt his cheeks redden.

She had been humming the jukebox tune. Now she softly sang the tag line of the Steve Allen song: *'This could be the start of something big.'*

'That's it!' Pierce shouted. He jabbed his finger at Pat. 'Did I tell you!' He rounded on the redhead. 'I believe in fate. I believe in gross coincidence as the hand of God. I believe in overpoweringly gorgeous knockers and Bette Davis eyes. Just for that, girl, as a special incentive, this week only, girl, when you deliver your pitcher you and Beth get to *share* it with us.'

Cautiously, she pushed aside his pointed finger as if it were a gun. 'Sold,' she remarked quite calmly.

Four

The General Aviation sector of Boston's Logan Airport is devoted to smaller jet and prop-driven light planes tethered there, staked down with rope ties like the kills of a particularly lucky hunting safari.

The afternoon of 24 December Pat Rossi sat looking at one of the newer telephones with card-sized computer screens. He wondered how it worked but wouldn't ask Jack.

They had become inseparable, sharing the same rooming-house bedroom, the same girls. Midterm grades had not been bad. Jack, whose bullshit was dazzlingly oral, did best in discussions. Pat, with the power to replay a lecturer's own hallowed words, formed a foolproof base. Together, they were invincible.

His call went through. 'Good afternoon,' Eileen said.

'Pregnancy Clinic?' Pat asked. 'Do you deliver?'

'Where are you calling from?'

'Boston, where else?'

'It's Christmas Eve. You get on Amtrak and by the time you get to Penn Station here, catch the 34th Street crosstown bus and then the Second Avenue bus, it's too late for dinner.'

'And what if I tell you I'll be there in an hour?' He paused for a moment. 'And with a surprise.'

'Go for it.' She gave the telephone a kiss and hung up.

The privilege of being away at college had almost happened to her. Her graduation from high school had been delayed a year because of classes missed. 'T'will do you no harm in heaven,' Mother O'Malley explained, 'losing time caring for your Da.'

She presided over an all-girl school beside endless Second

Avenue truck traffic. Eileen referred to her as Our Lady of the Perpetual Monoxide. 'Mother O'Malley is putting you in for a scholarship,' her father reported.

'And what lucky girl gets my job here?'

'I've asked in the family. We'll get somebody.'

'At what salary?'

They looked at each other for a long time. Then she tapped out a number on the phone and tucked it under his ear. 'Call off O'Malley,' she said. 'I've grown accustomed to your face.'

Eileen's eyes got the shiny look that preceeds tears. She had opened the front door to find Pat standing there with a blond young man who had to be the much-spoken-of Jack Pierce.

'Eileen, say hello to Jack.'

'His more intelligent but uglier roommate,' Jack added.

Pat had wrapped his arms around his petite sister and lifted her off the ground. 'Not that way,' Pierce complained. He tilted Eileen's chin and planted a light kiss on each cheek. 'How's that?'

'Fellas, call me crazy, but there *is* a difference if the guy isn't your brother.'

The three of them stood in the doorway, eyeing each other to record this first encounter for posterity. The December wind howled out of the north down Second Avenue, short, angry diagonals of pale sleet. When they hit skin, they burned.

'Hey!' Former Detective Sergeant Michael Rossi bellowed from inside the tiny house. 'You guys are freezing me to a block of ice. Come in, shut the door, break out the booze.'

The meeting of Rossi and Jack Pierce, two highly conversational types, looked to Pat as if neither wanted to venture beyond the usual 'heard a lot about you.'

Watching the ice cubes rattling in the young people's drinks, Rossi remarked: 'You're too young to see the ice man cometh? He had a horse and wagon. My folks had a sign from the ice company. On each edge it had numbers. If you wanted a 50-pound chunk you put the card in the window with the 50 edge on top. The ice man wore a thick leather jerkin. Using a long icepick any hit man'd be proud of, he chipped a hundred-pound cake of ice in two, grabbing half by the tongs and slinging it over his shoulder. Fifty pounds was nothing to him. The chill to his shoulder was insulated by the heavy leather. The kids would scramble for slivers of ice to lick like popsicles. He'd slip the chunk into my mom's ice box and take fifty cents from her.'

Eileen came over and tipped her glass to his lips. 'Thirsty work, boring the young.' His glance flashed around at each face. 'Jack, you're staying over, right?'

'I don't want to put you out.'

'Put me out? They can't even budge me.'

'Then we're on. But I have to see my folks tomorrow. And I'd like to bring Pat with me.'

'Why not?' Michael Rossi was silent for a moment. 'I guess you guys took the shuttle flight down?'

'A private Citation II,' Pat explained. 'And he had a limo waiting for us at La Guardia Marine. Beats how I got back here in November?' He gestured with his hand. 'Five hours by thumb.'

Eileen pushed open the front door and beckoned through the sleet. The uniformed chauffeur arrived, stamping ice from his boots. 'Would a coffee help?' she asked.

'Jimmy never turned down a coffee in his life.' Jack Pierce was on his feet, making gestures of introduction. 'These are my friends, Mr Michael Rossi, Mr Patrick you already know, and Miss Eileen, Guardian Angel of Chilled Automobile Drivers, who might even have an ounce of brandy to brighten up your coffee?'

He escorted Eileen and the driver into the small kitchen. Michael Rossi eyed his son. His lips barely moved. 'Smooth moves,' he muttered sotto voce. 'Rich, huh?'

'Pop, he's a good guy.'

'Wears a white hat?'

'My best friend.'

His father's face settled itself into the flat noncommittal look every cop knows. 'He'd like to be Eileen's, too.'

'What?'

'Paddy, me boy, you'd never make a good copper. He's smitten with her.'

'Come on. Five seconds and he's smitten?'

'How much longer does it take?' his father asked.

The mechanics of having a friend sleep over in the small house had long ago been worked out. Tim Groark had staked out the living room sofa where Michael Rossi spent his days. That was where Jack Pierce tried to spend the night.

It was a foot too short for him. Second Avenue, right outside the wall, proved to be an all-night thoroughfare of heavy transport and crazed-siren ambulances. An old Manhattanite like Groark never even noticed.

But it was more than that. Jack sat on the edge of the sofa and stared at his J. Press blazer, hanging on the back of a chair. He had bought cigarettes, now that he was a graduate student. Although they made him sick, he longed to smoke one.

In his predicament he was open to strange feelings, an aura of . . . danger?

In this place? Among the Rossis? Indomitable? Wisecracking? Courageous?

He picked the cigarettes from his jacket pocket. No beginning smoker remembers matches. He looked around him for some time before realising he was being watched.

Pale, feral green eyes regarded him unblinkingly. He nearly jumped a yard. 'Eileen?'

'Paleface no smoke-um. This cig-free zone.'

Jack returned the pack to his blazer pocket. 'Can't sleep. There's a . . . an aura about this place.'

She sat down beside him, legs folded under her long white robe. 'Second Avenue is where all of Brooklyn, Queens and Long Island traffic enters Manhattan. It's a gate to hell.'

'But there's more.'

He felt her daunting gaze move slightly across his face like a targeting laser. She moistened her lower lip and the gesture quickened his groin.

'The house? It's an anteroom to hell. It's the house of a

murdered man,' he heard her say in a hushed voice. 'Murdered but still alive. In such places Satan makes his home.'

'But, surely – '

'He knows we're tracked by killers waiting only for the order to finish the job. Did Satan send you?'

'I mean, this was years ago.'

'Fifteen. Bad guys live. Bad guys die. The maf rearranges its priorities. One piece of business still remains open, a stand-off called Michael Rossi.'

'It's hard to believe that.'

'It's easy to believe if you grew up on the potty or washing your toes, knowing people were watching every move.'

Miming, she extended one bare foot and pretended to be washing it. 'At this moment they're laser-reading vibrations on our front window.'

The room went silent, as if neither would ever speak again. She suddenly grinned, mischievously, and extended her toes to him. He kissed them. Then she disappeared.

Until the room grew light at dawn, he sat there, trying to understand why he had done that. Had they sealed a contract? Why had she asked if Satan had sent him? Was it sheer sexual tension? Was it the threatening aura of this place?

From deep inside him he knew Michael Rossi had not yet paid his debt, nor had those who wished him dead. That was the taint in the air. That was the smell of dread.

And to the unavenged debt he and Eileen had just added a promissory note.

Next morning the helicopter was waiting for them at the Lower East Side landing pad across town from the World Trade Center. Christmas had dawned sunny but much colder. The big-rotored aircraft hauled itself aloft, tilted its nose as if snubbing Manhattan, and headed due east.

Staring down at the view, Pat said: 'I wish Eileen could take this trip.'

'As a replacement for you? Any time. She's a great girl.' The words sounded automatic. 'I sort of got the idea she liked me, too. I hope she didn't mind me dropping in that way.'

'Get the note of surprise out of your voice. You made a nice break in her routine.'

'And your Dad's quite a guy, too.'

'You should've known him wh–' He stopped cold. 'What'd you think of him? Some battler, huh?'

Pierce stared ahead to the wintry sun flashing off the Hudson River. Finally: 'Doesn't think much of me, does he?'

'You're nuts. He's a man who rarely sees a new face. Mostly relatives, buddies. He takes his time sizing up someone new.'

Pierce nodded a second time. 'Not too happy about the Pierce family fortune.'

Pat was silent as he chewed at the idea. 'You know the Rossi family fortune. He gets a police disability cheque. He's too young for Social Security. I get my allowance from Frontier. The rest? Eileen scrapes. I think –'

He paused again. 'I guess he might resent a guy who can command a jet and a limo at the snap of his fingers.'

'It's only natural.' Jack Pierce's pale grey eyes looked him over as if meeting him for the first time. 'Your Dad is a hero. Every day he puts in more sheer thought and guts and perseverance than all of us put together. That's because he refuses to be martyred. My Dad . . .'

'He teaches, right?'

'He teaches history at Yale. He manages the family portfolio. His idea of a hard day's work is proctoring an exam after a couple of sets of lunchtime tennis. He's never had a crisis in his entire life. And neither have I.'

Pat grinned at him. 'And neither have Eileen and I. Pop didn't raise us to think we had a crisis to handle.'

'Hey, you and Eileen raised *him*. In the shadow of death.'

The green in Pat's eyes grew darker. Then he looked out the window to patches of greenery below, tracts of trees now separating each house. Pierce cleared his throat. 'I don't have any business judging a guy like that. He impressed the hell out of me because he doesn't carry a grudge.'

'Against Tommy Uschetti, who did his back? Tommy bought it years ago in a shoot-out. Vinnie Sgroi, who paid Tommy to do the job? Vinnie was massacred in that freight shed battle out at La Guardia Airport a month after Tommy copped it. The guy who had Vinnie chopped? Big Mimmo Caccia, King of All the Airports? He was never part of the original hit.'

'Pat, this is Jack you're talking to. Somebody laid down political protection for the original hit man. He and his capo walked the streets of Manhattan free as doves, killing at will. When they got punished it wasn't for crippling Michael Rossi. He's never been avenged. And it's too late now.'

It had grown terribly chilly in the Plexiglas cockpit-cabin of the helicopter. Up ahead, glinting coldly in the meagre sunlight, the great land mass of Long Island had bifurcated. Ahead lay the Montauk branch, its lighthouse delineating an eastern edge of America around which the Gulf Stream detours.

Pierce's glance tried to read his friend's face. But Pat seemed frozen. Never been avenged, he thought. Never will be. Another of Manhattan's prize examples of injustice.

Suddenly, with a ducking motion, the helicopter banked left and began to lose altitude as it headed north over Long Island Sound to the icy coast of Connecticut.

'Sorry I said that,' Jack Pierce muttered. 'Sorry. Sorry.'

Pat gave his friend a soft punch on the forearm. But he said nothing.

'Sad.' Michael Rossi watched Eileen reading the *Times*. 'No more homework for me to supervise.' When she nodded but failed to answer, he added: 'Jack Pierce?'

Reluctantly, her eyes lifted from the newspaper. 'Jack Pierce?'

'Is he a plus or a minus?'

'Butter wouldn't melt down the centre of that blond hair. Still, we get so little company, anybody's better than nobody.'

'What I'm asking: is he good for Paddy, or bad?'

'Is that what you're asking, Mr Detective?' He should have seen the temper spark igniting, but he didn't. 'How about asking why they've started mail surveillance again?' Her voice grew higher and louder. 'Vinnie Sgroi's long dead. What in God's name keeps them watching us?'

'Nice Irish temper there.'

She managed to lower her voice. 'When someone from the outside world visits us, like last night, you suddenly realise what a weirdo life we lead. What a feeling this place must give them. It's like walking into the House of Usher.'

He gave her an ironic grin. 'So you liked Jack Pierce.'

'I'm surprised I could have any kind of normal reaction. Always someone watching. It's a good thing I have a hard shell. It's a good thing I'm not the sensitive type. Or else I would be GOING BATS!!!'

Five

Déjà vu is usually undetectable, like the early stages of tuberculosis. One really couldn't say that the moment he saw the offshore island of Athens Landing Pat Rossi felt the same sense of dread his best friend felt when he'd visited the Rossis. It's only long after hindsight that foresight kicks in.

Nowadays, when he tries to recall that helicopter approach and landing, Pat instantly remembers the clammy feel of tension. It has never left him.

And this is without his knowing what actually happened there. The horror that spread outwards from there. Only Jack knows, and Jack isn't telling. He's well aware of what the police would do, but he's even more frightened of what Former Detective Sergeant Michael Rossi would do.

Jack is bound to the Rossis until death. There is no amnesty. Unconfessed guilt can never be forgiven.

Athens Landing appears before a new arrival so quickly that it's difficult to take it all in. The copter pauses a thousand feet above what seems to be a deserted island just off the Connecticut coast. The aircraft hangs there for a moment.

There is a change in the rattle and clack of its overhead rotors. As Pat looked down, wind-driven waves crashed along an almost straight coastline.

The rest of the island was shaped like a half-round clam shell. Maps from the late seventeenth century show it as Clamshell Isle. But, to quote from the booklet Pat found on the side table of his bedroom later:

'... Transcendentalist groups around Ralph Waldo Emerson at the end of the Civil War collected the sum of two hundred dollars, mainly in gold doubloons, to buy the uninhabited island. Several hundred more were spent building the seven-mile circumference seawall, great portions of which were made of two-foot-wide locust trunks driven six yards under and still, a century later, effectively holding back the winter storms.

'The Reverend Crispin Cotton, his wife, Tansy, and their twelve children, took up residence at the newly built church in 1868. After the first school was founded a year later, Cotton rechristened the island, redolent of ancient Greece.'

The helicopter made a rough landing. The wind had freshened to near gale force, driving snowflakes with the force of buckshot. Pat and his friend ran for the parked Jeep. Jack Pierce switched on the engine.

In later years, after many such visits, what Pat still remembers most clearly of this first arrival is its being steeped in the gaunt, nameless danger of winter malevolence. But that is mostly an intellectual recall.

Once the Jeep entered into heavy woods, the wind moderated. The windshield wiper was enough to clear off the snow. Order reigned. Dread retreated. The plain Yankee mind that had laid down this path had obviously sworn never to let it continue in a straight line for more than a few dozen yards.

'Because it's the Circumference Road,' Jack explained. 'Originally the caretakers used it to mend fences and bulwarks. That's all electronic security now. So we just use it as a handy way to reach any part of the island.'

'I don't see any fences.'

'No, you wouldn't. All secret stuff. State of the art.'

'But is that a good idea?'

'My dad's proud of the fact that there are no fences at all on Athens Landing. Everyone's free to go where he wants.'

'How about intruders?'

Pierce's thin lips tightened in what might have been a smile. 'I told you: state of the art.'

In the bedroom brochure, Pat read:

'Main House, where some bedrooms are located, and the two nearby guest houses, are all found at A on the map. At

B is Storage and maintenance, where standby generators and a radio shack are ready for emergency power failures.

'Tennis courts, swimming pools etc. are found at C and D, while the garage and workshop at E and . . .'

Pat switched on his bedside lamp. Out of doors, dusk had fallen. A city boy, he had never before in his life been in such a quiet place. The thick forest of firs, lit here and there by white birch in clusters, muted even this fierce Christmas wind. Finally, far away, he heard someone poking at a piano.

He squinted at the brochure, illustrated with elegant line drawings like the expensive promotional folder for a luxury resort. Pat's eyes started to close. The last thing he read clearly was the facsimile signature of Jack's parents, Paul and Serena Pierce, also parents of Jack's younger brother, Cummings, and kid sister Paula.

Nice, he mused. No danger here. Reassuring. Friendly. He knew he was supposed to change for dinner at eight. But sleep overtook him.

It was a great, predatory bird, gigantic, broadwinged like a condor, with the true raptor talons of a hawk, bladed to slash and hooked to cling.

One claw raked inside his spurting windpipe to release his life, the other slashed sideways against his eyeballs to blind him.

He twisted on the bed and came awake, hearing the heavy beat of its wings. His door opened and a blond head poked inside his bedroom. The heavy beat slowed, stopped. 'That's Dad's copter. Dinner's ready.'

'Yuck, what a dream.'

'Let's go.'

'I have to change.'

Pierce looked him over as he got up from the bed. 'You're fine. You should see how my kid sister, Paula, comes to the table.'

'But it's Christmas Day.'

'For Catholics, we're not all that religious.'

'I wasn't aware we mackerel-snatchers had a dress code.'

'Come on. Dad hates for dinner to start late, especially if he's the one who delayed it.'

Pat followed him along a wide corridor off which other bedrooms led. They clattered down a flight of stairs suspended in space by an intricate stainless-steel framework. Ahead, a long table glittered with lighted red candles and an army of silver forks, knives, various spoons, flanking and surmounting each person's plate, napkin and three glasses.

'Yay!'

A girl of eighteen, skinny, with messed-up hair of a shade even blonder than Jack's, launched herself at him from the near side of the table. 'Squeeze! Squeeze!'

They took turns lifting each other up. 'Getting fatter, Jackson,' she shouted.

'Not everybody can handle anorexia the way you do. This is Pat Rossi. Say something polite and decent.'

Before he could defend himself, Pat was lifted off his feet. 'You're just the right weight,' she told him. 'Are you engaged?'

'You pick 'em by the pound?' Pat made a gesture of writing on the palm of his hand. 'There! You're on my waiting list.'

'High up?'

'I'm as corrupt as the next person. Will I get on your waiting list?'

Abruptly her face went bright red. From the far end of the table, a tall woman, her black hair done upward in a swirled knot, called out: 'That'll teach you to trade repartee with the big people, Paulie.'

She came to meet him, her hand outstretched. 'We've heard so much about you, Pat.'

He had the strange sensation of having seen her before. She had a model's figure. Perhaps approaching the age of fifty, she remained very much a long-stemmed professional beauty. 'Mrs Pierce, it's a real pleasure.'

'A bit daunting, I should think.' Her voice had a stage-trained way of coming up powerfully from beneath her lungs and rising at the end of a sentence. 'I know Jack was thrilled to be able to meet your family yesterday. I hope he wasn't too much trouble.'

It was the kind of conversational opening he and Pierce loved to get because it demanded a quick 'no, ma'am, we all fart at the table' or words to that effect. That was a staple around the sawdust tables at the Climax, where Didi, the big redhead, and her pal Beth, got laughs just as gross.

'We Rossis don't daunt easy,' he said at last and was relieved to see her smile.

'Pat, this is Jack's brother, Cummings.' He shook hands with a taller, weedier version of Jack. 'And this is my nephew, Carrington Pierce, and his fiancée, Dinah Branch.'

Faces came forward. In all, he shook hands eleven times. If Mrs Pierce hadn't been by his side, he would have panicked. As it was, he felt on display, laid out on an oak tray like a side of smoked salmon awaiting the slicer.

Pat soon realised the table was missing a major participant, he whose helicopter, with its great beating rotors, had put him through a major anxiety nightmare. Perhaps that was why no one had actually sat down yet, but milled slowly about, making a point of ignoring him. He supposed that was good manners.

One of the younger people plinked a Christmas carol on a small Boston spinet. Pat's command of classical music was limited to the operas his father doted on. ''Tis the season to be jolly...'

Several people sang along. One soprano rose clear and full for just a bar or two, as if not wanting to show off. It was Mrs Pierce.

Inside Pat's head, her face clicked into place immediately. When his father watched opera cassettes she would crop up in mezzo roles. Because she was tall, she often got the 'trouser' parts, miming a young man. She was... she was Serena Wainright.

Around her the young faces seemed to glow either from the many candles, or the excitement of Christmas, or of hearing her voice.

'Brava!' someone called in a rich basso. He clapped his hands three times.

Every face turned to the last steps of the staircase. Paul

Pierce paused, a tall, slender man, good looking in a dark way. When he grinned, his teeth glistened darkly. Something jagged, caught at Pat Rossi's heart.

All the lights went out.

'Oh, damn!' Serena Pierce muttered. 'Jack, get on the phone to the power company.'

Outside the wind grew abruptly harsh. Candles flickered wildly. Paul Pierce's shadow danced madly on the wall. A few candles guttered and died.

Eventually, they all would.

Six

By the start of the spring, 1984, semester, Pat and Jack had moved to a two-room flat his mother had found. She had installed a phone/fax and paid the rent for a year. She, his cousin Carrington or his father seemed to keep in daily touch with cryptic, vaguely financial, messages.

Both Didi and Beth had begun leaving books, clothing and douche-bags in the rooms. The young women had been close friends since high school in California. After a casual try-out period – this was an era when even doctors hadn't heard of AIDS – Didi voted for Pat. Beth, thin and strangely fey, let Jack know he was second choice but not at all bad.

On either side of the big room there had been twin beds. Now the desks and chairs from the small room had been brought in and one twin bed banished to the privacy of the small room, known now as Pat's.

Pat found it strangely exciting to share a narrow bed with a girl as big as Didi. Naked, she absolutely awed him with the power of her body, its balanced masses, the grandeur of her breasts and buttocks. She would hold his hands behind him as she bit his nipples.

He loved to roll her on top of him, head to toe, her warming bosom slowly smothering him in musk. 'You have no idea,' she would murmur. 'You're saving my life.'

'Mmf?'

'If you think I have a low boiling point, Beth is truly oversexed.' She began rubbing her breasts across his open mouth. 'She's a very religious girl. Did you know that?'

'Mmm.'

'After her Stanford BA she actually signed up for an M.Div.'

'Mf?'

'Master of Divinity. Then she switched here to Law School. It's made her randier than ever. I have to fight her off some nights.'

'Yuf?'

'Like most people, she's bi-sexual.' She lifted herself. 'Breathe!'

Pat inhaled her perfume. 'You mean she – ?'

'As long as she gets off on Jack, I'm safe,' Didi explained. She settled her great body like a womb around his face, shutting off sight and sound and movement, but not taste or scent.

As they became more accustomed to the bed, they wore no night clothes, squeezing up into each other's cleavages, armpits, groins. She taught him how to hold until she had teased off the last of her orgasms and brought him to a noisy, lid-shattering explosion.

They didn't speak again about Beth's sexuality until Jack announced that on the coming weekend he had to attend a family get-together in Athens Landing.

That night, Didi lay beside Pat, idly scratching and massaging his body the way apes groom each other. 'I . . .' She seemed to have trouble getting something said. 'Look, she's . . . Beth's going to spend the weekend here with us.'

'As always?'

'Not exactly.' Didi began softly squeezing his penis to slowly pulsing life. 'Can you handle a threesome? Be frank. About sex Beth can be very demanding.'

The prospect – shocking, tempting – weighed on him all Friday. Used to sharing every secret with Jack, he felt strange keeping quiet about what might . . . might . . .

Friday night, after Jack had caught the plane to Connecticut, they brought home the normal weekend provisions, six-packs of cheap strong beer in chilled sixteen-ounce cans, library books for required reading, sliced cold cuts and rye bread.

Beth's lanky body, clad only in a long beach shirt that came down to her ankles, lay curled on the floor at Didi's feet. Pat watched her and decided she was tame, harmless, her so-called voraciousness a myth. She clapped the book shut and began sucking Didi's big toe.

'C'mon, Pat, she's got another one.'

'Well, in that case.' He crawled over and began sucking Didi's other big toe. He found the whole thing rather foolish until Didi began to moan, very softly, encouraging them both.

'God,' she muttered.

'God-given,' Beth amended.

Just before midnight they had him bring in the other bed and tie it to its twin. On this great plateau, in the warmth of a May night, he pleasured one, then the other. Then the landscape shifted. Both of them attacked him, nibbling, biting, licking.

One would imprison his arms and the other would savage him with her teeth. They would begin, each at a foot, and work their way together until they had to stuff their sweatsox in his mouth to muffle his shouts of pleasure and pain.

Beth crouched over his face. 'I give you communion, Pat. Take, eat, this is my body and my blood.' She lowered herself onto him and they rocked slowly together.

'Now me,' Didi cried. She was gasping for breath, Beth's religious imagery igniting her. She crushed herself down on Pat's face. The beds began to creak in sexual agony.

'Oh, God!' she screamed, sobbing.

None of them ever told Jack, of course. The evening was never mentioned again by either girl, although Pat had no idea if they spoke of it to each other. He found this ladylike reserve both incredible and terribly exciting, like a supposedly dormant volcano. When would it all happen again? Or was the idea that it only happened by chance?

In any event, it wasn't until grades had been posted and the semester was at a close that the matter came up again. The Climax had a tiny dance floor nobody ever used. Dancing in mature sawdust was an unknown and possibly risky art form. The four of them sat at a table trying to feel celebratory. All had got A's for the semester.

Jack had been drinking boilermakers, a shot of Seven Crown

blended whiskey with each stein of beer. The rest of them, content with beer alone, never seemed to reach such a high shelf of merrymaking.

As a result, this night, he took Beth's hand and escorted her quite formally to the dance corner near the jukebox. He took her in his arms with a cruelly possessive grasp, like an Apache dancer, and bent her backwards to begin a tango. It was, perhaps, a tribute to boilermakers as an ecumenical force that the tango was being danced to Elvis's 'Blue Suede Shoes'.

'Hey,' Jack growled later after several more boilermakers, 'for a cerebration this is a fucking wake.' His blond hair, parted in the middle, kept falling down over his forehead and eyes. One of his arm garters had slipped off, leaving that sleeve puffed out and quite unrestrained.

'Celebration,' Beth corrected.

'Straight fucking A's,' Jack persisted. 'Is this the best we can do to cerebrate?' He stared challengingly at each of them in turn. 'Wha'bouta norgy?'

Didi ran her long, orange-tipped fingers through Jack's bright hair, combing it down over his face. 'Norgy? Something new and different?'

Back at their apartment, Jack pulled the belt from his jeans and, reuniting the twin beds in the same room, strapped them together. It took a lot of effort because his hands had turned fumbly with drink. His jeans slid down to his knees.

'What's the idea?' Didi asked demurely

Pat sat back and watched, fascinated. Amazing how these two post-graduate women of the world had never considered, barely heard of, an orgy. 'Is dropping your jeans a norgy?' Beth asked in the same voice of innocence.

'You broads are – !'

Didi twisted the loose lower legs of the jeans in a square knot. Pulling hard she locked Jack's knees together. 'Naughty norgy. Shame on Jack.'

The two women pulled his underwear briefs down over the knot and rolled him on his stomach. They pinched his buttocks to a rosier hue. 'Mooning becomes you,' Didi sang.

'It goes with your hair,' Beth continued, tweaking his rear

growth of bum-beard. This should have been excruciating. Instead, face down, Jack began to snore.

'Shame on Jack,' Beth mused, turning towards Pat. 'How could he make such a lewd, crude suggestion to two straight-A scholars like us?'

'Maybe if you'd kept him awake . . .?' Pat reminded her.

'Keep a civil tongue,' Beth warned him, 'or we'll truss you up into another June moon.'

Didi hiccuped. 'His tongue is more than civil.' She struggled for words. 'It's . . . prehensile.'

Beth pulled off her T-shirt and draped it gently over Jack's bare buttocks. 'Now, then,' she went on, massaging her nipples thoughtfully, 'as long as we're a quiet and pious congregation, we can worship in the other room without waking up Jack.'

'Take communion,' Didi added thoughtfully. 'Give it, too.'

Each young woman lifted Pat up by an armpit and guided him into the other room. They shut the door, turned the key and propped a chair under the knob. 'In the name of the Father,' Beth intoned, stripping off the rest of her clothes.

'The Son,' Didi continued, undressing.

Pat unhooked his belt and slid his jeans down to his ankles. 'I guess that makes me the Holy Ghost. But why are you shutting the church door on poor old Jack?'

'Not holy enough,' Beth said in a low, thoughtful voice. 'Too satanic.' She knelt beside Pat and pulled off his briefs with her teeth. 'Now there,' she said, 'is Godhead.'

Didi knelt beside her. 'I can't tell you how holy this makes us feel, Father Pat.'

The end arrived by fax, abruptly, next afternoon. 'Dear Pat and Jack, please send our stuff air express. Beth's got us both back at Stanford, in the law school. The weather can't be beat, my family's nearby and fully understands my decision to "come out" with Beth. It makes life much easier for me. Her, too. Much love.'

There followed an address in Palo Alto, California.

It called for boilermakers at the Climax. 'I just can't believe,' Jack muttered over and over again.

'That they're gone?'

'That we were just camouflage. For their lesbian kicks. I mean, hey, I eat women, too. Why didn't we get in any jolly-box lunches, then?'

Pat remained silent. Would he never see Didi again? Beth he wouldn't miss, with her spooky churchiness. What a partner she'd make in some California law firm! Dingbat, Airhead and Flake.

But what he and Didi had had was passionate and very pure. He couldn't face the fact that she had chosen to opt out, as thoroughly as taking a female lover three thousand miles away could make it. Turn her back on something that pure?

Maybe that was the lesson to learn. Nothing is pure. And, therefore, was it worth thumbing his way three thousand miles to Palo Alto to fall back into that soft dual womb again?

He shook his head. 'What?' Jack demanded.

'Nothing.'

'Thassa very doleful look.'

'Nothing.'

'Hey, this's Jack you're talking to.'

'Jack-You're-Talking-To? Indian name?'

'Hup. We drown heap firewater. But it no beat pussy.' They raised their shot glasses, clinked and swallowed hard. The cheapo faux-bourbon burned for only a moment before beer flushed it all gutward. Jack got up and went to the bar for two more shots.

Pat watched him move, lurching slightly. He was always ahead in drinking and always would be. Nothing mysterious about that. But why hadn't the girls ever let him in their circle?

Pat's head dropped onto his crossed forearms. He realised he was crying, quietly, no sobs but rivers of tears. He realised now he would never see Didi again.

No, never.

Seven

After a cool June, Manhattan began warming up. By Eileen's birthday, Bastille Day, the Fourteenth of July, the little brick house in Mulberry Bend was in dire need of air conditioning. Pat spent an hour in the cellar, cleaning out air ducts and filters before switching on the cooler for the first time since the previous September.

That hour was a quiet boon. The year of heavy studying, demonic note-taking and hyper-sexuality – never alone, never relaxed, always aroused – had made him treasure the soot of the cellar.

He came upstairs and asked Eileen to join him where his father sat watching TV with the sound turned off. 'Idiot,' Former Detective Sergeant Michael Rossi told the video tube. 'Moron.' The man on the tube-face shook both hands furiously.

Eileen showed up in shorts and a halter top. Her body reminded Pat of a scaled down Beth, with padding where it counted. He and his father nodded and beamed. No need to exchange information. It had always been a compote: joy that Eileen so closely resembled her mother, sorrow that her mother had died eighteen years ago, not in childbirth but two weeks later of septicaemia.

She had left them this small, bright, lively replica, with a Celtic delicacy to her face that resembled a fourteenth-century ivory carving, the planes and folds incised firmly but lightly.

'Well?' Eileen demanded.

'*Happy Birthday to you,*' the two men began in uneasy

harmony. Pat adjusted up a half-note and they finished a third apart, drawing out the last *'tooo you-hoo.'*

'She was just eighteen,' Pat revised the Beatle song, unaware that his nose carried a broad swatch of duct dirt. *'You know what I mean.'*

He gave his sister a small cube-like package. 'Tis from the both of us,' he said, unconsciously slipping sideways into his mother's Irishisms. He had been four when she died, but there was no way he would ever forget her.

'Hey! Whoof!' She had peeled off the wrapping to disclose a pure white cardbord box carrying the Van Kleef and Arpels logo. 'Hey, you shouldn't have.' On opening the white box a dark leather one appeared. She unsnapped a catch and swung open the top to disclose a long pearl necklace, coiled around a black velours stand.

Her fingers were shaking. She swung sideways to a mirror and slowly adjusted the pearls around her neck. 'Look,' she began. 'I mean . . . I couldn't poss– '

'I know, my beautiful daughter,' her father announced. 'In response to your unspoken question, yes, they are cultured because, no, we are not yet zillionaires but what we wish you is a zillion zillion years of happiness and good fortune because we love you, Eileen.'

She burst into tears and knelt beside him on the sofa. 'You guys are absolutely untrustworthy. I was expecting a carpet sweeper.'

They began laughing so much they failed to hear the doorbell for a long time. 'Whoops!' She went to the front door. 'Yes, who is it?'

'Western Union.' A muffled voice.

Her father's eyes went flat: 'Western Union hasn't delivered telegrams since – '

Pat went to the door, 'Identify yourself, please.' His low-pitched voice was reined in so forcefully it made the wooden door buzz.

'John Abercrombie Pierce, future attorney-at-law.'

Pat swung open the door. Jack stood there with a huge

mailing folder hand-decorated like a telegram. 'Is there an Eileen Rossi here?'

She swung the pearls in a lasso loop around her neck with a certain Bea Lillie abandon. 'Ah, the satanic Jack Flash. Yes, young man? For it is I to whom you must address your inquiry.'

But the Pierces, Pat remembered, were sticklers for protocol. Jack stepped inside the small living room and addressed himself to Michael Rossi. 'Permission to deliver birthday message, sir?'

There was something less than pleasure behind the outwardly friendly look in Rossi's glance. 'Sure. Lay it on her.' Eileen withdrew an immense greeting card that, when freed of its envelope, sprang open a bouquet of brilliant mylar-glittering flowers.

They settled down to catch up on news. Jack had been out of Pat's life for more than a month. He handed over an envelope the mailman had delivered up in Cambridge after Pat had returned to Manhattan.

'And how long are you in town?' Michael Rossi asked.

'Till tomorrow morning. I'm at the St Regis. Can I take you all to lunch?'

The Rossis glanced at each other. It was possible to get their father kitted up for a wheelchair expedition. He did it every six weeks to the doctor's. But it made a difficult day, very tiring for the father and for Eileen.

More to the point, as king of his own living room couch, his true condition rarely reminded Michael of how handicapped he really was. Lunch at the St Regis would be an acute form of rubbing it in.

'Not this time, Jack,' Eileen let him down gently. 'Some day. Maybe when Dad sees the doctor. There's a deli he loves just down Second from the medical centre.'

The look on Jack Pierce's face was unreadable. His sandy complexion had gone red. 'Look,' Pat suggested. 'I'll stay here with Pop. No reason to cheat Eileen out of a birthday lunch.'

'And we could spend the afternoon shopping,' Jack added.

'Shopping, is it?' she asked.

'What the hell, it's my birthday treat.'
'Go on, Eileen,' Pat said. 'Show the world your pearls.'

For him, the day went with the same slow leisure as his hour cleaning air ducts. Doing nothing suited him to a T. But he noticed his father had for some reason ceased his normal round of activity, reading, combing the TV channels.

He got him on the wheelchair and took him to the bathroom for his lunchtime pee. Pulling up his father's trousers again and fastening his belt, he caught the look of grim stoicism on the older man's face. It took a lot to distort Michael Rossi's features. He had trained himself never to give clues like that.

'Seeing you slopping out your dear old Dad,' he said, 'just reminds me of how hard Eileen works around here. I mean, a lunk your size can handle me easy, but a slip of a girl like Eileen...'

'That's why I wanted her to grab a day away from here. Jack will lay on the goodies. He likes her a lot.'

Rossi said nothing until re-seated on the TV sofa. 'Does he, now? Did he rehearse this with you beforehand?'

'What?'

'Along the lines of "the second Eileen's legally of age, you're helping me get a date with her." '

'You're crazy. Jack thinks of her the way I do, as a kid sister. He's got one of his own, Paulie.'

'You're suggesting incest as a form of rehearsal?'

'What the hell?'

'Sorry.' But the cop's pale green stare showed no contrition. 'And you needn't remind me that Eileen's got a level head on her shoulders and wouldn't fall for the first would-be rapist who swoops down on her.'

'You are in a very ugly goddamned mood.'

'Maybe.' The silence between them grew. 'Maybe it's the voice of scepticism. Maybe I ask myself why we haven't seen the handsome, well-to-do young man since Christmas, right? And what we get instead is remote-control largesse, a grand apartment for you two, rent-free, right? A family with its own island nation like a diamond as big as the Ritz, right? And he only shows up to take Eileen away the day he legally can, right? And if you – '

'Shut up, Pop.'

'Right.'

'I'm sorry, but you're way off base with accusations like that.'

'Right. Right. Right.'

'What did you mean, satanic?' Jack demanded.

They had finished lunch in the hotel's dining-room and were having espresso. 'Just what you think it means.' Eileen produced a maddening smile.

'Every girl I ever date calls me a blond bombshell. Where's my dark skin and hair? How about the Dracula choppers and the curvy horns?'

'Just because everybody falls for you, the way Pat did, doesn't mean you don't peroxide your locks and part your hair down the middle to hide the horns.'

Jack frowned, pulled off his right shoe and sock. He elevated his bare foot to the table top. People turned to watch. 'See? No cloven hoof.'

'Plastic surgery.' She turned to smile at the onlookers. 'Six toes,' she told them. They immediately looked away in perfect Manhattan unison.

'I mean it, Eileen. A crack like that gets your Dad upset, believe me. He starts asking himself, "Satanic? what's going on?"'

'You think this lunch excites suspicion?'

She wore a plain black silk dress, cut above the knee and suavely showing off the pearls. Her short-heeled black silk pumps were tucked under her chair. Her knees, slightly tanned, had the powdery glisten of a pale coral-hued plum.

'It certainly excites me.'

'Why? I distinctly remember you promised me a birthday lunch back in March or April or whenever we had one of our clandestine telephone calls.'

'Which your Dad must suspect.'

'Not sure. He thinks of me as having a sensible head on my shoulders. He doesn't realise I'm in the grip of fate.'

'An absolutely gorgeous head.'

'That, too.' She began tickling the sole of his foot. He bent over and put shoe and sock back on. 'Agreed I'm gorgeous, though brainy. So Dad assumes I am not about to serve up my cherry the day it's legal to pick it.'

Jack blushed. 'Well, not to just anyone.'

'You're not just anyone? That it?'

'I'm not,' Jack protested. 'First of all, I'm your brother's best friend. Second, fate has sent me to you.'

'That cuts several ways.' She sipped her coffee, frowned and tipped a few more grains of sugar into it. 'This coffee is also satanic.'

'And third,' he went on boldly, 'I treasure your cherry. Picking it – no, licking it into life – would be a long, leisurely act of worship. It would have – ' Jagged flashes of Beth's churchy talk surfaced. ' – a sanctity, a holiness, the sweet discovery of your God-given – '

'Jack, I wasn't aware that cherry fondant needed that much milk chocolate coating. You actually do have a room here?'

'A suite.'

She nodded approvingly. 'Give me the key, partner in fate. I'll go upstairs. You tell the desk you've gone for the day. Then follow, rehearsing acts of contrition, ten Hail Marys and whatever sleazeball erotic tricks you've picked up over the years from women less gorgeous but more experienced than I am.'

'That's more like it.'

'I warn you, Satan, since the day destiny and Pat delivered you to me I have lusted after you. This puts me in a pre-occasion of cardinal sin, while still undefiled. If it turns into a crumby afternoon of virgin worship I'll never forgive you.'

Eight

'Let's face it, Pat, just how well do you know the guy?'

It was dinner time. In the continued absence of Eileen, Pat had opened up two TV dinners and was heating them in a toaster-oven. The aluminium/cardboard aroma of frozen cornstarch and MSG had begun to fill the kitchen and work into the living room.

'As well as anybody I've roomed with for nearly a year. Somebody I've studied with, chased girls with, got drunk with, visited his family, shared lecture notes, crammed for exams with and, in the end, got A's with.'

'Drop in the bucket. What kind of character has he got? How does he treat his women? His family?'

'His mother – ' Pat stopped short, realising this would be a trump card. 'What's that?' he broke off, pointing to an advertisement his father had painstakingly circled with a felt marker.

'It's the computer I want to buy some day.'

'For that dream project of yours?'

'Right now I have memorised so much data my head's bursting.'

'You keep it in your head?'

'Where else? It takes me ten minutes to write one sentence. I can memorise it in ninety seconds.' His father's frown began to build up. 'You were saying something about his mother?'

'Whose mother?'

'Stop yanking my chain.'

'Jack's mother? She dotes on him. He's the oldest so he's the favourite. And she . . .'

'Stop building it up.'

'When God made tough cops he started off with you, huh, Gonzo? Take a deep breath. Mrs Pierce is Serena Wainwright, the soprano.'

Michael Rossi sat in silence for a long moment. 'She's a brunette.'

'So's his father and brother. His kid sister's a towhead. What is this, genome research?'

Again his father was silent. Then, reluctantly: 'Serena Wainwright. The best goddamned mezzo the Met ever had. And his old man?'

A bell went off in the kitchen. Pat brought out two open trays, each containing a thin wedge of possible chicken breast, a dollop of mashed potatoes and a lot of diced carrots in a kind of thickened arrowroot paste.

He cut the chicken in small squares and switched on Channel 13. Without speaking any more, the two men sat facing each other as Pat lifted food to his father's lips. The public service news programme droned on, with Pat spearing mouthfuls for himself so that both trays emptied at the same time.

'No dessert, Paddy, thanks.'

'Tea?' He handed his father the remote control.

'Listen, get on the phone and call the St Regis, will you?'

'No way.'

'She's been gone since eleven this morning. She may have reached the age of consent but that's eight hours spent with that bargain-basement Beelzebub.'

'One thing I know about Jack and women. He's resistable. I thought they'd keel over like wet wash on a line. But they have their ways of saying no to him.'

The key rattled in the front door and Eileen swept in. 'Pat'v'y'got a finnif?'

'He didn't give you cab fare?'

She slowly revealed a hundred-dollar bill rolled in her fist. 'The hackie can't change it.'

Grinning, Pat went outside to pay the cab driver. Inside, Eileen stood in front of her father and flicked the bill onto a nearby table top. 'I'm putting this in your kitty for buying a computer. Did you eat?'

45

'Yep.'

'Watch MacNeill/Lehrer?'

'Yep.'

She kicked off her pumps and sat down beside him. 'You don't look too deprived.'

'Only of feminine company. What did you and Joe College get up to?'

'Lots of window shopping,' she lied. 'Apparently, in his social class, that's what women do. All afternoon.'

'Class? *You* got class. Pat has class. Jack Pierce has money.'

'Sure does. If I'd let him buy me half the stuff we looked at I'd've had to take it home in a Mack truck.' Neither of them spoke for a long time, digesting the suggestion that, though tempted, she'd returned home unbribed, therefore un-anything.

'As if I could let him buy me things. Clothes. It's out of the question,' she summed up in a no-nonsense tone.

'Didn't he buy you dinner?'

'I finally had to explain to him that the kind of place he liked to eat left me cold.'

'You let him off easy, huh?'

'Big Mac and a Diet Coke. Hold the fries.'

'This guy pinches pennies till they squeal.'

'No.'

'No?'

'No.' Pat agreed, coming back in. He closed the door behind him and double-locked it. 'Jack isn't in any way cheap. He's a very serious customer but he's not ever going to show it.'

Eileen's pale green eyes flashed up at him. They locked into his glance for a long time. 'Dad's concerned that I was such a cheap date.' Then, appeased by whatever she found in her brother's glance, she got up and waved as she left the room.

Pat nodded smugly at his father. 'Satisfied?'

'As soon as you get that C-note back to Mr Ethical,' he growled. 'I don't let guys like him buy me a computer on the first date.' Former Detective Sergeant Michael Rossi fixed him with his Number One stare.

'Satisfied?' he said at last. 'Where Eileen's concerned? Never.'

Nine

'French, French and Underwood, good morning.'

Pat felt his throat close up. Of all the heavyweight law firms, FU2, as it was called, was the most prestigious. Two Presidents of the United States had come from among FU2's partners. Republicans, of course.

'Mr Ludlum, please?'

Pat glanced at his wristwatch. Ten a.m. was an okay time, wasn't it, to call a partner as senior as Daniel Ludlum? Later he'd be too busy.

'Mr Ludlum's office. Good morning.' A low, dark voice, more of a hoarse purr, not yet sexually differentiated.

'Good morning. This is Patrick Rossi. In late June Mr Ludlum sent a letter to me at Harvard Law. I just got it yesterday. Is... am I...?'

'Is his signature initialled RM? or RB?'

Pat's fingers shook as he unfolded the letter. 'MJ.'

'Oh, good. I'm Maria Jenner. Can you read me the letter?'

Female, Pat registered, one of those low-pitched old-time tough Manhattan secretaries. 'Dear Mr Rossi... just, you know, uh, call for an appointment.'

'Ah! Just think, Mr Rossi, if you'd managed to work that in after Good morning.' She laughed teasingly, her voice rising from tuba to bassoon. He had no idea what she looked like, except that he would not have expected her to flirt. 'What does today look like for you? Today at four p.m.?'

At three p.m. Pat left the Donnell reference library on 53rd Street across from the Museum of Modern Art. A firm as antique as FU2 had left behind it a lot of history.

Always involved in corporate law, it seemed in recent years to specialise in the shotgun marriages created in the dusk of the twentieth century as American capitalism concentrated itself into fewer, larger bastions of profit.

Since World War II, an article in *Fortune* had revealed, one hundred top corporations had condensed into fewer than thirty, washing out trade unions, long-term work contracts, fringe benefits and small stockholders.

Most of these companies had been swallowed live, python fashion, and then digested. In this period no one built businesses. One looted a business and stuck its stockholders with the debt. Of these cannibal feasts, FU2 had masterminded nearly a third.

Of Daniel Ludlum, senior partner and, in the parlance of the trade, 'rainmaker' who brought in business, the library's files were crammed. Most senior partners lead shadowy lives except when their wives were fleshed out in bizarre dresses at charity events. Ludlum was made of different stuff.

To Pat, if one could believe the photographs, the charisma began with craggy good looks of the New England variety centred above a jaw upon which, as his Maine ancestors put it, 'you could hang a lantern.'

Early pictures, when he was part of the Harvard tennis team, showed a tall, slim lad who looked athletic even simply standing there with a glass of iced tea. He'd married his first wife right out of the Air Force and law school. The next three Mesdames Ludlum were neatly spaced over intervening years.

After such documentation, including two sons and three daughters, came the gossip, the actresses, female artists and musicians. It looked, Pat saw, as if Ludlum rarely had to make do in bed with just any ordinary housewife/hooker.

It was perhaps because of this informal streak in his character that FU2 had directed Ludlum to make subtle but deep changes in the firm's own corporate image. It remained the plutocrat's law firm, but Ludlum, for example, had raised money for Adlai Stevenson and Jimmy Carter. As law firms must do, eventually, it took on non-paying cases, known to attorneys as *pro bono publico* work.

Pat went down into the IRT at 51st Street and changed to an express at 42nd Street. Awed by Ludlum, he'd lost track of time. He would reach FU2 half an hour too soon. What he needed most was to talk to Jack Pierce.

That morning at breakfast Eileen had been no help as to where Jack might have gone. She seemed barely to remember who Jack Pierce was.

As Pat walked upstairs into the Wall Street area at half past three, he stepped into a telephone booth and spent quite a lot of time placing a collect call to Jack's mobile number. 'Jack, this guy Ludlum, at FU2? He wrote me that letter? I'm seeing him in fifteen minutes.'

'Fast work. After first grades are in, big firms start to recruit. Good luck.'

'That's all you've got to say?'

'Except that I truly enjoyed yesterday. Always love talking with your Dad. What a hero that guy is. And Eileen!'

'Dad grumbled. I said the son of Serena Wainwright could not be a successful rapist. That shut him up. He's always had a crush on mezzos and her in particular.'

In the 44th Floor executive offices of FU2, Maria Jenner turned out to be overpoweringly statuesque. Probably old enough to be Didi's mother, she wore her dark hair as short as a young boy, setting her oval face in strong relief without much hair to surround and soften it.

Standing, her focus was long legs below a short skirt. When you're forty, Pat mused, and you've still got it, flaunt it. Her terribly low voice seemed to vibrate somewhere deep in his groin. She gave the 'i' in Maria a hard, Old West pronunciation. Mar-eye-ah.

'Did anyone ever tell you, Mr Rossi, that you look quite different from the way you sound over the phone?'

A flirtatious opening requires answering in kind. 'And I, too, had a completely different idea of what you looked like.'

'Domineering dyke, heavy smoker?'

He grinned. 'I wasn't prepared for ravishing good looks. The rich man's Mary Astor.'

'Oh, that.' She gave a wave of dismissal. 'Come with me,'

she said, smoothing her navy blue blazer down over her breasts. She strolled ahead of him at a leisurely pace, he noticed, so as not to rush his close observation of that much leg.

She seemed to be leading them out of the building. On Wall Street, forty-four floors below, a taupe Bentley limo pulled to the kerb and they got in. 'Mr Ludlum's schedule's very flexible,' she said, crossing those legs as she relaxed on the rear seat. 'Ishmael,' she called to the driver, 'let's try the tennis club first.'

The long auto surged north for several blocks. As it neared the South Street Seaport area, it eased towards the East River. Pat saw one of those inflatable tennis buildings, a bulging green and white balloon kept erect by forced air.

The limo drew up to the kerb. Maria Jenner recrossed her legs while Ishmael – a stocky Puerto Rican – came around to open the door on her side.

'Check the shower room, Ishmael. Find clues.'

'Kay, Miz Jenner.' He trotted off.

Her briefcase slid to the floor. 'Mr Rossi, would you be a dear?'

Pat bent over, his face at her knees, to retrieve the case. As he looked up she recrossed once more. The swells and curves, the indentations and deadly sharp places interwove with the hiss of nylon. Her scent surrounded and embraced him in a dense erotic zone.

He felt locked in by flesh that had yet even to touch him. The resemblance to Didi seemed to lift his heart. Not the face. Not the hair. Just the entire body and the lush odour it exuded.

'I see you like big women.'

He handed her the briefcase. 'Everybody has a weakness.'

'Dangerous to let me know it.'

'You'd take advantage of me?'

'I already have.'

She turned to watch Ishmael trotting back to the limo. 'He's gone on?'

'To Americano.'

51

'Más allá,' she ordered. 'Onward.'

In the streets around Park Avenue South, between 34th Street and the upward reaches of Greenwich Village, lay the new landscape of publishing, currently moving there for lower rents. Where publishing exists, there endless expense-account restaurants arise to give editors something to do.

Americano was this year's flavour, featuring dishes from tasteless Sioux-blue cornmeal fritters to overspiced Argentine marinade charbroil.

From almost its opening day, Americano had been overbooked in the usual rude forty-five-minute-wait-for-strangers mode. Once the film-TV people who bought novels in manuscript began arriving, celebrities seemed to emerge like mushrooms after a damp night.

At four-thirty Americano should have been populated entirely by busboys setting empty tables. Instead a small line had already formed for the privilege of an after-work cocktail hour. Since the bar was already crowded, mainly with actors, and tables were reserved for diners later on, the line grew dense, a self-advertising come-on.

Maria Jenner swerved past them, Pat in tow. She spotted the maître d' homing in on her. Firing the first rudeness ICBM she strode past his very nose without seeing him and led Pat to a corner table.

Barbra Streisand was just getting up. The man who remained took her hand in his and gave it a good, hungry kiss, not the usual knuckle-brush. Maria Jenner cleared her throat. 'Mr Ludlum, this is Patrick Rossi.'

The man behind the table had been a P–51 fighter pilot with the USAAF Eighth Air Force based in Britain. So he had to be late sixties, Pat told himself. He'd shot down three Messerschmitts and four JU–88s, bailed out over Schaffhausen and escaped from Stalag Luft III to fly again.

'Thanks for dropping in.' Ludlum was an inch or two taller than Pat and looked in much firmer shape. 'Maria, hold Ishmael to take Mr Rossi home. I'm here till God knows when.'

The famous jaw jutted like the prow of a clipper ship. The

eyes glowed milky blue. The nose would have been too big, except that the jaw balanced it. Around the thin-lipped mouth two parentheses had been carved in the suntanned skin.

They shook hands and Ludlum indicated the banquette. The gesture had a proprietary look, as of someone used to being the centre of the universe, enjoying every moment of it and pleased to share a bit. It may have been his satisfied look that gave him a quick resemblance to Punch.

Pat sat down. He tried not to watch the intricate play of Ms Jenner's legs as they slashed hautily past the maître d', once more cutting him to shreds.

'The one thing,' the older man began, 'I do remember from law school is the solemn lecture about the responsibilities of the legal profession. Like doctors, balancing profit with enough voluntary work to ease the croak of conscience.'

'They still give that lecture.'

'Why change it?' Ludlum smiled, an awesome movement of lips and teeth. Pat got the feeling that in the dark it would be even scarier than Punch.

'I understand FU – ' Pat choked. 'French, French and Underwood has been doing much more pro bono of late?'

'When you've done zero, anything becomes much more.'

'Mr Ludlum, I didn't mean – '

'And it's perfectly all right to call us FU2.'

Pat watched a tall, substantial gent in a $3000 suit stroll in past the maître d' as disdainfully as had Maria. He kept an oddly small head turned from the Ludlum table. But as he sat down nearby, Pat recognised him as Big Mimmo Caccia who had engineered the execution of Vinnie Sgroi, not for having reduced Mike Rossi to a potato sack, but for trying to muscle in on Mimmo's airports.

Ludlum observed the newcomer for a brief moment. If he recognised Big Mim nothing in his face gave it away. But the adjoining auras of power gave Pat the feel of being between two high-tension electrical generators.

'We may be a very ancient firm but we operate on very modern lines,' Ludlum said, taking a small brochure from an inside pocket. 'Trying to, anyway. Take a look at the personnel list. Tell me the most notable thing about these people?'

He lifted a hand and two waiters came forward. 'Drink?'

'Uh.' Pat thought fast. 'Club soda.'

His eyes swung up and down the columns of names, hundreds of them. Ludlum couldn't, he thought, mean what was so obvious. The older man produced another of those ferocious smiles, Punch swinging his killing bat. 'Say it, Rossi.'

Pat winced politely. 'In a town of two million Italians and two million Jews . . .'

'Exactly!'

'But other firms have . . .'

'Exactly. We're entering the next century with all our dinosaur genes intact. No Rossis. No Cohens. How can we survive?' He took a heavy, dramatic breath.

'We have a start, with pro bono. But poor people, black people, Latinos, single mothers, old folks, the sick, these are traditionally serviced in New York City by lawyers, social workers, doctors, therapists and nurses of Italian, Jewish and Irish origin. Tradition! It long ago reached the point where kids who came out of Exeter and Choate, via Harvard and Yale, with their White Anglo-Saxon Protestant souls intact, couldn't be diverted to pro bono use.'

'Too valuable buttering up corporate people.'

Pat blinked. Had he actually said something that stupid? His drink arrived and he was too paralysed to touch it.

'Exactly!' Ludlum barked.

They stared at each other. 'Is that why you asked me to come in?' Pat wondered, 'Because my name's Rossi?'

'Pat. Pat. Even a dinosaur has to start somewhere.'

A short, rodentine man, white-haired, arrived at the table, his right hand clamped like a soggy claw into the armpit of a tall blonde in her late teens. Ludlum rose to his feet. 'Abner, you just missed Barbra. Is this the Miss Drew you mentioned? What a nubile young thing. Say hello to my young friend, Pat Rossi.'

Abner, whom even Pat knew to be one of Hollywood's

most powerful talent agents, gave him a meat-rack glance, assuming him to be an actor. 'Nice face power. Where'd you train?' he asked, seating Miss Drew beside Pat as if setting up a doll display.

Not exactly Barbie and Ken, Pat thought, but when you placed as carnal a blonde as Miss Drew next to anybody, the nubility pulsed outwards in waves of heat. All this, he noted, was closely followed by Big Mimmo, as it was by most men in the place. Did it partially answer a question some observers had asked about a bachelor like Mim, in his late forties and still unmarried? Probably not.

'Harvard Law,' Ludlum explained. 'He's not your kind of meat, Abner. He's mine.'

Ten

'Everybody says the same thing about law school,' Jack Pierce remarked.

The November weather still had a touch of Indian summer in it. He and Pat Rossi, in bleached denims, had carried the two-man scull sideways to the bank of the Charles River. 'Everybody says the second term is easier than the first.'

They stepped into the rowing shell and set it afloat. Then, with a thrust from each of their two-ended paddles, they forced the scull to lunge forward, sharp prow leaping, into the chill central current of the river.

'The first year,' Jack went on, 'you learn the tricks. The second year you find out that's all there is.'

Now their paddles dipped and swept in unison, slicing the water, leaving small rings of ripples like a water bug scampering across the surface.

Ahead, a flotilla of sister sculls came at them, five or six craft, seeming to move twice as fast because they were closing on them. Pat, the forward rower, deflected his next downstroke very slightly and the boat slewed out of harm's way.

'Is that why we've been taking so many weekends off in Manhattan?' he asked. 'Not that Pop objects to attention.'

'And Eileen's grateful,' Jack reminded him, 'for getting some time off from nursing.'

'By the way.' Pat's arms relaxed. He let the paddle lie flat on the thwarts. 'She and Pop really appreciate that computer.'

'Nothing. It's an oldie my Dad was getting rid of.'

'Eileen says it was damned near brand new. And would've cost damned near the Earth.'

Jack laughed. 'In the computer business, you're old and out of date the day they manufacture you.'

'So, maybe,' Pat went on, 'you could take back that hundred-dollar bill I put on your dresser. It's only been there since July.' A thin gust of damp chill shoved past them. Pat shivered.

His friend was silent for a while. The flotilla now swooped back on a return run. It closed silently and was gone in a second. 'You Rossis are an independent bunch.'

'Pop has to have it that way. Otherwise he'd've caved years ago. But if he feels he's making it on his own, it keeps him charged up.'

'Excuse me, Pat. Maybe this is too personal a question. Charged up for what?'

This time the silence seemed endless. A flight of Canada geese, reminding Pat of the suicide flotilla of sculls, flew high overhead, its leader honking in an irritated way as if trying to keep the formation lined up neatly. The afternoon sun turned their white wings warm yellow, sweeping up and down like candle flames.

'Even quadriplegics have plans,' Pat said at last. 'Without them,' his voice got hoarse, 'they die.'

'Plans for what?'

Pat turned half way around on his seat. 'I guess they're Pop's plans. If he wants to tell you, okay.'

'I'm not asking for details. Whatever he's up to it's all a part of the . . . the aura of his place. Eileen mentions it a lot. The House of Usher, she says.'

'Meaning?'

'Meaning doom and gloom and all those Edgar Allan Poe things like being walled up alive or dancing with the Red Death.'

'My kid sister has a morbid imagination.'

'No, she's on target. She says that a man half alive, half killed, is an unfinished case. It can only be finished by something drastic happening. She says he could hardly wait to download thousands of items he's been carrying in his head.'

57

'For years. Decades. To you it looks weird.' Pat said. 'To me it seems your average daily routine.'

'Soon he and the computer will start generating strategy, plans. Some mobile person has to execute his plans. And that person is you.'

'We've never discussed it.'

'It's bred in your bones,' Jack pounced.

Pat frowned. 'Eileen takes a dim view of Pop's planning. But the Italian side of me can see his point. Wasn't it you who first pointed it out? To a goombar, any unanswered injustice requires revenge. Pop hasn't been avenged. The guys who wronged him know that.'

Unpaddled, the little scull was drifting towards a deep patch of weeds. The two young men gently dipped the water for a moment with their cupped hands, sending the narrow boat back out into the mid-channel current.

'He seems above all that,' Jack mused.

'Above punishing injustice?'

'When you put it that way . . .'

'What other way could you describe what they did to him?'

The quiet calm settled around them. Suddenly it was broken by the sound of a great, sad sigh from Jack Pierce. 'I've been trying to avoid this ever since we got to be friends.'

'Don't tell me. You're crazy about Eileen.'

Jack blinked. 'Who isn't?'

'You're nuts about her and she's the same about you.'

'What's she told you?'

Pat snorted. 'I don't need words. Every weekend you fly us down to Manhattan and just sort of drop in at Mulberry Bend to say hello, I see your face. I see hers. A blind man couldn't miss it. Pop knows the whole thing.'

'So I'm in deep shit with you?'

'Not me. If Eileen sees something not totally hopeless in your wasted life, who am I, your best friend, to throw stones? But Pop is not your best friend.'

The same sigh welled up a second time. 'That's what I'm trying to tell you.'

'About Eileen?'

'Eileen? For Christ's sake. I have something to tell you about us Pierces. It . . . it requires a few boilermakers.'

'First of all,' he touched his shot glass to Pat's, 'the name isn't Pierce. My father's called Paul Pierce, right? He was christened Gianpaolo Persico.'

He and Pat downed their shots and rapidly followed with sips of beer. 'You telling me, with that mop of straw-coloured hair and those pale eyes, that you're a paesano like me?'

'Un paesano Siciliano, si. Lots of blondes in Sicily, left over from the other Norman conquest. Let's face it, you lousy half Mick, I am fifty per cent more Italiano than you.'

'Your Dad changed his name?'

'Everybody in his generation did. And they did it for all the kids. The last time any Persico went under the name of Persico was . . . I don't know, some time in the early 1930s.'

The alcohol, chilled by the beer, seemed to mushroom out in Pat's gut. He sat back, eyes intent on the line of bubbles in his glass of beer. It seemed important to keep something clear and known in front of him.

Then he laughed, softly. 'When you reminded me that Pop lived on without revenge, I should've known I was talking to an Italian.'

'It's our biggest weakness. And what about the Micks?'

'Worse,' Pat agreed. 'They never forgive. But it's dumb to let the past run your future. You Persicos had the right idea. Change. Even the name.'

'Total change,' Jack promised. 'Some of those old-time Moustache Petes were bad guys. I mean, there were Persicos on the FBI's hit list.'

'Woof.'

'But, hey, I have an uncle who's a senator, three cousins are congressmen. An aunt's a judge and a cousin's a police chief. Another uncle is an executive veep at General Motors. I mean, show me a Pierce and I'll show you a solid citizen.'

Pat nodded, lapsing again into that ruminative stance he had when furiously thinking and re-thinking. 'What about . . .?' He paused abruptly, as if his windpipe had clamped shut. Slowly, he sipped more beer. 'I mean, they never relax their grip. What about the maf?'

'Not since Prohibition, Pat. Guaranteed.'

'Shit, you had me fooled. You have the Waspiest cover I've ever seen. I figured, if anybody dotes on white bread and mayo sandwiches, it's the Pierces. But you all know, deep down, your hearts are carved out of mozzarella.'

Jack produced a tentative smile. 'No, we don't all know. My kid brother and sister don't. Any famiglia their age doesn't. Persico's an unknown name to them. Some of my father's younger brothers don't even know. Don't have to know. It's a dead issue.'

'How come you were let in on it?'

'Because I'm meant to get into a different line of work, one where somebody might use it against me if I didn't know.'

'The law?'

Jack produced a sideways slanting gesture, as if sloping off from the entirely true to the nearly so. Pat realised it was a subjunctive gesture every one of his Rossi relatives knew by heart. When he said nothing, Jack spoke up again:

'Nobody wants me to follow in my Dad's footsteps.'

'Teaching?'

'Teaching is his day job.' Jack's eyes flickered sideways to Pat's face, then away. 'There is a huge family estate portfolio, a lot of property and investments. It requires close supervision. He does it all. I'm expected to relieve him one of these days.'

'That's his night job?'

'One of them.' Jack looked off into the nearby patch of weeds. Behind them, behind the high-rise office buildings of Boston to the west, the sun was setting in long rays, horizontal as fiery missile tracks. Another breeze swept past them, warmer, more friendly.

The orange sunset seemed to Pat to make everything right again. He gave a contented sigh.

'I'm expected to marry well and end up managing the portfolio.' Jack's face looked suddenly hollow. 'I told that to Eileen from the start. I said I was like some turkey born into a royal family. I couldn't pick my wife or my job or even the dressing they stuffed in my gut.'

'Royalty, huh?' Pat grinned at him. 'Pop always expected Eileen to marry some prince.'

Jack's glance swivelled sideways again to judge the effect of what was coming. 'He's also chairman of a philanthropic trust.' His voice went flat and boring. 'It finds worthwhile Catholic youngsters and finances them through college.'

A stream of icy air swirled around them, river mist, dank and chilling. Pat shivered. His face felt frozen, his glance locked on Jack's face.

'You're talking about . . .?' He could hardly move his lips.

'The Frontier Foundation.'

Eleven – 1987

'Yeah,' Former Detective Sergeant Michael Rossi grumbled. A portable telephone sat in his lap, its volume control turned high. 'Yeah, fifty years old.'

'Today?' a craggy, elderly voice demanded, a voice used to barking questions.

'Today,' Rossi admitted. 'Don't make something of it, Timmy. I even discourage the kids from making a fuss, okay?'

'That might be okay for your kids,' the other man muttered. He managed to get a heavy, admonitory feeling to the words. 'But this is Timothy Groark. If I want to make a fuss over your goddamned birthday you can't goddamned stop me.'

'What ever stopped you anyway, you hotheaded old fart?'

The voice from the telephone cackled, wheezed and began coughing. In the quiet of Rossi's living room, as he sat propped up before his TV and computer screens, it sounded as if someone had stepped on a dog's tail. A big dog.

'Anny-way,' Groark went on, out of breath, 'happy fiftieth to you, paesan. What I really phoned for was Pat. He's passed his Bar?'

'A month ago. You calling about a job?'

'There's damned little joy working for the District Attorney's office, Mike, as well you know. But there's an Assistant DA slot opening up around Thanksgiving. Tell Pat to call me.'

'Is this the Mick mafia speaking?'

'Tell him not to call me over a cellular telephone.'

Rossi produced a mirror-image of Groark's throaty cackle, without the tobacco-induced sound effects. 'You're a pal, O'Groark, sure and that's what you are.'

'Anny-thin for the widower of sweet little Eileen Callahan.'

God, Rossi thought as he worked his left hand up to the telephone and managed to switch it off with his thumb. God, but people have long memories. Especially the Irish.

His dear wife Eileen had been gone now some twenty years. But people like Timmy Groark still remembered her as Lieutenant Callahan's little daughter who married that guinea bastard Rossi and conferred honorary Gaelicity and police complicity upon him.

Not that Lt Callahan had been any less corrupt that Capt Feeney, who had run the 119th like a cross between a bookie joint and a retreat house for pimps.

He groaned and worked his fingers sideways towards the keyboard of his computer. His work-pace was terribly slow, since he moved his hand by using the two fingers to crab-walk on the keyboard. What took another computer operator minutes often took him hours. But, he thought, it beats having to memorise the stuff. And in the end, what else have I got but time, endless time?

He had been running a spreadsheet of a special kind. Police cronies had given him a complete rundown on Vinnie Sgroi, the capo who'd sanctioned Tommy Uschetti to do the Rossi spine.

Long dead, Vinnie had produced a grand spreadsheet of arrests, acquittals, near-convictions, held-on-suspicions, affiliations, aborted trials. His entire MO was laid out as a pezzo novanta of the family that handled Manhattan from Canal Street north to 110th Street.

Interfaced with this record was everything Rossi had ever learned about Vinnie's financial life, thanks to pals in the Securities and Exchange Commission and District Attorney's office, buddies like Timmy Groark.

Nobody believed he had everything, every deposit, withdrawal, CD, courier shipment to Zurich, mortgage, promissory note, accounts receivable lien, securities buy or sell or property syndicate. But he figured to have entered onto the spreadsheet more than half of Vinnie's widespread activities.

The inventory power of Rossi's computer – quite expensive

when new – was such that the master spreadsheet could easily absorb more levels of intelligence. Vinnie's family tree, for instance, going back to great-grandparents along the northern shore of Sicily, west of Palermo in the Castellammare del Golfo area, was cross-indexed down to the youngest infant cousin.

A kind of daily diary also existed of his movements and whereabouts on Mother Earth, with whom he'd been seen at lunch or dinner, or just watching the bocce game. Rossi's earliest entry was Vinnie's baptism – by Father Greco in San Gennaro's on Eighth Avenue.

His last was the coroner's report on Vinnie's cadaver, chopped to sushi by assault-rifle fire in an Eastern Airlines freight warehouse off Runway 22B at La Guardia Airport. All in all, a monumental, unique set of records.

A lot of work for a man long dead.

But Rossi had a theory. He knew there was no magic to this, just simple superimposition, first, and then a lengthy search for coincidence. Computers were better at this than humans, expecially ageing quadriplegics with vendetta on the brain.

Whoever had been tormenting him all these years, boxing him in, firing cruel and abrupt warning shots, didn't need him dead. Sure, Rossi knew too much, but all you had to do was show how easily he and his kids could be wiped away. Maybe the old Rossi had been foolhardy-brave. But Quadro-Rossi knew better. Kick him and he turned into a pussy-cat.

Now all that had changed. The micro-bits inside his computer changed Rossi from passive to active. Electrons gave the sad sack of cement a new, dangerous life. Once his persecutor realised that, he would stop playing and go for Rossi's jugular.

Computers could, for instance, put Vinnie in a lawyer's office the morning he took possession of a thirty-two-storey office building in foreclosure, who had owned it, why the mortgage had gone bad, how the bank offloaded it to Vinnie, who in the bank, how much he took under the table, when he next steered a crooked profit Vinnie's way.

Littering these reconstructed aspects of Vinnie's life would be ghostly coincidences. What title company? Which insurance trust? The broker who handled the pay-off sale? One day, there on the computer screen, something would *click*. Vinnie would be tied in firmly to another piece of Establishment America, some entity without a police record, some underpinning of organised crime sunk way out of sight in the primordial slime.

Vinnie Sgroi was worms. But the Vinnie Project would teach Rossi the real foundation of the organisation that called every shot, owned every hood, operated every corrupt politico, profited from every corporation on the make.

Because it duplicated existing records and its chances of producing that *click* were marginal, the attempt had never been made by a law enforcement unit with a hundred times Rossi's computer power. So this was a labour of . . . love?

Rossi choked on a laugh. His head was almost immobile but there was a tiny bit of movement, a tight nod, that signalled his certainly: one day, one great and victorious day, something would *click*. A labour, truly, of hate.

One day soon, when he could find the money, he would add onto the spreadsheet Artificial Intelligence software that accepted, tested and rejected until it actually produced something original, a direction, a trail that said: 'He went thataway!'

Then whoever Vinnie had served, his invisible master, would face the vengeance of Pitiful Cripple Rossi, red in fang, thirsting for blood.

Meanwhile, Rossi existed on the charity of others. Good guys like Timmy who took a chance to offer Pat the job. Assistant District Attorney – God knew how many of them Manhattan had at the moment, dozens? – was a prime stepping stone for a recent law school graduate with his eye on politics.

Too bad Pat's eye wasn't aimed that way. No, Rossi, reminded himself, it was his ambitious, scheming, quadriplegic old man – with his spreadsheets – who had great political plans for Pat Rossi. For those plans, an ADA was a perfect starting place.

Pat was a good son. It wouldn't take too much counselling to get him to accept the post. He'd always do what his father suggested. He didn't really question it, the way Eileen did. In her own petite way, she was the orneriest of the Rossis, always poking holes in her Dad's advice.

He smiled slightly. In his scheming, he envisioned getting Pat placed first, then Eileen. But she had leapfrogged ahead of her father's plans. She was already a rich kid's mistress.

Rossi's smile went lopsided. Not easy, trying to steer a maverick daughter when you had to pretend you didn't know what she was up to. Pat would be easier.

Rossi was in one of his rare free periods when nobody was keeping watch over the pitiful cripple. Eileen, after making sure he was well propped up with everything readily at hand, had scooted out to the grocery store for some ten-minute fast-lane shopping.

Before she got back, was there anything he had to attend to that she shouldn't know about? She had got wind of the Vinnie Project because he'd had her buy him certain software. She took a dim view of the idea that a human being could be reconstituted in full virtual life, wheeling, dealing, cheating, lying, killing, being killed.

No, that wasn't it. What she didn't like was that her father was thus learning how to avenge himself. 'It's overkill,' she would warn him. 'You're too good a man to waste your time bringing some dead slob to justice, playing the vendetta game.'

'Excuse me. Righting injustice isn't a game. But, if it is, it's the *only* game.'

He heard a key in the front door. Expecting Eileen, he saw Pat enter, grinning broadly. 'Pop! Where's Eileen?' He displayed a half-bottle of sparkling wine. 'Not champagne, but we have to celebrate.'

'I told you. No fuss over my birthday.'

Pat's green irises glinted mischievously. 'Oh? Is that today?' He put the bottle in the refrigerator. 'You've heard me talk of FU2?'

'Yes. Fine language for an innocent father's ears.'

'And F you, too.' Pat sat down beside him. 'I mentioned this partner, Dan Ludlum?'

'A year ago. He still sniffing your butt?'

'He's just hired me, Pop! Five-o per annum! We're rich!'

Rossi's face, normally non-committal as a cat's, went even deader. So much for the ADA job, which might have paid half that in salary.

'That's terrific, Paddy.' It took an effort but the face slowly came to life. 'Marvellous.'

'Good pay, yes. Marvellous, no. He's got me on pro bono work, strictly. In fact, he almost said the magic words, but choked them off.'

'What words?'

'We're hiring our first goombar specifically to handle poor people.'

Pat relaxed on the sofa and went into his chewing mode, working over again in his mind the scene at FU2. It had been loaded with unasked questions, with connective tissue that never got plugged in.

'He did have the chutzpah to compliment me on being the first Frontier Foundation fellow they'd hired. Is that coded language or is that coded language?'

'Meaning what?'

'FU2 handles Frontier's legal work, pro bono. That means it handles Jack's father's stewardship of the Foundation.'

Rossi produced a short, bitter laugh. 'Talk of coded language. When was the last time you had a heart-to-heart with Jack about that? About how he got to be your best friend. About how Frontier kept paying your way through good grades and bad.'

'I know about that. I asked his father.'

'When?'

'When we passed our Bar, Jack and I were having a quickie dinner at the Climax.'

'First I heard that rathole served anything besides boilermakers.'

Pat shrugged. 'The world's worst chili con carne? Their cook thinks chili is a bean dish. Anyway, Paul Pierce came in with little Paulie in tow. After a few libations, my Fenian gene always surfaces. I just asked him straight out.'

'And he dodged and weaved.'

'No, he levelled. He said grades are never a first criterion in awarding fellowships. Potential comes first. Making a friend of his worthless son counted for something. Saving him from women and drink. Making sure Jack graduated counted even more.'

'He was ribbing you?'

'No, levelling with me. You have to remember both of us nearly failed our second term. Only last-minute cramming got us both passing grades.'

'You save the son from perdition. And now, the big pay-off, a job with FU2.'

'Is that how you see it?' Pat turned sideways to face those angry green eyes. 'Just who you know? Favour for favour?'

'And just when I would've got you Manhattan ADA.'

'Through Timmy Groark? What's the difference? Either way I'm a cut of tenderloin ready for grilling.'

His father was silent for a long time. Then his keen hearing picked up Eileen's arrival at the front door. 'You're right,' he admitted, about-facing instantly. 'Why not sell yourself dear? Why the hell not?'

He watched the two of them exchanging news, setting up glasses and a dish of munchies. Pat began peeling the foil off the sparkling wine.

It was a character fault, Rossi told himself. Just when his scheming took a big lurch forward, he would view the event as a step backward, Pat into servitude, Eileen into white slavery.

Rossi blew out a silent whistle. Learn to look on the bright side, kiddo. You're weaving your webs and you suddenly find both your kids caught up in them? Both in the camp of the enemy? Is that such a bad thing?

The doorbell rang. Eileen let in Aunt Ruby and Uncle Eugene, carrying a willow picnic basket. 'Buon compleanno, cáro Michele!' Uncle Gene shouted. He unveiled the dish-towels that covered the basket. 'Eileen, baby, this is enough

Bolognese sauce for a month of penne. You should freeze most of it, capeesh?'

Wine creamed up the throat of the opened bottle. Pat deftly caught the foam in glasses, then filled them fuller. 'This is not,' he announced, lifting his drink, 'a birthday celebration for anybody we know.'

'You mean,' Aunt Ruby asked, deadpan, 'nobody here is fifty years old today?' She leaned over and kissed her cousin Michael's cheek. 'That's for nothing, cugino mio.'

'Kiss Pat,' Eileen urged. 'He's got a job.'

Pat lifted his glass as high as he could and said:

'So here's to a decent salary propping up the relentless rise of Clan Rossi. Cheers.'

'And if anybody around here is also having a birthday, good luck to us one and all.'

Rossi surveyed him with a broad, disarming grin of pride. Was it bad planning to have two agents in the enemy's camp? Two spies reporting from inside deep cover?

What other kind of opportunities did life present, but poisoned ones? Never mind the morality of it. And especially don't blame that particularly Manhattan atmosphere that tarnishes any metal in the world, that changes a pixie into a call girl and a defender of justice into a Wall Street pimp.

Harsh? Bitter?

He closed his eyes, trying not to see his children as they were but as he'd pictured them becoming over the years. But nobody forced Eileen to match up with a rich boyfriend. Nobody held a gun to Paddy's head and made him take a big starting salary covering for rich shysters.

No, they'd made that choice all by themselves. Who was he to call them names?

'To my two beautiful children,' he said. He made a lip gesture and Eileen touched his drink to his mouth and tilted it. Slowly the foamy wine eased down her father's open throat.

You have to swallow what comes your way, Rossi thought. Bitter or sweet, you can't let it choke you. Painfully, he tilted his head back.

'And give it back to 'em, right in the eye!'

A thin jet shot upwards from his pursed lips. He hadn't felt this happy in years.

Twelve

The two slim, middle-aged men came off the tennis court dripping sweat, their big, bright, capped teeth bared in grimaces. Since the acceptable facial expression after either a tennis victory or an abject tennis flop has been identical grimaces, neither man's face showed joy or despair. Just teeth.

Enamel-crowned teeth lived in pared and stitched gums, electro-brushed and flossed. Dan Ludlum's teeth were blocky, spade-like. Paul Pierce's teeth were narrower, longer. Both seemed well able to bring back to the lair most of the edible parts of any carcass.

Pierce had come into Manhattan for his three-monthly medical check-up. The tennis game was a bonus, designed to reaffirm what his doctor had already told him:

'How do you keep the ladies from devouring you?'

Ladies? As the doctor well knew, being a nephew, Paul Pierce was notoriously faithful to his beautiful and talented wife. 'Sickeningly so,' Dan Ludlum often added, trying to stir up mischief. 'Paul, one morning you're going to awaken and it isn't. Before that sad moment, get it in.'

'Get it in? That's the Ludlum motto, eh, Dan?'

'Also God's.'

Despite being an airtight construction of neoprene-impregnated rip-stop nylon, the inflatable tennis building channelled chilly drafts where least wanted, such as the shower room. To keep warm, both men doused themselves mightily with hot spray, lathered and then rinsed in icy droplets.

Ludlum, finishing first, watched Pierce daintily drying his toes. The Pierce jewels clenched in a chill-shrunken knot, half subsumed into the body. Then Ludlum saw the penis rise out of snow and ice, its wrinkled shaft upthrust as arrogantly as a sabre, a banner with a strange device: excelsior!

Ludlum looked thoughtful. As far as he could see into Pierce's character, having Serena Pierce's tall dark beauty to himself should have been enough. That, in the teeth of a cold shower, his penis suddenly awoke, was ominous.

He was a friend, Ludlum mused, and a client. But one never knew about these cerebral types. Often they didn't take to physical kidding of any kind. The erection, nominally joyous, did not fit the handsome, intense, almost obsessed face.

'Did Jack tell you?' Ludlum began abruptly. 'We've incorporated Pierce et Cie in Delaware. He can begin taking deposits in thirty days. The brokering must wait till we've bought him a seat on the exchange.'

Pierce put his toes up towards the electric heater. 'We're completing connections before the end of the year. London. Frankfurt. Headquarters in Basel. I'm glad you're giving him attention. I had the idea you were roosting in the top branches with show-biz birdies like Streisand and Redford.'

'That's my fund-raising posture.'

'Still financing the horrible Democrats?'

'As you finance the ghastly Republicans.'

Pierce's high forehead, ending in a frieze of pre-baldness wisps, wrinkled horizontally. He smoothed down the fly front of his trousers. 'I hope we know what we're doing, Dan.'

Pierce had buttoned his shirt, brilliant vertical stripes of royal blue, white and sky blue, each half an inch wide. 'This computerised "expert" system has been tried before. After endless, costly interviewing, we drain the brains of some veteran market traders. We record each one's personal way of operating. We record *him*, every trick, cautionary warning, stop or go signal. We make him into a program that shows a computer how to think like a successful broker. Then we put the machine to making decisions. Suppose it improves market performance over a human by – what? – ten per cent? Is that too much to expect?'

'No. Even fifteen.'

'Since the rule is "for someone to win, someone must lose", the system degrades back to Square One.'

Pierce's hand went to his fly again, but stopped short. He encircled his collar with a four-in-hand tie of brocaded silk, shimmering somewhere between chartreuse and taupe. Slowly, he tied and slid the knot upward against his Adam's apple. With his dark, diabolic good looks, he resembled a hangman at work.

'Paul, I hope Serena realises how many female glances her hubby gets.'

Pierce's sallow complexion darkened in a blush. 'My doctor thinks I'm some kind of lady-killer.'

'With that schlong? Naturally.'

All this was said in the calmest of Ivy League lockjaw-mutter. 'Jack puts a lot of faith in elementary precautions.' Pierce centred the tie carefully. 'He is, after all, my son.' For the first time his forehead cleared of its washboard frown.

'I've pulled all the right strings. He's on his own, truly. He's been positioned for maximum effect. He's been given funds, polish, connections, even a best friend. The very first decision he made was brilliant.'

Working with great care, Pierce fingernailed his forehead fringe a quarter of an inch lower, hoping it would stay there.

'Jack went the recorded-expert program one better.' There was a veiled note of pride in his voice. 'His computer takes a million-dollar trade, minces it into separate buys under ten thousand dollars. This produces one hundred small trades that can't trigger an IRS or SEC computer alarm.'

'Well done.'

'He's cut back the exposure of these transactions to very few people, all quite young. His cousin Carrington. My sister's son, Carter. The rest of his staff, as of now, doesn't exist.'

'But he'll need more people later on.'

'Fewer, not more. He'll outgrow the best friend. I've never been happy about Pat Rossi's father.'

Pierce examined himself in a full-length mirror. It seemed to shiver slightly as a gust of wind outside rattled the building. 'Dan, listen to me.' His voice sounded peevish. 'What is the use of automation if it doesn't make humans excess baggage? Humans make mistakes, betray you, cheat you, rat to your enemies.' His eyes slitted sideways. 'They even criticize your cock. But a computer is your slave.'

Ludlum slipped into soft leather street slippers with easy-on-the-instep laces. 'I can see that someone has given this bank a lot of thought.' He rubbed his immense chin, producing a rasp. 'Are you telling me that Pierce et Cie can promise a client total confidentiality? In the US?'

A faint smile distorted Pierce's thin lips, a dark ray from a far distant, dead galaxy. 'We're all counting on Jack's dexterity,' he said. Outside, the rubberised building shuddered faintly. 'And we're all watching him like scientists with microscopes.'

'Poor Jack! I don't envy him.'

Thirteen

'That's a very suspicious piece of software, Eileen.'

It was one of their stolen afternoons, a slightly undercleaned cheapo hotel between Madison and Park – with a once-famed name – where busloads of Italian tourists now cluttered the lobby, but not the bar, on cut-rate Alitalia charters.

Jack had booked a registered nurse to baby-sit former Detective Sergeant Michael Rossi from noon until six o'clock. She was a nurse they had used before. Michael tolerated her. Choosing a hotel gave them a lot more trouble.

It had to be a place nobody they knew would ever use. Since they knew all sorts of people, the choice wasn't easy. All this preparation, together with its risk-taking, worked up an amazingly aphrodisiac head of steam. They would crash onto the bed, yanking off each other's clothes in an excited frenzy.

Only after the first fornication would they lie in quiet and exchange news. The words had nothing to do with the sexual demands they made on each other. What they said was meant only to let them recover that heat all over again. The affair was still in its early stages. Chagrin had yet to set in.

'Why suspicious?' she asked.

'Most hackers don't get involved in AI. It's beyond their budget or their need. What's your Dad need AI for?'

'What's AI?'

He stroked her back, along the vertebrae from the hollow in her neck to the three fingerprints where her buttocks began. He knew that such a formation was common to many women but hers seemed amazingly erotic to him. Were they somehow deeper? With an even more delicious aura of musk?

'Artificial Intelligence.' He could feel his blood begin to pound in his throat.

She made a deprecating noise. 'My father is the most intelligent man I have ever known. Including you, Jocko. Why does he need some horrible little robot to do his thinking?'

'Sometimes because the job at hand is too boring for a human. Sometimes because he's seeking a connection a human would never think to make.'

A moment later he was fast asleep. In Jack's shirt she went to the hotel window and stared at a featureless crosstown street in the 30s. The shirt, much too large for her, came down around her small body like a cloak. Fine affair, she thought. Jack, all passion spent, napping.

'Ain't misbehaving,' Eileen mused. 'It takes two for that, both needing to remain awake.'

Misbehaving gives me a personality of my own, she thought. Those drab earlier manifestations: Little Sister, Dutiful Daughter, Housekeeper/Nurse. Yech.

Now I take my place next to Hero Dad and Handsome Brother. My own title: Rich Kid's Whore. She turned away from the window as if someone had caught sight of her. 'Jack? Wakey-wakey.'

'Mf.'

'Jack, who on earth would have spent all these years keeping a twenty-four-hour plant on Rancho Rossi? Surely a man couch-potatoed for the rest of his life cannot be a threat?'

'What?' He sat up in bed.

'When I was a little kid it didn't matter. But now it feels like every time I take a shower or get dressed or undressed some peeping Tom has his binoculars on me.'

He frowned. 'Get away from that window.'

She came back to bed, dropping his shirt on the floor.

He began wriggling the tip of his tongue in the three fingerprints where her buttocks began, as if trying to mould them deeper. Yes! The aroma. The taste. This part of her small, neatly made body always carried a stronger scent, as if summoning him to a more animal enjoyment.

'Careful, Jack, you're on dangerous ground there.'

'Mm.'

'I remember when I was small, ten-eleven years old. I took out a book from the library by an Irish writer called Edna O'Brien. I expected great things of such an Irish name. I wanted to know what grown-ups did, so I never told Sister Clare I had a card to the public library. Sure an' begorrah I didn't have long to wait. Edna up and describes having sixty-nine with some fellow, she on top sucking him as dry as an old bone. But the feeling that nearly rocks her off her feet is that she has him at her mercy. While he is working hard to bring her off she could shit all over his face. Can you imagine how that struck a ten-year-old girl?'

'But weren't you always a horny little devil?'

'At ten?'

'My apologies for such a stupid remark. But it's been my experience women like to eat their cake and have it too. Did she actually shit on him?'

Eileen looked thoughtful. 'It's never that open a thing. Women . . . I mean we don't brag about conquests as men do. Besides, you have to assume O'Brien was too nice a girl to get the poor man all messed up. Although doing it to him would have been extremely exciting.'

'Women.'

'What's that meant to be?'

'She's too nice to shit on his face but not to enjoy the expectation of doing it. That's the same person, the same brain producing her conflicting thoughts. And also capable of putting it in the pages of a book for you to find. It isn't two different women, one nice, one not.'

'Are you complaining?'

He bit one of her buttocks. 'I'm as horny as you are. I wouldn't have it any other way.'

'And as for being shat on, they're not allowed to write a porno book without it. And those sleaseball want ads where they're looking for some raunchy female to humiliate them. Men.'

'What's that meant to be?'

'A general across-the-board indictment. In one and the same male brain we find the sadist rapist and the masochist victim looking to be shat on. At close range.'

He fell silent for a while. 'It's no wonder we hand over the big jobs to AI.'

She giggled. 'Seriously, do they sell AI software?'

'I seriously don't know. If I locate some, should I get one for your Dad?'

'If it costs under fifty bucks.'

She wriggled around, got on her knees and mounted him backwards. 'Attention.'

'Oh, God, don't pull an O'Brien.'

'In the fine careless heat of passion? How would anyone know, in advance? How could I issue a safe-conduct pass?'

'You wouldn't actually do it.'

'Why?' She began brushing against his lips. 'Because I'm a nice girl?'

Fourteen

The moment the helicopter touched down at Athens Landing, Paul Pierce leaped off, teenager style. He felt his disadvantaged hairline collapsing in the chill rotor backwash. The copter lifted up and away towards Manhattan again.

All invisible, insubstantial, floating on air like the windborn tennis court, no foundation, no support. Not really there, any of it, shimmering nothingness. Like his goddamned hair.

It may have been his doctor's clean bill of health. A natural worrier sees joyous low tidings – low cholesterol, low blood pressure, low prostate size, low blood sugar – as clearly forecasting a highly dire fate just around the corner.

Don't let's forget his doctor's smartass comment: 'How do you keep the ladies from devouring you?'

Before switching on the Jeep engine he sat in silence, trying to piece out the rest of his day. He was not yet fifty years of age, still keen enough to have noticed his own asinine by-play, his heightened attention to hair, that embarrassing erection in front of Dan Ludlum, ridiculous comments about his fictitious prowess with women and, sadly, the weakening of his short-term memory.

Instead he had given up his wafer-thin electronic diary with its miniature keyboard. He would discipline his balky memory by forcing it into overdrive. But without a diary he felt a tremendous blankness ahead, as if he were still flying in a copter but in complete darkness.

Some of his schedule he knew: he and Serena had to attend a rather formal dinner up in Stonington tonight near the big submarine bases and fitting yards. One of his financial subsidiaries was getting a bronze statuette of Neptune, trident and all, for its services to various admirals and ex-admirals currently operating the overrun scams.

But that was four hours from now. Paul Pierce would never let four hours go to naps or idle rumination. He stared down at the Jeep's steering wheel. He had a reputation for active, hands-on management. His father and his great-uncles would never have entrusted the top-to-bottom makeover of the Persicos to anybody less enterprising.

He started the engine and slowly drove the circumference road. Circumnavigation always calmed him. It confirmed his hegemony over this enchanted place.

The office he was heading for he had built twenty years ago as a spare guest house. Betty Ankrum, who had become his secretary when the office started up, still ran the place. There was no one else, not counting his hospitality staff and his security honcho, Carmine Onofrio.

But for Pierce Industries, no driver, gardener, janitor. No computerhead. No fax savant or personnel handler. No physio coach. No Number Two, Three or Four. Consequently no absenteeism, calls for unionisation, demands for regular merit increases, employee hangovers. Yet here in this unassuming cottage lived the nerve centre of the Pierce empire.

Betty, hired in the 1960s for her high IQ and pert looks, had been paid a small, constant percentage of company profit as salary. She currently banked over a hundred thousand a year, after taxes.

He parked under a broadly branching apple tree. You couldn't run a business this way if you had dozens of employees, all of them curious about you, trading gossip, being suborned by the press or business rivals.

Not only was this a self-sufficient nerve centre, it was provisioned that way, too. In case of emergencies – not minor ones like power outages but major events like hurricanes or civil uprisings or atomic disasters – the entire attic of this place was stocked with canned and freeze-dried food, even down to one-litre aluminium cans of drinking water. No idea how long they might hold out. Years?

He let himself into the two-storey cottage, sheathed in

cedar shakes that had long ago turned silver. The office's high-peaked roof had a faintly Alpine look to it. As he entered he got the feeling of a ski lodge's casual rough-sawn timbers. Betty waved from her desk but remained seated at her monitor screen. Twenty years in this place had barely aged her short, dark hair and round face, with high pixie cheekbones.

'Who won? You or Ludlum?'

'Classified information.'

'I'm sorry. Too bad.' She tapped something into her keyboard.

'Does that imply that I lost?' he asked.

'You never imply. I have to infer.'

Underhanded, he chucked his briefcase to her. 'Low and outside, Ball Four. Most of that is Pierce et Cie stuff Dan left with me. Just commit it to disks in your normally flawless manner and transfer a copy to Jack.'

He and Betty needed very little adjustment to lock onto each other's wavelength. He stood there, hoping her short-term memory would unveil a few items to refresh his. Eventually she deciphered the body language.

'Frankfurt opens in five minutes,' she said, examining her watch. 'And Milan. Mm?'

He smiled slightly. She had a smooth, cushioning way of reminding him and the plump, reassuring, full-breasted pouter-pigeon figure of one's favourite pillow, cuddly, forgiving, comforting, just to look at, not to fondle.

He realised he was staring at her. She frowned very slightly, her kewpie face broad and confident. 'Admiral Christian and Lt-Commander Elgin are due here at five. They want to do a run-through of the ceremony tonight.'

Ah! The missing item. Perfect. Her glance dropped slightly. He realised she was staring at his crotch. He glanced down and saw to his horror that he had developed a full-fledged erection. 'Sorry,' he mumbled, turning away.

'Never be sorry about that,' Betty called after him as he shot up the stairs. Her giggle sounded too loud.

Fifteen

Pat Rossi's office at FU2 was as small as any other new employee's. He shared a secretary with three other newcomers. But there was one difference. His office had a window.

He stood at it this early evening, looking north and east towards the Brooklyn Bridge's Victorian ironwork, and wondering at his luck. Sunlight fell on him. The city sparkled. The others had dank cubicles of despair. He, with his window, was a human being, not a worker bee in a dark, sticky cell.

God knew, he reminded himself, he was busier than a bee. This week he had appeared for twelve different defendants, all poor, black or Latino, caught in the gears of big city injustice, mangled by inability to pay fees or to understand the English of what they were supposed to have done.

He hadn't won all twelve. But he'd got three appeals, two dismissals and four acquittals. Good enough to make pro bono work seem rewarding.

He had started a kind of diary. 'Annals of Injustice' would be a good name for it, he thought. In an age of computerised data, he had chosen a very nineteenth century way of recording his cases. He had bought a bound daybook ledger at Woolworth's for the vast sum of eighty-nine cents.

In its lined pages he would write a brief summary of a case of injustice, often fifty words or less. Not all his cases were recorded because not every one involved a raw injustice. Often they were simple errors or mistakes. Often they were not.

This week, before Judge Craven, a black second offender caught stealing a $150 TV set got three years. The week before Craven had heard a broker who had scammed his customers of nearly two million dollars. He got ninety days and a fat fine.

Pat stood there as the setting sun bathed his face. He could see himself in reflection, his face superimposed over this rich uptown view that had sustained his spirit all this past year. That and his battles against injustice.

His hair was shorter. It now cost him twenty bucks at a barber Jack had suggested. His neck was now encased in high Brooks Brothers button-down collars of thick, wondrous long-fibre cotton that had a posture of their own. His ties spoke with the reassuring elegance of muted colour that told the world: 'Trust me.' Jack had picked them for their resemblance to the neckware Dan Ludlum wore.

As if agreeing to this upwardly mobile change, his telephone produced its self-effacing cricket-chirrup. 'Rossi here.'

'Patrick Michael Rossi?' It was a woman's voice, not the deep-throated sexual tease of the leggy Maria, but a warm voice he felt he knew. It held no note of cajoling but, somehow, it also asked confidently to be trusted, like his ties.

'Speaking.'

'Who appeared for José Jesus Muñoz in Magistrate's Court yesterday?'

'Yes. Who is this?'

'Enid Bart, Channel Three.'

'I thought I knew your voice. You do the . . . um, "News is Made at Night" show?'

He felt suddenly excited, with only her voice to go on. It spoke with easy confidence and, mirror-wise, of the confidence one could legitimately place in that voice. You would, he realised, buy a used car from this voice.

'Mr Rossi, your next line is, "I'm your greatest fan."'

'I'm asleep at that hour. But you can count on my Dad and my sister.'

'But I can't count on you? Then how did you know my voice?'

'I don't. You could actually be your own assistant pretending to be you.'

'Everybody knows: Enid Bart skins her own skunks. Could a mere assistant sign-up the kind of VIPs I do?'

'What is this, some kind of loyalty oath?'

'It certainly is. I'm proud and egotistical, Mr Rossi. To watch me is to be my fan. Stop denying it. You stay up watching me till all hours because you can't help yourself. Say yes?'

'No, but at breakfast I get a full report from my sister. She can remember every word and also what you were wearing.'

'I'm trying to pin down something vital. You *have* seen me on the tube.'

There was a long pause. 'I get it,' Pat responded at last. 'You're beautiful, right? But brainy. A force for good in this sin-sotted city. Your TV programme is a bright arc light of justice in a dark after-midnight of corruption. Yes, Miss Bart, I have seen you.' He paused again. 'Okay?'

'Well done. Now, listen. We had a crew in court who happened to tape your summing-up. You're great, visually. Are you interested in some one-on-one wrestling? We do an open-ended, phone-in debate in the one a.m. segment and I'm always looking for articulate people to argue with each other.'

'On what?'

'It's different every night.'

He had sat down on the edge of his desk to do the usual Pat Rossi moment of re-think. She had a lovely voice, not a harsh note in it, projecting deep interest and a high-speed brain that thought rings around whoever was lucky enough to be talking to her. She would be formidable in court. But her late night news/talk programme wasn't a courtroom.

'Miss Bart – '

'Enid.'

'Enid, I'm a new boy down here at FU2. I'd have to run this past my boss.'

'It's Dan Ludlum who suggested I call you.'

'You mean there is no tape of New York County vs. José Jesus Muñoz? Since movie cameras are forbidden anyway? You mean you made that all up?'

'Um, is that important?'

'You mean you haven't actually seen me in court?'

'Please, Mr Rossi – '

'Pat.'

'I have heard terrific things about you from my contacts, including Dan Ludlum. And I did see a news photo of the Guitterez acquittal last month. The one the *Times* ran across five columns. Where you closely resembled an Irish Paul Newman. So I know what you look like.'

'And on that basis . . .?' He let his voice die away.

'Pat, it's only a TV show. I'm not asking to marry you.'

He burst out laughing. 'For a proud and egotistical beauty, you have very shifty moves. Are you open to negotiation?'

'Like what?'

'Like ask me on the show when you have something I know about. Give me that much of a break and I'm yours.'

Tiny pause. 'What about tonight at quarter to one a.m.? The topic is "Chasing down delinquent fathers". You game?'

He knew the only reason she'd phoned was that she had a slot to fill with a last-second talking head. No assistant of hers would have the bravura chutzpah to try that trick. He suspected the debaters she'd scheduled had let her down.

But he had no solid background in the many delinquent-father cases that clotted up the courts. Fathers went missing owing not only child support but debts the mother was stuck with, serious rent and finance-company debts.

'Who will I be up against?' he asked at last.

'Don't have anyone yet.'

'You ask a lot of your last-minute guests. It's like jumping off a high-dive tower in the dark.'

'That's it. Real live-TV excitement. You game?'

'I – '

'Just this once? Please?'

'Enid . . . I'm yours.'

Sixteen

Paul Pierce's face felt on fire as he mounted the stairs, his swollen penis noosed by the sudden tightness of his trousers.

He went to his bathroom, lifted the toilet seat and peed. It always reminded him of Onan, spilling his seed. A bossy Catholic gene controlled this part of his character, a deep-seated fear that, once having dedicated one's spermatozoa to one's wife's ova, any other fornication diminished a man.

With a few emendations, this was the Pope's view of it, too. But not always Pierce's. On the few occasions, early in their marriage, when Serena had been touring with the opera and away from him for a month at a time, he had fallen from grace.

The angels who helped him fall were motley birds of passage, targets of opportunity, usually married, looking for the tall, dark stranger. But how he had paid! After the sin something bad always happened. A business setback, a boil on his neck, Serena finding out and leaving him.

A magnificent thing when a soprano exits! Sonic, tonic, air-clearing, blasting loose redundant earwax. Temporary, of course She always returned, sotto voce.

It wasn't that his secretary Betty wasn't attractive in her upholstered way. But, Pierce reminded himself, zipping up his fly, a promise to God is the most solemn commitment a man can make, more solemn than marriage vows or the baptism of a child.

He prepared to place some late calls. Before he could begin, a pale green telephone attracted his attention, its tiny emerald lamp blinking silently.

It signalled some important relative whose attention to

telephone security was magnificently faulty, a certain royal carelessness. Why be a Pierce if you had to be as careful on the phone as any other citizen of the Republic?

'Paolo, tesoro, come stai?' A rough voice, but cultivated.

'Harry?'

'What else, your Aunt Harriet? Have we been swept?'

Paul winced. This line was tested every morning – by him alone – for eavesdropping devices. But, still, he hated someone to refer to this, especially on the line in question.

'Yes. Carry on.'

'It's this gift I have from Providence.'

'Patriarchal manna?'

'If you say so, Paolo. You're so phone-shy I'm afraid to open my fuggen mouth when I talk to you.'

Pierce decided to award this a small chuckle. 'Your sense of humour's improving. What's up?'

'Guido Smaldone. Conosce questo stronzo?'

Pierce let out a tight, controlled sigh. 'Okay, Harry. Always nice hearing from you. Ci vediamo.'

He hung up and sat absolutely still for a minute or two. He hadn't had one of these requests for disciplinary action in months. He could feel it fizzing in his blood vessels.

A request like Harry's validated Paul Pierce's authority. Only he could settle affairs by life or death. Once a matter for a committee, in the pared-down managerial structure of the new era this authority rested with just one member.

He taught his history classes that the sovereign state was a lineal descendant of the divine right of kings. To the state, all its own behaviour was legal; executions, assassinations. Rarely did he remark that certain families – Medicis, Morgans, Pierces – also considered themselves sovereign.

Though it celebrated his authority, Harry's request also bothered him, not coming in a flawlessly secure fashion, a lunch, a pre-dinner drink, a whispered word, face to face. Not a phone call, no matter how secure the line.

Okay, Pierce told himself, he was truly, as his wife and even his son Jack had pointed out, a control freak. As if strict control was something to be ashamed of. 'Thank God,' he had snapped back, 'somebody pays attention. Somebody fixes up mistakes. Somebody takes the concern of the family to heart.'

He was struck suddenly by a thought: the great trove of emergency provisions stored overhead included no alcohol. He scribbled a note to himself. 'Case of Scotch.' Damn. Clearly the act of a control freak. So what?

As requests went, the Smaldone one was trivial. Somewhere in Providence, Smaldone's own turf, lived a young high school teacher of history called Herb Applebaum. He had been Pierce's pupil five or six years ago at Yale and had been helped out of a tight place when the Feds had collared him for dealing snow.

Some profs are just naturally caring. A bond had been formed, a lock on Applebaum welded into total control when the careless, luckless Applebaum had been nabbed for drunken vehicular homicide. One of the Pierce specialists created evidence that said Applebaum's wife had been at the wheel. Her innards tested clean. These things are very difficult to stage. But not in little old Rhode Island.

Pierce dialled Applebaum's telephone. It rang seven or eight times. The cooperative wife answered in an unsure rasp.

'Gretchen, let me speak to Herb?'

She had reason to know Pierce's voice and to owe him as much as her husband did. Pierce lawyers had got her off with an accidental manslaughter rap. 'Not home, but – '

'Tell him to call me,' he cut in. She, of course, had no idea her husband's IOU had come due and the price was Guido Smaldone. That could only be transacted face to face.

'This is cash, Gretchen.'

'I'll m-make sure he calls.'

He hung up, picturing Applebaum's wife, one of those lanky New England beauties, long sinewy neck and calves, with pale blonde hair so fine the wind was always sweeping it in her face. She had been one of his early cheating partners, absolutely in awe of a Yale professor.

He gently patted down his own hairline as he pulled over to the desk in front of him a flat box with tiny lamps and swing-needle meters. He dialled his own office number and waited for Betty to answer. 'Pierce Industries?'

They chatted as Pierce set and re-set the meters, watching their dials for any drop or rise that indicated an electronic device had been shunted on or off the line.

Control freak at work. He felt tightness grow in his crotch, looked down and saw his erection taking outline. It was the Applebaum bitch, wasn't it? He pictured her long, horsey face so excited by pain that it brought her to climax.

He went back to his bathroom, unzipped and let his penis emerge. It came out like a brontosaurus rising to tree-top. Big enough for Ludlum to kid him about it.

He could feel a thickness in his throat, as if his own rushing blood was choking him, as if he had somehow stuffed his own penis down his throat. Control affected him that way.

He wanted to cry out, bring Betty running up the stairs to take one look and fall on her knees.

He wanted to swarm all over her, spouting great jets of semen. But Paul Pierce cannot be out of control. Paul Pierce *is* control. Paul Pierce is in command of an empire eight-fold larger than the old Persico holdings.

Paul Pierce controls in his hands the power of life and death, as did his father and great-uncles. In his left hand, the life of Smaldone. In his right . . . his penis. He gave it a great, controlling upstroke that snapped his throat shut. He began to gag as his orgasm tightened within him.

Christ! The male menopause is not for cissies. He clenched his eyes so tightly shut that he saw stars. His teeth gritted as he milked himself into the basin. Teenager! The shame of it! Overpowering!

Poor, Pubic, Potent, Pathetic Paul Pierce. On the fast track to crazy.

Seventeen

Medical Exam Day.

An old pal, Gino Frenese, arrived in his ancient Checker cab. It had as much rear-seat room as a limousine. He and Eileen loaded Michael Rossi onto a wheelchair, then down the steps and into the Checker.

It was a routine they had both memorised over the years, even though it only happened once every six weeks. Today was chilly, about to rain.

'Gino, you feel it?' Eileen whispered. 'Somebody watching?'

'Somebody is always watching.'

The bulky Checker trundled down Second Avenue at a slow pace. Raindrops dotted the windshield. Only one wiper worked. Gino muttered imprecations.

At the medical centre on Second Avenue, the staff looked shamefaced, as always, as if it were their fault that this hero-martyr had been reduced to such a state. They crowded around, trying to appear unusually concerned, offering useless help, a glass of water, a handkerchief pat.

Eileen sat in a corner, spurning out-of-date magazines or conversation with Gino as ways of passing time. Instead she tried, not for the first time, to understand her father's relationship to Manhattan.

People her age barely knew who he was. People of his generation, in the fifties age bracket, knew only too well that something about this town, some sewer virus, had all but killed this hero cop. They made the right mental connections, too.

Killing good cops, they knew, produced an overage of rotten ones. So, if you wanted to chart the city's downward slide, you could date it from Vinnie Sgroi. It was he who had introduced random murder. Once, in the old days, the mafia had rules. Crooked cops got no mercy. Straight cops were untouchable.

It now suited mafia strategists to create a society without rules, where casual death was the next person in line.

After the medical exam, the hero cop looked morose, as he always did when circumstances reminded him he was a quadriplegic. As usual the tests took time to process.

He waited, meeting no one's glance, as if ashamed of being the icon of Manhattan's downfall. Eileen took his hand and squeezed it. He failed to look up.

The results arrived: no new problems. Eileen and a nurse bundled him back into his wheelchair and rolled him outside, like a bag of rice. They installed him in Gino's Checker. He kept his glance away from them.

Gino took First Avenue nice and easy, fifteen miles an hour gliding uptown. Traffic slid past with only a few irate horn honks.

Then something came up from behind at thirty. It rammed the Checker hard, twisting its rear bumper.

Eileen lifted off the back seat and slammed into the rear window. Her father slid sideways onto the floor.

The back of Gino's head banged so hard against his Plexiglas protector that the plastic shattered.

Eileen got the first three numbers of the Isuzu Jeep-clone. Pat got somebody in Motor Vehicles Bureau. Half an hour later they had a make: stolen yesterday up in Darien, Connecticut. End of the line.

The way the three of them reacted was instructive. The back of Gino's skull leaked blood . . . not much. Michael Rossi shivered with rage . . . just a little. Mature New Yorkers, they knew how to handle violence.

Eileen sat in youthful catatonia. She had lived in Manhattan fewer than two decades. She was nowhere near desensitised. Yet.

The parcel looked like a book mailed in a padded envelope. Because of the bubble-paper lining, it made no noise as it came through the front door slot of the house on Mulberry Bend.

Former Detective Sergeant Michael Rossi, whose hearing remained acute even when the rest of him didn't, failed to hear the sound. It was a shower of smaller envelopes that alerted him. 'Eileen? The mail's in.'

She came out of the kitchen, removing the apron she wore when doing household chores or cooking. In the past year, her father saw, she had suddenly shifted sideways from being a girl to being a woman. Nothing had altered in her face or figure or way of dressing. It had to do with the way she looked at him.

As a girl, her glance usually plotted mischief, a wisecrack, one of the routine medical events of his day, something concrete. Now, as a woman, her mind was... elsewhere. Her glance swept the room almost idly.

It seemed clear she had been, in the trick language of the law, emancipated from primary allegiance to a parent. Her thoughts, Rossi felt, were probably working out some new way to see Jack Pierce without Pop knowing it.

She suddenly shot a glance directly into his. 'Impactron Inc.? Ever hear of it?'

She held up the book-like padded envelope. 'Impactron?' he mused. 'They're a software house. Just to approach Impactron and tug at your forelock costs an arm and a leg.'

Something changed in her face, a sudden disappearance of doubt, leaving a just-as-sudden knowledge. She hefted the package. 'It's very light.'

'You mean lighter than four ounces of dynamite, some shrapnel and a timer?'

She made a turned-down-mouth face. 'Not much chance of dying together. Want me to open it?'

Her father frowned his Number One Cop Interrogator frown. 'What kind of idjit question is that to ask of a young lad with only a fifth of his fingers on line?'

Her cheekbones produced a pale blush. 'I'm sorry. I'm not completely on line myself this morning.'

He refrained from wondering aloud what she'd done on her

half-day off yesterday, free time she'd expanded till long after dinner. He watched her remove from the padded envelope a smaller packet containing a spiral-bound booklet and two three-and-a-half-inch floppy disks.

'Logic Synthesis, 3.07,' she read from the label. 'Adventures in AI.' She looked up. There had often been a faint blush to her cheeks when she didn't quite tell the truth about something. It was there now, a lovely peachy hue.

'It's the new stuff they're asking half a grand for,' Rossi announced. 'I hope you weren't foolish enough to – ?'

'They may have sent it on approval.'

And pigs, he added silently, may fly. He watched her crack open the tight cellophane wrapper that protected the disks. His computer, which stayed on all day, accepted the A disk and produced a two-beat note of thanks.

'Welcome to Adventures in AI,' his screen read in rich blue letters on a pale yellow background. 'To begin this tutorial, press ENT.'

Eileen reached out a finger. 'No, let me do it, honey.'

She steadied his posture with an extra pillow and put the keyboard near his left hand. Rossi worked his thumb over until it could punch up ENT.

Immediately the screen reversed colour. Violent yellow letters seemed to burn on a blue backdrop.

'HEY, CRIP! DON'T
SHIT WHERE YOU EAT!'

Neither of them could quite take it in. 'That's me,' Rossi finally said. His voice had a growl to it of a suspicious cat. 'They're talking to me as sure as if they called me by name.'

'Dad, you saw me open the wrapper. Nobody could have got at the disks and changed them.'

'Not nobody. Somebody.'

'But how?'

'Never mind how. Somebody wants to warn me off... what? Off using this software? Then why send it? Or off the whole project? More likely.'

He seemed to settle back in deep thought. Although it

barely moved, his body seemed to condense like a cat making itself small. 'But that means . . .?' He fell silent again.

'That means they may know about the Vinnie Project,' Eileen guessed. She turned away, not ready to face her father again.

His mind kept pushing ahead, but to himself. She knows who sent this, Rossi thought. Could it be lover-boy Jack Pierce? That would mean he knows what I'm up to. Or could it be someone else in that fine financial First Family of Pierces?

He studied the back of his daughter's head. The Persico-Pierce change, decades ago, had escaped a lot of law officers who depended on the FBI to do their thinking. J. Edgar Hoover's FBI had covered it up because the Persicos of New England were allied with Hoover's head boy, Frank Costello of Manhattan.

It had not escaped Rossi. Studying the back of Eileen's head, from this angle she still resembled the teenager he loved best, not the kept lady of a guy he would always consider a Persico scrubbed with steel wool and caustic.

He had analysed the thing between Jack Pierce and Pat Rossi so many times. Which had come first, Pierce's interest in befriending Pat or the accident of friendship busily exploited?

It scared him, before Eileen entered the equation. Where was it engraved, on what marble slab, that two good-looking guys, rooming together, don't start taking showers together?

'Eileen, honey?'

She turned back slowly to face him, as if delaying the moment when their fiercely green glances tangled. 'You know what I have to ask you?' her father said.

She nodded. 'Who knew you were into AI?'

'Smart girl.'

'Too smart to lie to you. I only told one person. Jack.'

He nodded in the same way she had, as if pressed down by fate and yielding unhappily to it. 'How long ago?'

'A month or two?' They both fell silent. Then, abruptly, she was talking fast: 'He had nothing to do with that electronic message. Jack isn't like that. Jack stands in awe of you, Dad. He considers you a hero. In a million years his mind would never conceive of such a . . . a . . .'

'Such a clever threat.'

'Not in a million years would he . . .'

'Or a shove from behind at thirty miles an hour?'

'Never!'

'But what's left isn't believable.' Rossi drew in a long breath. He could feel it tremble in his upper chest behind his ribs. 'You're asking me to believe that whoever Impactron is, or some mail clerk in their shipping room, they got wind of this when Jack placed an order and they recorded that threat before wrapping the disks. On a believability scale of one to ten it doesn't even make the needle flicker.'

Rossi was dozing in front of his computer screen when Pat came home from work. Eileen pulled her brother into the kitchen and, in a low whisper, reported what had happened.

'Jack's not like that,' Pat responded. 'Listen. I know his whole family. His parents treat me like a son. I even keep a change of clothes in one of the guest bedrooms.'

'None of that cuts any ice with Detective Sergeant Rossi.'

Pat's face went grim. 'You don't have to tell me. Pop has always played for keeps. Now that I'm bringing in a little money, he's itching to get ahead with his life project of reconstituting a dead mobster.'

'And giving him a proper burial. The ultimate revenge.'

'But he's frustrated by the idea that both his kids are hooked into the Pierce family and he doesn't trust the Pierce family. A major difference of opinion. And I'll tell you something else, kiddo.'

'Don't glare like that.'

'I'll tell you what bugs him the most. He loves you and he isn't able to sound off in the open about you and Jack.'

Her cheeks went pink. 'What am I supposed to do? Give him a licence to harangue me? He's too smart for that, anyway. Play the irate father out of the comic strips? Not him.'

'Cut out that whispering!' their father shouted from the other room.

'We're just admiring your hearing,' Pat called. 'If you can stay up till one tonight, you get the chance of a lifetime. You get to watch me on TV.'

'Doing what? Phone-in sex?'

'It's that "News is Made at Night" show on Channel Three.'

'Ah-ha, I was right. It's that Enid Bart cookie, the thinking man's whistle-bait.'

They joined him in the living room, Pat sitting down beside him on the sofa, Eileen sitting on the floor. 'I hope you aren't turning,' she told him, 'into one of these puritanical fathers who wants his kiddies kept pure.'

Their father rarely laughed, even when making a joke. Such physical activity tired him. But they saw his face slowly constrict into a grin as two barking, coughing bits of laughter escaped into the room.

'I have two beautiful children. Keeping them pure in this corrupt city would be the miracle of all time.'

His pale green eyes darted from side to side, checking the glance that passed between brother and sister. Once again his body seemed very minutely to grow smaller, more compact, more . . . coiled to spring.

In thrall, he thought. The phrase came to his mind suddenly, an old-fashioned phrase. Both of them in thrall to the same person. It proved that God wasn't the only one who worked miracles. So did the Devil.

Eighteen – 1990

FU2 had become a cave of rumours. Ludlum was breaking up Marriage Four. Marriage Five was a lanky, rawboned Texas blonde in her early forties, Madge Headley, widow of T. Gordon Headley, chairman of Headol International, the nation's seventh largest oil company.

Madge was almost as tall as Dan Ludlum. Quite bright, she had already made two mistakes. She had retained FU2 to handle managerial arrangements for control of Headol. Mistake Two was using FU2 to draft her pre-marital agreement with Dan.

That, and originally agreeing to marry him, left this big, powerful woman as defenceless as a kitten, without knowing it. The illusion of having won something she shared with Wife Four, who had been bought out with stock tenders Ludlum reckoned would go bust before the end of the year. The tenders made her believe she was mistress of a fifty-million-dollar fortune. And, for the moment, so she was.

'It's the Ludlum style,' Maria Jenner murmured thoughtfully in that deep cello voice of hers. She sat on the edge of Pat Rossi's desk and ground out a cigarette in his ashtray. She had crossed her legs in order to swing one back and forth in a wide, dangerous, scything arc.

'What he offers looks good because it *is* good. But the shelf life is short.'

Pat knocked the ashtray clean in his wastebasket. The only person at FU2 who ever used his ashtray was Maria. Anyone who needed to smoke would go to a power-ventilated room on the 45th Floor, set aside for tobacco addicts. But Maria had long ago staked out Pat's office as her smoking lair.

During the year he'd been here, Maria had left her spoor every working day. Her arrogant strategy was to leave a butt with Pat early in the morning and again at quitting time.

Now she got off his desk, smoothed down her miniskirt and strolled to his window. The sun was sinking in the western flatlands of New Jersey, giving every Manhattan building a sharply three-dimensional vertical stripe of orange yellow and a contrasting stripe of shadow on the east side of each facade.

Pat remained seated, watching her in silhouette. Maria was something of a mystery to most of the men at FU2, particularly as to how much sexual service Ludlum demanded of her.

But the women, partners and staff alike, detested her, not so much for being promiscuous – she wasn't any more than the rest of them – as for being Ludlum's.

'That's why I'm still here. Whore Number One, while Wife Five is warming up in the bullpen,' she explained to Pat. 'I mean, Dan Ludlum has two other secretaries. I'm the one who does his pre-marital agreements. I actually like the former Mrs Headley.' She stared northward at the great view.

'She's more your size.'

She looked back at him, a withering glance. 'I am only five-ten. That lady is six sinewy foot tall.'

'But without the gorgeous Jenner looks.'

'Ah, yes, beauty like mine is rare.' She turned to him but her face remained in shadow. Her voice grew more serious. 'So is yours. That appearance on Enid Bart's show! I hear the phone calls are still coming in, a week later.'

She reached for his hand and scratched his palm for a long, sensuous moment. 'You're not fated to linger here at FU2 forever, Young Patrick. You're built for bigger things. But always keep a soft spot in your heart for me. Promise?'

'Will you keep one for me?'

'Men don't want it soft,' she snapped. 'Do you speak any Italian at all?'

'Si, un po.'

'I had a boyfriend once. His father had taught him the four

best things in life: vino claro, cazzo duro, acqua pura, fica stretta. He said stretta meant tight.'

'Heavy stuff, Maria. You Italian, way back?'

'Only,' she said, strolling to his door and throwing it open, 'by injection. Night.' She started to leave.

'I wanted to ask you something. Ishmael, the driver. His uniform has some sort of doodad badge.'

'PPP. They're the security outfit we use.'

'I guess that means they're pretty reliable?'

Her motion froze. She pivoted on the ball of one foot and examined him more closely. 'Why do you ask?'

'Come in. Close the door.'

She sat back down on the corner of his desk, crossed her legs thigh-high and lit another cigarette. 'Tell me,' she murmured, breathing so that smoke got in his eyes.

'You know my father's situation. He gets a medical checkup every six weeks. I want my sister to start using a bulletproof limo with an armed driver. Is this PPP the firm I need?'

Her lips opened slightly and more smoke arose past her eyes. The room had been turned into some kind of Sybil's temple of truth. 'Well?' he repeated, in a softer voice.

'Well,' she echoed, 'how much do you love me?'

'Insanely.'

'Then I have to say: find another security outfit.'

She took a tiny inhalation and ground out the new cigarette. The new aroma, that fetid, fungal, wet-dog odour, took over his office. He dumped his ashtray again.

'Nick Jenner, my dad, is no hero,' Maria said in an abruptly lower voice like a tuba with a velours cushion stuffed in its horn. 'But if I had to pick a security outfit to take care of him, PPP would not be anywhere on my list. Does that yank your cazzo duro hard enough to get your full attention.'

He took her hand as if to shake it, but kissed it instead. He knew she had subtly shifted office loyalties by bad-naming the security firm Ludlum used. She had thus bad-named her boss's judgment, or exposed it as devious. And she had done Pat Rossi a great favour.

'Anything you do has my full attention,' he told her.

She got off the desk and straightened her blouse and skirt as if she had just been rolling on the floor with him. 'When it comes time for me to call in that IOU, young Patrick, I promise to treat you gently.'

She gave him a mischievous look and departed.

Nineteen

The two friends were surrounded by the highest magic Manhattan can weave, its vistas endless, complex, baffling. Access to Manhattan was easy; bridges and tunnels fed it like arteries and veins. But the life-fluid that flowed through was made up of humans, a vastly mysterious collection of corpuscles barely known even to themselves. Only television seemed to bridge all gaps.

The third time he appeared on 'News is Made at Night', the after-midnight news-and-chat programme that accounted for a lot of Manhattan's insomnia, Pat Rossi suddenly understood the power of television.

'When a newspaper runs a photo of me,' he told Jack Pierce at lunch, 'I get a snide wisecrack from my cell-mates at FU2. But when Enid Bart has me on for an hour while the town's supposed to be asleep, I get fan letters, phone calls, handshakes on the street. A professor at NYU wants me to lecture.'

'That's the difference between being merely competent and being a celebrity.'

Jack had established his small merchant banking firm on Park Avenue but when he lunched it was downtown at Bridges. This was a mile-high dining club from whose picture windows one could see every bridge, from the Verrazano up through the Brooklyn, Manhattan, Williamsburgh and Queensboro Bridges, right to the Triboro and George Washington.

On clear days, if one's geography were up to it, bridges could be discerned as far away as the Bronx Whitestone, the Throggs Neck and even the Tappen Zee. What flowed in and out over these bridges remained obscure. It was part of

Manhattan's bloodstream that the corpuscles rarely met face to face.

The two friends saw very little of each other these days. It bothered Pat that they had such busy schedules. But it worried him more that Eileen's affair with Jack had begun to assume such dire significance. The business with the AI software... Damn!

Still, here they were at lunch, quality time indeed. Pat's long, aquiline face, handsome in a classic brunette way, gave off an aura of concern for his friend. Jack's sandy look, everything symetrically in order, hair middle-parted, collar buttoned-down and big, tie like a central anchor, did not seem to need concern. But warmth was always welcome.

'Terrific lady, Enid Bart.' Jack poked at a Caesar salad that had too much anchovy in it. He signalled a young waiter with bushy hair, who took his time arriving. 'She's very special,' Jack continued. 'You ought to get to know her better.'

'How much better? Every time she calls I lose a night's sleep. That show sometimes doesn't go off the air till three-four a.m.'

'I can't think of a better way to lose sleep than with that lady.' Jack gave him a Groucho Marx leer, heavy on the eyebrows, as the waiter finally arrived. Jack smiled pleasantly at him.

'Too much anchovy,' he announced, handing him the plate of salad.

'And?' The young man showed no sign of taking the salad from him. Come to look at him, even his heavy head of hair bristled with attitude. The newest meaning of attitude was the desire to maintain both an appearance and a mindset at odds with the rest of society.

'Ask the chef to do it again. Right?'

'The Caesar is his specialty.'

'Mine too,' Jack said. 'Take the plate, please.'

'But I –'

Jack let the salad crash to the floor. 'Oops.'

He and Pat watched the man bend down and painstakingly brush the salad back onto the plate, muttering something just the other side of audibility. Then he left, hair protesting all the way.

Pat looked curious. 'You used to dote on anchovy.'

'That was before I grew powerful and nasty.' Jack sipped his glass of pinot grigio. He glanced casually around him, then arrogantly, as he saw that most of the other diners were older, senior partners and executive vice-presidents. Any women they invited were powerful in advertising and finance and, therefore, just as old.

'This pre-cemetery is a membership club,' he said then in a low, aggrieved tone. 'If a member can't get what he wants, what's the point of belonging?'

Pat nodded. 'The sensitive palate is a new thing, isn't it? I mean, when you consider that your previous choice was the Climax Bar and Grill?'

Jack flushed, first red and then, more disturbingly, white-faced. He seemed to be having trouble saying anything or even, in fact, breathing normally. Then Pat watched him get his rage under control. The whole thing, from fury to laughter, took only a few frightening seconds.

'You mean, the man who could digest that slumgullion they called Climax Chili shouldn't balk at too much anchovy?'

'You remember when Didi found a cockroach in the – ?'

'Oh, God, do I!'

They began stifling their laughter, trying not to become the centre of attention again. After a while the elders around them went back to their own conversations and the hairy waiter brought a less anchovy-tainted Caesar salad. He served it, without a single word of attitude, and left.

Although the Bridges was a membership club, some tables were obviously 'better' than others. A corner one with a view west and north, for example, was occupied by three men in expensive suits. Pat frowned. The one with the small head . . . Ah, Big Mimmo again. Which reminded Pat of Eileen's demand.

'Jack, we had another scare with Pop. You remember the time his Checker was rammed. This was subtler but scarier.' He repeated the story of the software with the hidden threat.

'Clever,' Jack responded. What do you th– ?'

'I think only you knew he was moving into AI.'

'How can we be sure?'

'So, like a pal, you ordered him the software.'

There was a long pause. 'And?' Jack demanded. 'And then tried to scare him off? Get real.'

'I know it makes no sense.'

'So, of course, the name Jack Pierce pops up.'

Pat reached across and laid his hand comfortingly on Jack's. 'We don't have any other names.'

Jack frowned murderously. 'Then leave this bastard to me. I'll find him.'

'You have other things to do. Just point me and I'll do the hound-dog bit.'

'It'd take time even to find the right direction.'

'A week?' Pat persisted.

Jack thought for a moment. 'About that.' For the rest of the lunch he listened with scrupulous politeness to some of Pat's grimmer pro bono stories. 'Crumby world,' he said then. 'It must give you a charge to set it straight.'

'Remember I told you I was keeping a ledger on some of the cases? Jack, I'm on my third ledger. They used to cost eighty-nine cents. Now they're two bucks.'

'Hello, Young Turks.'

They looked up to see Dan Ludlum, with Enid Bart beside him. Once again, their table was the focus of other diners' attention.

'No,' the older man ordered, 'don't smile. Don't get up. Just keep that grim, serious *purposeful* look on your faces. You guys are a lesson to us all.'

Jack, nevertheless, got to his feet, as did Pat. 'We guys might smile more,' Jack explained, 'if we had someone truly gorgeous to share our monastic lunch with.'

'Uh, that Caesar,' Enid murmured, 'what exactly was wrong with it?'

She came up to Ludlum's shoulder, a very slender woman Pat's age with long legs and dark high-cut hot-pants to demonstrate this fact. Her face was narrow, too, but her black hair had been ruffled outward to give her an intellectual top-heaviness. Under black brows, her dark, knowing eyes seemed never to stop moving, first to the younger men, then to Ludlum, then to someone at another table who waved to her.

'What Caesar?'

'The one that decorated the floor.'

'Butterfingers,' Jack explained.

'You see?' she asked Ludlum. 'That's why I can't ever use him on the show. He's such a perfectly believable liar.'

'Oh, that's unkind. You can't – '

'Whereas Pat Rossi has probably yet to utter his first prevarication.'

Pat smiled vaguely but he was watching his best friend's face. The action was identical, first a flush, then white rage. Then he mastered the whole mood swing. 'Nobody loves a rich, powerful and seriously handsome man,' he mourned.

'Oh, I don't know,' Enid remarked. 'Look at Dan here.'

'On which note we depart,' Ludlum added, steering his companion towards the exit.

The two friends sat down again. Jack took a long, deep, calming breath. 'God, what a fuck she'd make,' he groaned.

'You think so? You think Ludlum's having it?'

'Is that a question?' Jack asked in sarcasm.

'No, more a moan of envy. But you have to remember, she's getting to be a very powerful lady. Power appeals to power.'

Jack got a faraway look in his pale blue eyes. 'What was that wisecrack of Lord Acton's? Power corrupts?'

'Absolute power tends to corrupt absolutely,' the demon note-taker recalled.

They both fell silent. Jack looked at his watch. 'Christ, I'm off.' He grabbed the bill and scanned it at some length. 'Mine today.' He continued to examine its fine print.

'It's always yours.' Pat snatched it away from him.

'Okay.' Jack flipped through his pocket diary. 'On the proviso we lunch this time next week. I'll have some news about the creeps pestering your Dad. Okay?'

'Great.'

Jack said goodbye at the cash desk and went to the toilets.

When he returned, Pat had gone. He went up to the cashier. 'Can I speak to Larry?'

'Yes, Mr Pierce.'

The manager arrived in under a minute. 'Yes, Mr Pierce?'

'Does Bridges have a hairy waiter called Sam? His name was printed on the receipt.'

'Yes, Mr Pierce.'

Jack glanced out the nearest big window at the nearest bridge, the original linkage between Brooklyn and Manhattan, a complex triumph of wrought-iron and riveting. Poems had celebrated it. Lovers had immortalised it. It had, Jack felt sure, witnessed even shabbier events than the one he was now to unfold.

'Listen up, Larry. I don't want to hear he's working his way through medical school. I'm not interested if his dear old mother has myasthenia gravis. I'm lunching here this time next week. I want to hear he's no longer on the staff. Okay?'

The response came slowly enough to seem reluctant. A long, heavy glance carried across the room from the manager to the corner table where Big Mimmo was lunching. If something telepathic flashed between the two, Jack couldn't spot it.

Finally, Larry coughed discreetly. 'Yes, Mr Pierce.'

Twenty

'I'm only five years younger,' Enid Bart's producer-director told Pat Rossi, 'but Enid's from the classic era of TV. I'm the new grunge-fringe.'

She, too, was named Pat, a smiley candy-doll out of Vassar with a cropped-straw boy's crew cut and tin Mexican earrings that scraped her shoulders.

She first made Pat Rossi a herbal tea which he found disgusting. Then she tried to sell him a small vial of homeopathic aphrodisiac that also shrank the prostate. Now she was persuading him to do a TV show of his own.

'I've watched you, Pat. Sexy but non-threatening. You could be this channel's male Enid.'

The tiny studios occupied slope-roofed attic floors of an elderly but tall building on Madison and 53rd Street. It had once housed a pioneer station, now long gone. But the Eiffel-like transmitter tower still remained.

This do-it-yourself channel now existed mostly on mail-order and due-bill advertising for local restaurants and clubs, its staff pared down to union minima for camera operators and sound engineers.

When the studio clock hit two-thirty a.m., Enid signed off and the channel went to syndication tapes more ancient than 'I Love Lucy', creaky routines of Milton Berle or Morry Amsterdam. Enid scooped up the male Pat and left.

Later, after a major financial scam, female Pat disappeared. Six months thereafter she surfaced on a Spanish-speaking Caribbean island doing a Learn English show while moonlighting as the Generalissimo's Numero Uno Candy-Doll. She seemed, as always, able to do two things at once as long as one of them was piracy.

This night, however, Enid took male Pat to one of her late places near Lincoln Center called Chapter Eleven. It was a night-owl roost for eggheads, reform-Democrat journalists, maverick ad and p.r. people, closemouthed millionaires who operated their own portfolios and other perpetual Volvo owners and denizens of the West Side.

It seemed to Pat that they all made a thing of trashing consumerism. All shirts and skirts were pre-wrinkled non-press. Nobody bought things to stun the eye. Nobody evaluated themselves in terms of the auto they owned or the designer logo on their clothes. 'Natural' was the facade they worked hardest to create. Probably all owned stock in Gap.

In this curious time-warp, Pat saw enough beards to bankrupt Gillette, accompanied by heavy-smoking women who made ferocious Bogart faces when they forcefully exhaled. From things his father had told him and Eileen, it all might have been a scene out of the late 1950s.

Politically, Enid explained as she slowly reduced a small cheese omelette to shreds, the core of the Chapter Eleven crowd was a non-left left. Those in this category had inherited a global disappointment with communism but still loathed the sickness of their society. Unfortunately, no new antacid had yet replaced those teachings of Marx that had cast such long shadows over history.

'The fellow with the orangey beard,' Pat murmured.

'Teaches history at Columbia. That's his wife with him. She runs a consultancy that tells you what colours to wear.'

'Is that why she's dressed in ninja black?'

Enid's hoot of laughter drew no attention. A hi-fi amplifier with bass boost was taking everyone through Mahler's Tenth, chorus and all. 'The fat lady in the Paisley schmatta?'

'*New York Times* fashion, you total Philistine.'

'And the runt with her.'

'Hubby does a tremendously influential Contrarist column for a financial journal when he isn't trotting under her feet licking them.'

'And that striking couple in the corner?'

'Conrad Courtney III, prematurely white-haired property person de luxe. Melinda Courtney, oil heiress.'

'Couples, couples, couples. How do people describe us?'

Her wide mouth produced a clown's upturned grin. 'There goes Pat Rossi with one of his sexbomb-bimbos.'

'I have a hunch I'm unknown in this precinct, while you shape up as Queen of the Hive.'

'On the con– '

'This is the hot heart of the Enid Bart network, the people who feed you gossip, forecasts, new ideas, shifting slants. No one broadcaster, even as brainy as you, could do it alone. I'm looking at your back-up, right?'

'Plus heavyweights like Dan Ludlum.'

'That was a pleasant surprise, seeing you at Bridges.'

'He's your Number One booster.' She finished mangling her omelette and gave him a long, firm stare. 'Yes,' she said then, 'these are my pals. We either went to school together, or once worked together. If we have kids they go to the same schools. On Sundays we play baseball or touch football in Central Park. We go to the same concerts. We commit adultery only with each other. We summer in the same Hampton. We gossip endlessly.'

'And self-perpetuate the network,' Pat added. 'The p.r. lady introducing a new client can count on the journalist. The fund-raising politician can count on the property baron.'

'And the TV snoop counts on all of them, yes.'

Suddenly she took his hand in hers. Her fingers, long and wiry, had a strange coolness for someone whose thoughts were voiced with such warmth. 'You're a reader of faces, like me. That's why your own is so patently honest. I read it almost with my eyes shut. Give it up.'

'Give up my face?'

'You and I are not going to have an affair.'

'Now you tell me.'

'You're too damned honest and I'm too damned busy. I don't have time for a serious love affair. And that's the only kind you'd have, isn't it?'

He made a silent whistling gesture, as if letting off steam. 'Just because I'm crazy about you? Just because I think you're the most attractive person I know? That makes you think I want to have an affair?' He shifted his hand so it was holding hers. 'I bet your feet are just as cold.'

'Pat.' She paused as if searching for the right words, something she never did. 'I lie as much as the next person. But not when the next person is you. You're intimidating. For me, that's a rare, unsettling quality. Your buddy, Pierce, is another matter entirely.'

'He's also under your spell.'

'Jack Pierce? Mr Wrong?'

Pat grimaced. 'What is it about Jack? Women whose standards are perfectly normal, even relaxed, suddenly upgrade to Mother Superior purity at the mention of his name.'

She smiled. 'Then there's hope for women after all.'

Twenty-One

His Nevada divorce having come through in record time, Dan Ludlum and his Texas bride-to-be immediately sent out their wedding invitations ... by fax.

It was a simple message if you could decode it: 'Mr and Mrs Ransom Caldoon (bride's parents, alive and well at age seventy, parents of seven) take pleasure in announcing the marriage of their daughter Margaret-Anne Caldoon Headley (sprightly, rich, forty-ish, mother of three) to Mr Daniel David Jonathan Ludlum Jr. (on the awesome cusp of seventy but looking no more than $59.95, father of four).'

The place was Athens Landing, Connecticut. The guest list numbered a discreet one hundred, a mere dozen being Hollywood names the press would not allow to languish unphotographed. Hotels near the Landing were instantly booked out. Guests assigned bedrooms within the Pierce island enclave felt about the way a Nobel candidate must feel when he gets the phone call from Stockholm.

The best man was to be Paul Pierce.

Considering the Streisands and Redfords being bunked down inside the enclave, it was a mark of distinction that Miss Eileen Rossi and Mr Patrick Rossi were assigned a room with two beds. 'Promise not to snore,' Eileen muttered as she unpacked her overnight bag.

'Promise not to flash,' Pat responded in brotherly fashion.

'The man who gave me my bath till I was five years old? Afraid of a brief flash or two?'

He lay back on his bed. 'Our family has always been deep into bodily functions. Considering how we have to service

Pop's requirements. How sure are we that Miss Strang can handle him for forty-eight hours without us?'

'Nurse Strang,' Eileen corrected him. She had kicked off her shoes and was hunched up around a pillow, looking as small as a child. 'She knows former Detective Sergeant Michael Rossi's bottom inside out. Big Brother, Jack's warned me: one of the guests here is a lady he's planning to marry.'

'Miss Coventry Hascomb?' Pat frowned. 'Only offspring and sole heir to Hasco Re-Investment? What sort of advice are you after? Should you spill hot tea down her bosom? As long as it looks accidental, yes.'

'Jack tells me her nickname is Cunty.'

Pat gave her a long look. 'As far as Jack's concerned, that's every woman's nickname.'

In the vast dining-room of Main House, Dan Ludlum and Madge Headley were going over last-minute details with the Pierce caterer. It was late. Jack, standing by to mediate, yawned discreetly. He made three Scotch high-balls. When the caterer left, he and the happy pair lifted their glasses in a silent nightcap.

Ludlum sipped long and hard. 'You'd think a little thing like a wedding wouldn't throw me any more.'

'Honey, look at it thissa way.' Madge sipped briefly and put her drink aside. 'We don' nevah haiv t'do this agin.'

The strangely ominous undertone sent each of them into thought. 'Jack, I just must tell you your family are angels? Your Daddy has done us the greatest favuh? And your Mommuh. I mean, promising to sing "Because"? I mean . . . I mean . . .' She gave up with a helpless shrug.

In silence they all drank again. Ludlum's glass was now empty, but neither of the others looked more than barely touched. It was the bridegroom-to-be who finally broke the silence. 'Jack, have you had a heart-to-heart with Madge yet?'

'She already knows where babies come from.'

Ludlum appealed to Madge Headley. 'You remember me mentioning the kind of service Jack's firm can offer.'

'Ultra-private?' Madge recalled. 'Like a Swiss bank on

Mercan soil? Where money's concerned, Dearest, my mem'ry works full-time.' She turned to give head-on attention to the younger man. She had always been a handsome woman in a headstrong male way. Now she seemed to soften. Her voice went from bray to croon. 'Baby, have your smarties send my smarties in Dallas a pictuah of what haypins to my personal account in, say, one year.'

'Leaving your Headol holdings out of it?' Jack asked.

'That's right.'

'Is that wise?' Ludlum interrupted.

'This Pierce et Cie,' Madge pronounced with a flat accent. 'It's what, a couple of years old?'

Jack nodded. 'You're right. Don't put all your eggs in such a new basket. I will get my financial thrill just rooting around in your old golf sox.'

'Dear Jack. What a sexy idea.'

'Planting a seed.'

'My, yes.'

'Making it sprout.'

'Ooh. Mercy!'

'And then reaping the harvest.'

Madge's face glowed. 'Give me that old time religion, Hubby. If he's good for the Prophet Daniel then he's good enough for me.'

'Sing "Because"?' Serene Wainright Pierce exclaimed. 'Are you insane?'

Paul Pierce sat on the edge of their great king-sized bed. He wore only his underwear briefs. 'I like that song.'

'It's old-hat, cornball, lower-middle-class and utterly laughable when applied to two crocks joining in yet another marriage.' Her voice had the true carrying power of an opera singer, belting upwards from the diaphragm and making one particular window-glass buzz in sympathy.

She was wearing a pale heliotrope peignoir which she now discarded in a gesture of disdain. Her husband watched her breasts jut out against her paler nightgown with the strap top, hardly more than a slip. In the half dark of their bedroom, he massaged his groin.

'It's as vulgar as Gounod's "Ave Maria",' Serena went on. She unwound her long dark hair from its top knot. It fell about her shoulders. 'Only somebody from Texas would claim to be thrilled by it.'

'So. What would you rather sing?'

A mischievous grin seemed to break her up for a moment. 'How about "Get Me to the Church on Time"? No. No, wait. How about the bridegroom's anthem: "When I'm Not Near the Girl I Love I Love the Girl I'm Near"?'

'Come on, Reeny, be serious.'

She stood in front of a wall that was one huge mirror, brushing her hair into place for its nightly rest. She saw her husband get up from the bed and then, oddly, seem to disappear.

'I don't know. Kern is always a major tear-jerker. What about "All the Things You Are"? There's a chord change in the release that knocks them dead when a mezzo hits it.'

'Kern it is, then.'

She realised he was behind her, on his knees, lifting her mini-nightgown. 'And it's quite appropriate for a marriage,' she added then. 'Well...' She felt his tongue, hot and damp. 'Well, what isn't?'

By midnight almost everyone inside the enclave – celebrity, family, friend – had gone to bed. Paul Pierce listened to his wife's steady, heavy breathing.

Air was her milieu, he thought. As a soprano she shaped and sang it. Now, after having had his sexual favours for the past half hour, she was inhaling and exhaling great drafts of her post-coital breath. She was, to be frank, snoring.

And he had another damned hard-on. Teenager! What the h–? The emerald neon light on the green telephone began to wink slowly, silently. Pierce lifted it and muttered: 'Hold on.'

He rolled off the bed and put the call on hold, then moved into his bathroom-dressing room and closed the door. 'Hello?'

'Mr Pierce, sir. Red alert.'

He recognised the voice of Carmine Onofrio, his chief of security on the night side. 'She must've slipped in by boat is all I can figure.'

'She?'

'That Applebaum broad. Herb Applebaum? His frau.'

'She's somewhere here on the Landing? How do you know? Has she been seen? Talked to?'

'Johnnie Sporco spotted her on B Wharf. This is a big broad. She pushed Sporco in the drink.'

'Do you have her on infra-red surveillance?'

'Now and then.'

'Get her into our lockup cage. Carmine, we have a wedding tomorrow, for God's sake.'

'Right. If she gives me trouble . . .?'

'No rough stuff. Mace. Stun gun. Give her a needle of tranquilliser. Gag and chain her. Capeesh?'

'No rough stuff.' He hung up.

Replacing the telephone, Pierce moved to a walk-in closet devoted to surveillance equipment. His breathing had quickened. He switched on the monitors linked to infra-red cameras dotted about the enclave. After a while one showed a Jeep approaching.

Video without sound can be frustrating. In this case it was scarey. He was gasping now. Carmine jumped out of the Jeep. Abruptly, the woman was being dragged forward and handcuffed to the iron arm-rest of the Jeep's near seat.

Paul Pierce sat there, fondling his penis. Gretchen Applebaum had looked raddled, tormented, sexy. He smiled.

The caterer had provided a long breakfast buffet with bakery, coffee urns and steam table of bacon, sausage and scrambled eggs. Alcohol burners flickered brilliant sky blue.

Jack Pierce arrived at six a.m., as the caterers were setting up. He poured himself black coffee, grabbed a pecan schnecken and left for his Jeep.

He had had a rotten night. Both his all-time girlfriend and his putative fiancée had been installed under one roof. Eileen he couldn't visit, not without getting Pat riled up. Cunty was sharing a bedroom with her very social mother, Mrs Maude St Helier Coventry Hascomb.

As a duenna, Maude was fierce. So Jack's night had been spent alone, dozing off. Dreams were troubled, spotty, frightening. Men moving about in the dark. Screams, choked off.

He had never been happier than taking an early morning drive around Circumference Road. The sun was not yet up over the horizon but the eastern sky, looking out to sea, was brightening. A clear day for a magnificent wedding.

Suddenly, Carmine Onofrio with his pug-dog face sprang out into the road, holding up his hand like a traffic cop. 'Jack. Jack.' His voice was curiously low, almost as if he wanted no one else to hear him.

Jack braked the Jeep. 'Morning, Carmine. Wie gehts?'

The heavy-shouldered little man, once a welterweight contender, sat down on the Jeep's front seat. 'Drive, Jack.'

They drove to a small shed deep in the fir forest where intruders and occasional drunks were kept overnight. Carmine Onofrio glanced around before unlocking the shed door.

Inside were two cell-cages. One was empty. In the other . . .

Jack's face winced sideways as he tried to avoid the sight. She had been chained to the bench. Her legs had been pulled wide, most of her clothes ripped off. There were bites.

A nipple had been gnawed off. Part of her pubic mound. The blood had dried darkly on her and in puddles beneath her.

'Carmine!'

'It's how I found her fifteen minnits ago. They's no heartbeat.' He sounded as if he were crying. 'I locked her in myself at one a.m., sleeping like a baby.'

'Why did – ? Who is she?'

Carmine shut the shed door and locked them inside. 'Jack, we got maybe halfa nour to get her off the island and lost somewheres. Jack, you're my owney hope.'

Jack looked down at the pecan schnecken in his hand. He gagged and started to vomit.

'Jack, shape up. She has to disappear. Tomorrow, maybe, your Dad can figure out the next step.'

Jack fought back his nausea, 'Why my Dad?'
But Carmine avoided his glance.

When Serena Wainwright Pierce sang, her voice had a rich, husky tone that raised goose bumps on Pat Rossi. He'd've given anything for his Pop to be here.

Everyone looked terrific, Pat thought. The bride had managed to look demure. Eileen in a pale silvery dress looked like a wood sprite. The TV crews were well-behaved. The Hollywood people looked professionally pleased, possibly at not having to hear 'Because'.

Beside Dan Ludlum stood the best man, Paul Pierce, looking suitably grave, yet terribly in command. The rest of the Pierce family looked great . . .

No Jack? Fine time to cop a sneak.

Pat raised himself on tiptoe, searching the room for his best friend. But, incredibly, he wasn't there.

Twenty-Two

In fact, Jack reminded himself, everyone had an alibi. He alone had none. It now being the day security shift, Carmine Onofrio was long off-duty and theoretically home in bed.

'And Johnnie Sporco is a little simple. He never knew what hit him,' Carmine recalled. 'He'll remember somebody shoving him in the drink. But I sent him right home to dry off. I doubt he even knows it was a dame dumped him.'

'So you're the prime patsy?' Jack asked, not bothering to be diplomatic.

Carmine's punched-in face looked tearful again. 'He said, you know, take it easy on her. No rough stuff. She got a needle of pentothal and was sleeping as happy as a child. He said take it easy... and see what happens? But I swear on my mother's grave, Jack, I had nothin, nothin to do with whacking her.'

'He?'

They worked well as a team, silent and thorough. Carmine scrubbed down the detention cell with trisodium phosphate crystals while Jack wrapped Gretchen Applebaum's mangled corpse in a waterproof tarp.

He hadn't done much physical work – outside of a gym – for a long time. In denim, without a Jack Pierce broad-striped shirt or self-confident tie, without arm garters, with his centre-parted hair falling loosely about like a mop-head, he suddenly looked boyish, far too young to have such adult work as cover-up thrust on him.

They spirited Gretchen off the Landing in a covered pickup truck with Carmine driving and Jack crouched down out of sight. That was all the alibi he had, that no one had seen him.

'No rough stuff, he said,' Carmine echoed. 'Mr Pierce.'

'He was in on it from the start?'

'From the start.'

'But . . .' Jack almost gagged again getting the words out. 'But at the finish . . .?'

'Some maniac. She was raped.'

'How can y–?'

'Pussy oozing come. When it dries it has like a shine to it.'

They had parked the pick-up in the extreme interior of Makepeace Wilderness State Park, a small forced conifer forest thirty miles from the Landing. Tarp removed to help animals feed on her, Gretchen was loosely covered with year-old pine needles and clumps of humus, what Carmine called 'the old country way'.

Jack glanced at his watch. 'Ceremony's just over. Reception's begun. I have to get back.' He glanced at the denim jacket and jeans he'd pulled on early this morning.

'I run you back.'

'Shit you will, Carmine. Run me to the nearest train station. I'll find a cab. You have any money?'

Grateful for the reprieve, Carmine dug deep and produced two twenties. 'So whadda I do at midnight? Check in like always?'

'Like always.' They got back in the pick-up and drove slowly out of the park. 'If we're lucky,' Jack said aloud but really to himself, 'the crows and foxes and wild cats will finish the job for us. Whoever Herb Applebaum is, he may or may not report her missing. I'll try and fill in details from Dad.'

'Yeah.' A long pause. 'You do that.'

'And, Carmine, nobody ever said the Pierces were a bunch of pikers. How many bambini is it now, five?'

'And one in the oven.'

'Let's just say none of them will ever have to worry where the money's coming from for college. Or a good job. You know what I'm saying?' The two men shook hands on the bargain.

By the time the cab left him at Main House on the Landing, the reception was in full swing. Jack dashed upstairs, changed and returned to the guests in spotless, well-pressed formal attire, morning coat, white tie.

He had centre-parted and fix-sprayed his hair. It glittered as he moved through the throng, shaking hands, kissing cheeks. From having been an urchin in denims he was once again the very model of a modern major banker.

'Where the hell have you been?' his father demanded in a chilling undertone. His teeth produced the dark-stained grimace of a meat-eater.

The image of Gretchen Applebaum's savaged vagina gave Jack a nasty turn. 'I've been with Mrs Applebaum.'

His father blinked. Just once. 'You should find yourself a better class of companion.'

'Oh, you knew the lady?'

'Start mingling with the guests.'

'You can't just finesse – '

'I said mingle, damn it.'

Jack produced a beautiful, dutiful smile. 'How'd my favourite mezzo do?' he asked, switching sideways to greet Pat Rossi.

'Thrilling as always. What kept you?' His best friend's dark, handsome face, green eyes bright with concern, watched him as if he were back from some terrible accident. But to Jack it seemed as if Pat and his father stared gloomily at him. Feckless Jack.

'What is it they say?' Jack mused aloud. 'When in doubt, blame the missing.'

'The missing,' Paul Pierce added, 'or the dead.'

However other working stiffs returned to Manhattan that evening, Jack had laid on a Citation II for himself, the Rossis and Barbra Streisand with a companion. The latter two managed to sleep through the entire flight back to La Guardia Marine.

'Poor Miss Holcomb will lose all her teeth,' Eileen remarked to her brother, mostly for Jack's benefit.

'Hascomb is my fiancée's name. Hascomb.'

'She's anorexic and God knows what else. When she retches food, she damages her gums with her own hydrochloric acid. Give her five years and she'll need implants.'

'Jack can afford it,' Pat explained patiently. 'Can't you, Jack?'

Jack said nothing. He was watching as the Citation dropped to five thousand feet over the Westchester County area. Ahead the Bronx and Queens sparkled in the night like giant multifaceted zircons.

'I guess nothing's too good for, uh, Miss Holcomb,' Eileen surmised.

'Hascomb. Call her Cunty,' Jack growled. 'Everybody else does.'

'Not her mother.'

'In her day she was Cunty, too.'

Suddenly, as if kicked in the butt, Jack burst into hysterical laughter. 'I get a real high out of an old-fashioned wedding, don't you?'

'Was that what it was?' Pat wanted to know.

'You know the last thing the bride told me as she and Dan flew off to Cannes?' Jack's sandy colouring grew bright red with anger, but his voice went totally Ivy League lockjaw. 'She told me she'd called her Dallas bankers and told them to expect an official fax from Pierce et Cie.'

'You've got her account?' Pat asked.

'Isn't that charming? It was the most important thing on her mind as she left for her honeymoon.' His face had gone dead white. 'Don't you love an old-fashioned wedding?'

'I just wish Miss Charming,' Eileen put in, 'had thrown me her bouquet.'

The three of them started cackling but, out of respect for their sleeping guests, shut down quickly. Jack reached inside the faded denim jacket he had been wearing that morning. He made a horrible face and slowly brought to light a crushed, demented-looking pecan schnecken.

'Did I tell you? This is not a dinner flight?' He bit off a third of the pastry and passed it to Eileen. She took a bite and handed it to her brother, who finished what was left.

'You guys,' Jack said. 'Did I ever tell you guys I love you?' His words were distorted by the pastry in his mouth.

His eyes went vague and teary. And, suddenly, he was sobbing bitterly, helplessly, as if his heart would break. He dashed into the toilet of the plane and closed the door behind him.

'Now what?' Pat wondered.

'I think there was something holy about that schnecken. I think we just participated in a part of the nuptial mass priests never tell you about.'

'I've never seen him so upset.'

'Was it something to do with the bride?'

'Nonsense.' Pat turned to watch the closed door of the toilet. 'It takes something titanic to shake up Jack.'

'And some day,' Eileen sang softly, '*I'll know that moment divine, When all the things he is are mine.*'

Nobody wants to be seen breaking down in huge gasps of total despair, when your heart requires more oxygen than exists in the whole world. Especially not seen by influential Hollywood types who could easily wake up. But most especially not in front of your closest friend and his sister, your forever-sweetheart.

But that was the problem, right there. Jack Pierce sat on the toilet seat and stared at a wall placard in four languages imploring him not to flush his sanitary napkins down the plumbing.

The problem was that only somebody as close to him as Eileen or Pat could help him out. And he could never, ever tell them.

Christ, it wasn't his secret in the first place. It involved Carmine but it was his father's secret, something toxic and frightening that had leaked out of that end of the business. A character flaw you simply couldn't talk away. But the fucking amazing thing was that his father *was* going to finesse it.

Jack could stand a lot of abuse from the man to whom he

owed so much. Any Italian son would understand that. But to force him to clean up his father's sick, scarey garbage, faultlessly, beyond the possibility of detection, was too much.

The problem wasn't the cover-up itself. Jack felt sure he and Carmine had improvised that fairly well. No, the problem was that Paul Pierce had abdicated.

He wasn't playing the role of psychotic perpetrator, witness or even innocent bystander. He barely even knew the woman. Therefore he was abdicating other roles as well: insane mastermind, coldblooded manager, conspirator. So his son and his security chief were left hanging by their thumbs.

Who, me? No, them.

The heartless gall of him! Doing this to his own son. And just, Jack thought, when the new bank was starting to do well. When people like Ludlum were feeding it big business. Just when it needed Jack's total attention, to dip him in such a deadly bucket of shit.

Jack could feel the tightness in his ears grow much sharper. He groaned. The 'Fasten Seat Belts' sign was flashing. It was time to face the music.

He gave the toilet a flush, simply because it might have been expected by his audience. He got back to his seat next to Eileen and patted her hand. Could you imagine asking a girl like her into a family like the Pierces? As a lover, he was tainted. As a reassuring seatmate, he was grotesque.

He looked like death, and he knew it.

Twenty-Three

A year, which is normally assumed to begin with the first day of January, can be delineated in other ways. The year 1991, for example, for the purpose of tracking the soul of Jack Pierce, could be said to have begun with the June weekend when the Headley-Ludlum wedding took place.

There are several official photographs. The first, of the pair alone, was the normal cabinet-sized double portrait taken inside the chapel at Athens Landing, with several potted ferns on either side.

The second was grander. Taken on the broad stairs that lead up to the verandah and entrance of the main house, it presented more than twenty people, all of them Headleys or Ludlums or Pierces. Plus the minister.

Everyone in the photo got a colour copy. It was serviced in black-and-white to local newspapers in Connecticut and Texas.

The third was truly grandiose, taken of the same view and from the same angle but with a panoramic lens. Twenty more people now intermingle with family. Most are show biz faces.

This appeared as a double-page spread in the next issue of *Vanity Fair*. Eileen and Pat Rossi appeared in this grandiose version.

But, of course, Jack Pierce was in none of them. It was disturbingly like a forecast of bad luck. Until then all had gone well for Jack, in particular Pierce et Cie, his boutique merchant bank. His self-esteem and arrogance ran high. His health had easily survived the long working days and nights.

His client list, never too big, kept growing in importance. His courting of various IRS and SEC middle-management types bore fruit. His courting of legislators, too. His courting of daughters of the rich had progressed to two engagements, one called off.

His downfall began with the Ludlum marriage.

By mid-July the happy couple had returned to Manhattan and then to their cottage in Point O'Woods, Fire Island. Families like the Ludlums always referred to their beach or summer place as a cottage. This one had five bedrooms, two parlours and a library the size of a barn.

In the nineteenth century, once the railroad had reached this far east, a chunk of barrier beach off Long Island had been bought by Trinity Episcopal Church, guardian of souls in what was now Manhattan's financial district. It built and leased frame beach homes to members of the congregation.

Dan's grandfather Octavius Ludlum had been a senior partner handling clients in the ready-to-wear business. Making uniforms for the Union Army had been a watershed in American capitalism: businessmen realised there were also super-profits in peace, Federal contracts, secured by political lawyers like Octavius.

On Octavius's death before World War I, Harold Ludlum, Dan's political lawyer-father, illegally renegotiated the family's Point O'Woods lease to carry it into the twenty-first century.

This was Madge's first experience with the padlocked Point O'Woods regimen, a Trinity infrastructure of social events, sailing classes for the young, endless tennis courts, thrift shops for the passing on of decent Wasp clothing at bargain Wasp prices and, in either direction, adjoining communities of pagans from advertising and the arts, many neither Episcopalian nor heterosexual.

Some, in fact, who bore Jewish or Italian names, were from the same garment industry that had given Octavius his first big killing. Later such guests came from TV and the films. Once they were admitted through the sturdy Point O'Woods gate, they mingled like anyone else.

This was not a public community. Technically, a stranger

could wander in off the broad, white sand of the Atlantic beach, but before long would be asked to account for his presence.

On Labor Day weekend at the start of September, Jack Pierce and Pat Rossi lay on *chaises-longues* on the verandah deck of the Ludlum cottage.

'Are you eating?' Pat Rossi asked.

They examined each other's bodies for a long moment. 'I suppose,' Jack admitted, 'it's being engaged to Cunty that does it. She hardly eats.'

'You really getting married?'

'Next June, if I live that long.'

Pat scowled at him. 'Any reason you might not? Cancer of the wallet? Withering of the brain under Miss Holcomb's management?'

'It's fucking Hascomb!' Jack snapped. 'You and Eileen keep playing this dumb game. Hascomb. Hascomb. Hasc–' He stopped himself and laughed helplessly. 'I'm going right off the deep end, Patrick. Start composing a eulogy.'

'I promise never to mispronounce the hallowed name of the woman you love.'

'Ah, crap. It's a merger, not a marriage. Every time my Dad thinks about Hasco Re-Investment his chin starts to dribble.'

'How is he?'

'You know he's marrying Paulie to a fifty-year-old high-up in Citibank? Did I tell you? My little Paulie. Welded for life to some dumbass banker? And Cummings is already dating an ugly girl he met at Harvard who comes out of Basel's number one pharmaceutical family. None of us lead real lives. We just do what Poppa tells us to do.'

Both of them were silent for a moment as Madge Ludlum returned from the beach with her youngest daughter, whose size and figure reminded both young men of Didi. Pat sighed heavily. 'I still dream about her.'

'Didi? Have you ever heard from her?'

'Never.'

They lapsed into silence again. 'Tell me,' Jack murmured,

'do you still do those ledgers of injustice? I always thought they were a waste of time.'

'I'm on my eleventh ledger. And they're only a waste of time,' he added in a sharper tone, 'if you don't give a rat's ass about the world you live in. If you assume that all social contracts are bullshit and we have no responsibility for the old and the sick and the stressed-out and the used-up and people who can't speak our language or are too drugged to speak at all.'

'Jesus! Save me! I keep forgetting I'm talking to the son of a martyr-saint.'

'Since you're such a fan of those ledgers, here's the latest news: I'm including anything from the press that hits a nerve. White-collar crime for which the big boys go free.'

'You're downright dangerous, Patrick. What're you going to do with your ledgers?'

'I was thinking of asking Pierce et Cie to publish them.'

Jack emitted a wild cackle and lay silent for a while. Then: 'D'j'ever follow up,' he began in a drowsy voice, 'on that Artificial Intelligence crap? S'your Dad using it?'

Pat was silent for a long time. 'That's what I call cast-iron nerve. You were supposed to find out who implanted a threat on the software disk. You never did.'

'But, look – '

'Don't "but look" me, Jocko. You – '

Jack quickly interrupted: 'I kept hitting dead ends. I never did get a name. But your Dad's okay, right? Nothing happened to him as a result.'

'And therefore you're forgiven?'

'Lighten up, Patrick. We are both,' Jack said slowly, as if repeating an ancient adage, 'sons of dominating fathers. Yours tries to avenge himself. Weirdos try frightening him. We know he doesn't frighten. What could you do to a man you'd already brought right down to the edge of an open grave? How could you frighten such a man? My father is a different story . . .'

His voice died away as if fingers had tightened around his windpipe. Pat eyed him. 'He's okay, isn't he?'

'I'm the wrong person to ask.'
'Meaning?'
'Meaning we don't see each other much.'
'But isn't he one of your bank's trustees?'
'Does that mean I have to be polite to him?'

The Connecticut winter had not been very severe but snow had covered the ground well into March. In April of 1992 forest rangers started their spring inventory of downed trees. In Makepeace Wilderness State Park the review was handled by helicopter.

The maintenance budget having been cut severely, the decision was not to log out dead trees but to leave the forest alone for another year. The wilderness area had few visitors anyway. Most people preferred crowded parks with lots of radios going and other kids to play with theirs.

Carmine Onofrio mailed a small news clipping about it to Jack in Manhattan. His first son, Duane, had just entered Holy Cross at an annual cost of forty thousand dollars. A Frontier Foundation student.

The clipping reached Jack in June, the day he married Cunty. The next morning, at their honeymoon hotel off the Georgia coast, he telephoned Carmine Onofrio in Summerville, Connecticut.

No one answered.

Twenty-Four

'Fractals,' former Detective Sergeant Michael Rossi explained. He sat, propped up by pillows, on his sofa in front of the TV and computer.

His old pal Timmy Groark sat in an easy chair opposite him. Unlike Rossi, Groark had let middle age run him to a beer belly, a Buddha chest, a bull neck and forearms the circumference of five-gallon jugs. All this teetered on boyish legs and butt, remains of a once athletic youth.

'Frack what?'

'It's a maths thing, Timmy. No Irishman would be caught dead understanding it. It's the way my AI software operates.'

Slowly, but without grimacing, Rossi managed to manoeuvre his left hand palm-up. He made his thumb and forefinger vibrate to catch Groark's attention. 'You know how you ask yourself: "Is it yes or is it no?" It's like tossing a coin?'

'Heads or tails?'

'Right. AI keeps asking questions.' His forefinger flopped weakly left, right, left. 'It's trial and error, Timmy. You ask a question often enough and you build a pattern of yesses and noes into a system. If you did it yourself it'd take years, a lifetime. The computer does it in under ninety seconds.'

'And wha'd'y'get? Garbage?'

'Mostly.'

'Shit, Mike, I don't need no computer to come up with garbage.'

'But life *is* garbage. Like the fella says, you put garbage in, you get garbage out. Do it long enough, keep following down every blind alley, keep up the trial and error and eventually garbage gives you a brand new truth.'

'Come on, Mike, life's too short for that.'

'Life is exactly that. Even a good Catholic knows we all start as tiny worms inside our mothers. When the planet was young, all humans developed from worms. Now, from worm to a superior being like Timothy Aloysius Groark takes an awful lot of trial and error.'

Groark's tight mouth twisted into a grin. 'So tell me, Einstein, what have you tracked down about a worm like Vinnie?'

Rossi's glance went to the digital clock on his VCR. 'Mother of God, it's seven o'clock, Eileen was due back here at six. So is Pat, come to think of it.'

Groark gave his own wristwatch a fearsome frown. 'I can hang in till one of them gets here.'

'How are your kids doing?'

The ex-detective, still assigned to the District Attorney's office, produced a shrug of his massive shoulders. 'Tim Junior's just produced my first grandchild. Marie and Yvonne . . .' He repeated the gigantic shrug. 'You know, girls nowadays aren't that eager to get hitched and pregnant. Marie's just got her PhD in psychology. You can now call her Doctor Groark. And Yvonne's doing great down in Washington at Treasury.'

'You're right. Girls nowadays aren't that eager to get hitched and pregnant.' Rossi's voice had grown tired. He seemed to condense slightly, like a cat. 'Speaking of which.'

A key rattled in the front door and Eileen entered quickly, her heels making angry cracking sounds. 'Evening all. Evening Dad. Evening Officer Groark.' She put her tiny wrists together. 'I'll go quietly, so I will.'

Chapter Eleven, the eating place near Lincoln Center, rarely got going before concerts and plays ended at ten-thirty and diners arrived. It usually hit its stride after players showed up at midnight. Enid Bart didn't get there till three a.m.

She and Pat Rossi hadn't seen each other in some time. This was a Manhattan pattern everyone understood. One might consider oneself a close friend but months might elapse without meeting or even talking on the phone. Careers came first, so people led lives full of stops and starts.

This was especially true in television, Pat reminded himself, where flavours of the week were common. For a while someone was seen all over the tube and in tabloid feature stories. Then he or she disappeared, never to return to public view for years. He supposed, as far as Enid was concerned, that he no longer ranked even as flavour of the moment.

It was that way with his best friend. He really hadn't seen, or talked, or lunched with Jack for some time now. Jack was very busy, he knew. And so was he. But, still . . .

Dan Ludlum had asked Pat when he'd last seen Enid. The verb 'to see', as used by Ludlum, had its usual code sense of sexual congress. 'Are you still seeing Enid?' translated directly, if mistakenly, into 'still yentzing her?'

'Not for some time.'

'You're a big boy,' Ludlum chided. 'Even if it means three a.m., call her for a date.'

It had been that simple. Meeting at Chapter Eleven, she had managed a fleeting kiss before sitting down to her usual omelette. She looked distracted. 'Did you watch me tonight?'

Pat shook his head. 'I catnapped. My sister says you looked gorgeous, vibrant, glorious.'

Enid's narrow face grew pale. 'I know.' She stared down at the omelette and began dismantling it with slashes of a fork. 'I know,' she repeated in a sigh. 'One always does.'

'What's that supposed to mean?'

'I see you got the Hutchison brothers off with an unpremeditated manslaughter rap.'

Pat nodded. 'That's what manslaughter is, unpremeditated. The trick was to work the charge down from Murder One.'

'It reminds me of . . .' There was a long pause, during which she cut the omelette into jagged strips without bringing any to her mouth. 'It's a lot like abortion, isn't it? Unpremeditated is a classic state in our society.'

'A novel ideal.'

131

'But in your personal experience, haven't you found that to be true?'

Pat produced a sheepish grin. 'I haven't had that many girlfriends to know.'

'I've got a friend...'

This time the silence was longer. 'She's got a problem with a tipped womb. A simple d-and-c won't work. And she's very much in the public eye. A litigator, like you, so I can't describe her more specifically.'

She paused long enough to mince the strips of omelette and then move them all to the left side of her plate. 'She needs an abortion?' Pat prompted.

'She needs a very special doctor, because of the tipped business and also because she's in her fourth month. And also because he has to be discreet. Closemouthed. Utterly trustworthy.'

Pat watched her summon a waiter to remove her plate. At no time had she glanced up at him because reducing the omelette to trash had taken all her attention. 'Enid, are you asking me to find a doctor? I don't have any real experi–'

'But you work for a big, discreet firm that –'

'... deals all the time with abortionists? You must –'

'... people like Dan who know exactly the right –'

'... him directly yourself?'

This brought the cross-talk to a halt for a long, painful moment. Then Pat said: 'Enid, it'd be helpful if we could dispense with the friend in trouble.'

Her face went pale again. At some effort she looked directly at him. 'It's the end of my fourth month and Eileen could spot it even on the TV tube. And Jack's no goddamned help at all.'

'Jack!' Pat's green eyes went wide. 'Jack Pierce?'

'I think I warned you I had no time for a serious love affair?' She sipped her glass of water. The ice cubes in it rattled badly. 'So that leaves a non-serious affair. And this inevitably led me to Jack Pierce. Or, perhaps, led him to me.'

Pat took the shock on a sharp intake of air; his diaphragm

banged upwards into his lungs, rendering him breathless. He sat back and tried to soothe his breathing.

'But, look here.'

He stopped, wordless as well. How could he express the sleaze of this? In love with Eileen, married to Cunty, impregnating Enid! No wonder Jack was avoiding him. His business life might be a succession of victories. His private life was a shambles.

'Jack can get a doctor,' he finally managed to say.

'You'd think so, wouldn't you? Some upper-class, utterly discreet Harvard quack? No bent wire clotheshanger for him. And a fee large enough to replace the Jaguar whose ashtrays are dirty?'

Pat watched her, hoping his inner disgust didn't show. You couldn't blame Enid for Jack Pierce being a total prick. And what did it all mean to Big Brother? Wasn't family loyalty the highest loyalty? Wasn't it his duty to arm Eileen with this double-edged weapon?

'Pat, you look as if I just vomited in your lap.'

He smiled wanly. 'It's Eileen,' he blurted out.

'Eileen?'

'She and Jack . . .' He paused, watching the angry tears well up in Enid's eyes.

'The utter bastard.'

Pat nodded. 'I'll get you the right doctor. I'll get on it tomorrow morning. I mean this morning.'

'And you won't tell Jack.'

'I doubt if I'll ever see him again.' His glance focused on the middle distance. 'I always wondered why women never trusted Jack. I mean, never, you know, sort of let him into their private lives.'

'Oh? Look at me.'

'Look at Eileen. But he and I used to keep house with two girls up at Cambridge.' He stopped. 'Never mind. Ancient history.'

'Of course there's always me having the child and hitting Pierce et Cie for a lifetime annuity that would choke a horse.'

'You could change the name of the show to "Babies are Made at Night".'

He watched her mull over the idea, perhaps not for the first time. There was a natural publicity value to slowly bloating up on TV night after night. And then the climax at University Hospital, in glorious colour. And a sick-making contest to name the baby.

'It's precisely the kind of thing Donohue or Geraldo would do if they had been smart enough to be born female.'

'Calculated vulgarity,' Pat mused.

'Don't sneer, Counsellor. We live in an era where taste becomes something that would stink up a barf bag. Everything's on the skids, values, civility, language, morals. We're in a mafia age,' she explained. 'We live by mafia ethos.'

He looked quizzically at her. 'Is this one of your upcoming shows.'

'No.' She paused. 'Yes! Will you be on it?'

'If you explain what you mean by mafia ethos.'

She found a sad bit of omelette on the tablecloth and carefully conveyed it to the ashtray. 'It used to be that one negotiated demands and lived with the agreed compromise. Nowadays, if you have a demand you take a hostage. If you don't get your demand, blow her head off.'

Pat jabbed his forefinger at her. 'If you ran for office you used to argue the issues. Now you get a photo of your opponent naked with some bimbo and blackmail him out of the race.'

'It'll be a great programme.' She paused and her face went sad. 'Pat, I hate to hang this doctor thing on you. You just happened to be across the table when I blew. I'm slightly in awe of you, most of the time.'

'Don't worry. I'll find the right guy.' Without him realising it, his face mimed her sadness. 'That's easy compared to what happens next.'

She took his hand, her fingers icy. 'Telling Eileen?'

There are Summervilles all over the United States. This one, east of Athens Landing, serves as a bedroom village for married staff who live off the island.

Carmine Onofrio raised his family here, twice served as chief of the volunteer fire department, still heads the local Knights of Columbus. For twenty years he has collected the Sunday mass donation before communion.

He hadn't seen Jack Pierce for more than a year but was pleased to find him kneeling beside him at the altar. Father Carey, supplying the blood and body of Christ to such an august guest, was imperturbable. Only a slight smile showed.

Afterwards, on the church portico, Jack murmured. 'I've been trying to call you for a week. I broke off my honeymoon to track you down.'

Carmine took Jack's arm. 'Congratulations on your marriage,' he said as he led them off. 'I was best man in Providence. You know those old-time paesani weddings. They last a week.'

Jack's glance swivelled here and there. 'Where can we go?'

Carmine's Escort, fourteen years old, had developed a faint whistle over the years. He drove to the water's edge, then parked near a clam bar, closed on Sunday. 'My godson up in Providence finely got hitched. You ever hear me talk about Guido Smaldone?'

'No.'

'It's a family from Castellammare del Golfo, like mine. Guido's a good boy.'

'Right. Makepeace Wilderness,' Jack began without preamble. 'Does that clipping you sent me mean that nobody will be messing around in the park?'

'A few private hikers, maybe.'

'So we're still not safe.'

Carmine's pug face, flattened once too often by opponents in the ring, produced a peculiar look, part pride, part cunning. 'In April I paid her a visit.'

'Christ!'

'It's like any grave, Jack. You have to pay your respects now and then and keep it neat.'

'Jesus.'

'The animals did their job, like we figured. Something big messed the bones around. Maybe a brown bear. We goddem back in those woods. Whadya call those docs? Forensics? They look at dental work and bones with a healed break.'

'Oh, God.'

'She never broke no bone. I took the skull back to my workshop and sawed off the upper jaw. I made muesli of it and the lower. When I drove to Providence for the wedding that dental work got scattered over three states. You know what I'm saying?'

There was a moment of fervent silence. Then Jack took Carmine's hand in his and gave it a long, firm squeeze. 'You're a good man, Carmine.'

'Old country training,' his father's head of security told him. 'Let Nature do your work for you. In Castellammare my papa was town gravedigger. He did a nice side income in jaws.'

Twenty-Five

Manhattan supports several periodicals that deal in what seem to be secrets, sexual, financial and political. Believing in them is optional.

Pat Rossi had been given *Whispers* by Maria Jenner. Or at any rate he'd found it on his desk under an ashtray in which one scarlet-smeared cigarette butt sat upright and unrepentant.

It was the current issue, January 1993, but its cover was of the six-month-old wedding of Jack Pierce and the woman *Whispers* coyly referred to as Miss Unnameable Hascomb. Pat held it up to Eileen. 'Anyone we know?' he asked.

As far as Pat knew she hadn't seen Jack for some time. Nor had he. ' "His attorney, everybody's Dan Ludlum, has filed for Mr Pierce's divorce from Miss Unnameable. They were married in a civil ceremony last..." ' Pat looked up from the magazine. 'FU2 is such a hall of rumours, you'd think I'd've heard about this long ago.'

'It's dark outside and I haven't started dinner.'

'Jack's edge is super-privacy. But...' He searched down the page. ' "... originally capitalised at $150 million, privately owned and under no compulsion to publish results, Pierce et Cie today manages assets estimated at $11 billion.

' "While most of this is sequestered abroad, the bank has yet to turn down a client off the street with a paltry bankroll of $100 thousand. Most of these are invested in 'special situation' US scams like mineral rights that yield from 5 to 11 per cent depending on degree of risk." '

He looked up to find his sister not listening to him as she

thumbed through a cooking magazine of recipes. 'Jack's built his rep on abominably *rich* clients.'

'And this will lure homeless tramps with a hundred grand to blow?' Eileen got to her feet and tied on a apron.

'What do I smell?' a faint voice asked from the other room.

'I haven't even started cooking yet.'

'See how sensitive my nose is? Is it meat?'

She and Pat went into the living room. 'It's something new,' Pat assured him. 'It looks like meat.'

'And it tastes like meat,' Eileen added.

'And it's really hydrogenated sawdust,' their father concluded. 'But it's low cholesterol.'

A loud crash, blood-freezing.

The outside window explodes. Slo–o–owly.

Shards of glass scatter around them like buckshot.

Two sage-green fragmentation grenades, detonator rings wired together, float slo–o–owly into the room.

They thud on the sofa next to Michael Rossi.

'Hit the floor!' he shouted. 'We've got ten seconds.'

Neither son nor daughter move. Horrified, they watch their father tilting himself over.

On the strength of two fingers of his left hand, he topples himself sideways to the right.

He falls like a tower.

Like a dynamited smokestack.

His body falls on top of the grenades.

In Pat's eye the scene will last for the rest of his life. The motionless body, smothering the grenade blast.

The father's life for his children's.

Two grenades don't need to have their pin pulled.

The throw has already triggered at least one from the swinging weight of the other.

'It's more than ten seconds,' Eileen's voice is high, wavery. 'I've been counting. Honest.'

'So it is,' her father agreed. His voice sounded as high as hers. 'Eileen, fill a pan with cold water. Pat roll me off the damned grenades. Dunk them in water. We have to assume they're friction detonated, not electrical.'

His eyes seemed to bulge as he watched his son sink the sage-green eggs in water.

'Eileen, sweetheart, get hold of an all-night glazier. We need a plywood window. Paddy, find Jamie Kennan at FBI. We have to assume these are phoneys, not duds. But we need to be sure.'

'Feebs, no cops?'

Their father, still sideways, managed to produce a sobbing kind of nervous laugh. 'My beautiful kids.' His eyes were wet. 'I thought it was a fast goodbye.'

He coughed. 'Sure, the Feebs. Hey, this is Manhattan. Everything's a Federal case.'

Twenty-Six

Technically, it is always possible to run a major American city so honestly that no politician is ever disgraced, either in office or when he returns to private life.

But when that city is New York City, with a vast hidden economy controlled by organised crime, such virtue is odious and unnatural to many voters. Adjustments must take place.

For Republican Mayor Gary Garvey, as his first term reached its fourth year, a series of minor misstatements broke out like pimples. City Hall spokesmen blundered on key topics of racism and abortion. Democratic Party stalwarts began joyously calling Garvey 'fascist.'

He had the misfortune of not belonging to a race or ethnic group victimised by fascism. An old pro would immediately have diagnosed the obvious: a mayoral election was nigh.

But editorial writers and people who appear on chat shows tend to behave as bulls do. They lunge at red flags and waste their energy arguing Garvey's fascist taint.

It was a mark of their professionalism that Enid Bart's pals, often to be found at Chapter Eleven, recognised a feint when they saw one, knew that real issues were being obscured by smoke and wondered how the Democrats were choreographing the fatal goring of poor Garvey.

At this point Dan Ludlum's capework had been fancy enough to avoid being spotted, even by *aficionados*. Much later, as Pat Rossi tried to analyse how all this had gained momentum, he could find no trail between his father and his boss.

Devious Ludlum and Hero-Martyr Michael Rossi? It was

laughable to think of a link. If anything, it began with a change in FU2's structure.

'Patrick,' Ludlum explained. 'I know your father must be proud of your work here for our pro bono clients.'

'Yes, he is.'

'We've been trying to find a way of formalising that work.' Ludlum's spare body seemed to grow longer as he leaned back in his office chair and slowly lifted his heels to the top of his large, uncluttered desk. His great jaw, the lower mandible of a race that included the magnificent British villain, Punch, seemed to jut forward like a scythe.

'Since the poor we have always with us,' he went on magisterially, 'and since there is no way to make a profit on them, let's instead make hay.'

'Hay? You mean ... Brownie points? Kudos? Plaudits?'

Ludlum's grave eyes twinkled in a kindly way. 'I've asked the partners to establish a formal *pro bono publico* division. It's capitalised by our paying clients tithing one per cent per annum of their billing, tax deductible. This sum we devote to protecting the poor. Can you see the editorial in the *Times*?'

Pat kept a straight face. 'Not just kudos for us,' he said solemnly, 'but for our altruistic clients, once thought heartless bastions of big business, now shown to have a heart as big as the Ritz.'

'Uh, yes.' Ludlum gave him a pained sideways glance, as he did all sarcasm. 'I'll have our talented publicity lady use that in the press kit.' When he paused heavily, Pat realised this formal recognition of his effort over recent years was not Ludlum's prime target.

'There's more?'

This time Ludlum awarded a pained frown to the remark. 'I don't think you appreciate what this elevation in your status means. But, as a father, I know how your father will take it. I want to make this as formal a presentation as possible.'

'How?'

'Does he ever have visitors?'

'You're certainly welcome,' Pat said, flustered at last.

'Fine! Drink time tomorrow? Say, five-thirty?'

The first to arrive, however, as Eileen reported, was a television camera crew who started flirting with her at half past four. 'You may find Rancho Rossi a bit small,' she warned them. 'Dad, hold still for a little foundation.'

She dabbed at his face, bettering his complexion. 'Eileen, you're crazy. And so is Ludlum. What's so important that – '

'I promised Pat I'd keep it a secret.'

When Ludlum and Pat arrived at five-thirty they had Enid Bart with them. 'I hope you don't mind,' she told former Detective Sergeant Michael Rossi. 'We want some footage when I announce this tonight.'

'Announce what?' Rossi's normal tone would have been withering. But to be chatting with the attractive woman who kept him awake to all hours had taken the starch out of him.

She eyed the crew. Two lamps switched on. The sound man aimed the microphone. 'We're rolling,' the head cameraman announced.

'In keeping with this programme's pitiful attempts at culture,' Enid began smoothly, 'we begin with a little Latin: *pro bono publico*.' She added some fast factual background and then introduced Dan Ludlum.

'*In media res*,' he picked up, 'let me introduce you to the head of our law firm's new division, a face familiar to Enid Bart fans and to the poor of Manhattan in need of solid legal help. Pat Rossi, perhaps you can introduce the next guest?'

'*Morituri te salutamus*,' Pat began. 'Twenty years ago Detective Sergeant Michael Rossi made medical history, surviving an assassination attempt. He then made parental history raising Eileen and me. For beating the odds, there's no one like him. And, since what I do is help people fight the odds, my boss thought my Dad might like to be in on this. Dad?'

His father's eyes went as wide as two patches of grass. 'I'm overwhelmed,' he said after a moment. 'I only had one or two goals for you, Pat. One of them was to help the victims of injustice and God knows you're doing that. The other . . . ?'

The silence grew tense. The cameraman racked his zoom lens in tighter on the hero-father's face.

'The other is typical of a Manhattan guy like me. What I've always wanted, Paddy, was to see you *make* justice work. I've always wanted to see you, when he retired, step into Bob Morgenthau's shoes . . . as District Attorney.'

Eileen's face, off camera, registered pain. Enid Bart's registered puzzlement. Dan Ludlum's looked as blandly disinterested as a ventriloquist with a dummy. Pat Rossi merely looked stunned.

'Sergeant Rossi,' Enid picked up nervously. 'It's an honourable wish. But judging by the fan mail we've been getting whenever Pat appears on the show, we're looking at a future President of the United States.'

Pat shook his head with mock gravity. 'Enid, being DA of New York County is a much bigger job.'

'Indeed it is,' Ludlum chimed in. 'This is the financial capital of the universe. When the Manhattan DA starts investigating a scam, heads roll all over the planet.'

'You tell 'em, Dan!' the elder Rossi crowed.

'Cut,' Enid snapped.

'How do you suppose,' Eileen asked her brother after everyone had left, 'your boss manoeuvred Dad into this?'

They were, they hoped, out of their father's hearing. 'Had they been in touch?' Pat wondered.

'I can tell things from the phone bill,' Eileen said. 'When I'm out shopping, an amazing number of calls get made.'

'Not bad detective work for an amateur,' their father called from the other room. He waited till they joined him. 'Look at the two of you. Is this a wake?'

'You know what it costs?' Pat demanded, 'To finance an election campaign, even for DA? Do you know how much whoring it takes to get contributions?'

'That's what rich friends are for.'

'Ludlum?' Eileen's voice had grown scornful. 'He reminds me of Jack Pierce. Low cunning in high places.'

'That's as may be,' their father said. 'What's the Latin, may I ask, for the good old saying: money has no smell?'

Pat plumped down beside him on his sofa. 'If anybody knows how silly that is, it's you.'

'Oh?'

'In this town? Sitting on the biggest mafia shithouse in history? A town that has to breathe its life with the aroma of mob money?'

'Tell me about it,' Rossi murmured sarcastically.

'For years I've listened to you carry on about the DA's office. What a triumph if I got to be DA. You even had Timmy Groark setting me up for an assistant's job. But as a lawyer, I look at what Morgenthau has been able to bring into court, even with his degree of dedication, I see what he can lay before a judge and jury. Who he can bring to the defendant's table. I see what happens then. And I weep.'

His father was a long time answering. His immobile face had gone pale, not with anger but with thought. 'Then let's forget the whole thing, okay?'

'What?'

'Forget the DA's job. Just keep on doing that Band-Aid stuff you call pro bono.' His left fingers twitched as he managed to grasp the TV remote-control keypad. 'I'm going to catch CNN.' The TV set lit up.

'Turn that crap off' Pat snapped at him. 'Thanks to you I'm going to be touted all over town tonight. By tomorrow morning I'll be a candidate. Sure, I can withdraw, looking like a quitter, like a puppet, like a fool.'

'Get Miss Bart to kill the story.'

Pat felt speechless. 'She's – I'm – '

'He's trying to tell you,' Eileen explained, 'that she's already part of the Ludlum team.'

'Which is the Pat Rossi team,' her father countered. 'I never saw one guy who combined a suspicious goombar and an Irish donkey in one and the same head. These people are your friends, Paddy. Start taking their help.'

The flood of telephone calls didn't actually dry up till almost four a.m. Dead tired, Pat took Enid to Chapter Eleven for a nightcap and found the place closing.

'Take me home, then. I haven't had such an audience feedback,' she murmured sleepily, 'since we did morning-after abortion pills.'

'The callers sounded split down the middle. Half of them wanted me to drop out of the race and the other half wanted me hit by a Hertz truck.'

Her apartment was a few blocks away, on Central Park West, a long street that bordered the park and, in lesser segments of its existence, known as Eighth Avenue. 'Nightcap?' she asked as they got to her lobby.

At ground level the elderly apartment house was a museum-like display of the art deco design popular when it was built in 1928, just before the Crash. The top floor, actually the thirteenth but called the penthouse, held only four apartments, Enid lived in one of the two facing the park.

'You were wrong,' she said. They stood with their drinks before the broad stretch of windows overlooking a ghostly Central Park, invisible in the dead of night.

'Wrong?'

'Most of my callers were hoping you'd run for office. Most of them thought you'd make a good DA.'

'We already have a terrific DA.'

'Dan Ludlum expects him to retire soon.'

'Eileen made a funny after you left. She said Dan reminded her of Jack Pierce: low cunning in high places.' He yawned, cavernously.

She finished off his yawn, put her drink on the window sill and turned to face him. This focused him on her. He had been looking about her living room, a huge space bordered on three sides by ceiling-high bookshelves. To avoid the look of a library, he saw, she had alternated rows of books with shelf spaces for small sculpture, vases, pottery, framed photos and other knick-knacks.

It looked peculiarly hers, specifically hers. It felt to him like a display of the magpie choices a TV personality makes whose real life is elsewhere, before cameras and microphones.

'Or,' he said, as if he had already been speaking out loud, 'is this where the real Enid Bart hides out?'

She approached him, face to face, took away his drink and removed his jacket. 'I ask you, would I do something like that in a TV studio?'

'It would double your phone-ins.'

She slid his braces off his shoulders. Immediately his trousers began to slip down his hips. 'At this point, the switchboard would be blazing with lights.'

He surveyed her for a long moment. There was no piecemeal way to retaliate, since all she was wearing was a pale coral crushed-silk dress, cut low in front and back. Sliding it off her shoulders would be a penultimate act.

He slid it off. The slippery silk fell to the floor around her ankles. Her breasts, which looked small when clothed, now assumed control of his view of her. She extended her long arms to give his trousers a gentle tug. They, too, slid to the carpet.

'Consider that all of Manhattan would now be on the phone,' she said in a slow, sleepy voice. She stepped out of the pale silk puddle at her feet and watched him do the same with his trousers. 'Follow me.'

She took his hand and led him out of the living room. 'No cameras here,' she said in the doorway of her bedroom.

'No mikes?'

'This building is so old, my neighbours can't hear me even if I scream.'

'So, no more phone-ins?'

She closed the gap between them, face to face. 'That's right. I've got you where I want you.'

'Me too.'

'Mm.' They kissed slowly. '*Aut tunc,*' she intoned, '*aut numquam.*'

Twenty-Seven

Although FU2 occupied only six floors of the French, French, Underwood Building on Wall Street, it also leased the penthouse floor, known as the Partners' Room.

It was here the senior partners – twelve of them – met quarterly with an open agenda, or more often on specific cases. The room was roughly forty foot square with dormers that looked out in every direction but whose views of the city had long ago been curtailed by taller edifices. The FU2 Building was, after all, a mere fifty storeys high.

A century and a half of partners were pictured here, framed and hung on the green distempered walls. In addition to the two who had become President of the United States there were seven who had been Supreme Court Justices, three vice-presidents, twenty-seven congressmen, five senators, various governors and fourteen deans of university law schools.

The earlier pictures were often brush drawings in ink. Grave, silvery daguerreotypes memorialised partners of the Civil War era. August and sombre black and white photographs began later in the century. Actual smiles appeared only after World War II. Colour never.

A public event like this rarely took place in the Partners' Room. Few employees of FU2 had ever been inside, saving a secretary or two. Nor had the general public ever seen these walls. And, surely no journalist.

Yet here they were this afternoon, camera crews and all. Mayor Garvey and the District Attorney had been invited. profit over the last year – after taxes – than any of his goddamjudges, city officials and the heads of several trade unions.

To do Dan Ludlum credit, no one from show business had been invited, except Enid Bart under the heading of news.

Today would be the official announcement of the new pro bono department. Television viewers already knew of it. But it wouldn't legally exist until these clan heavyweights were told. Chastely printed informational brochures, again in black on fisticuffs. Then Jack produced one of his tormented sighs. Elderly waitresses in black and white passed among the sixty or so guests with champagne, mineral water or beverage of choice. Since most of those in the room were connected with the law and under the observation of fellow Solons, the fizzy water got a heavy play.

A canapé table did a meagre business in tiny triangles of anchovy pizza and, to round out the ethnic mix, slender bagel chips dipped in sour-cream dressing.

'There is nothing here,' Pat murmured to Eileen, 'no white-bread-and-mayo delicacy, for a Wasp to munch.'

'I always assume,' she whispered, 'with a jaw like Dan Ludlum's, that Wasps only eat human flesh.'

'He does have that piranha look,' Enid said in an even softer voice. 'But I assure you he's only dangerous if you're already bleeding.'

She had a hand on each of them. Her fingers suddenly squeezed. 'Here they are.' Her voice went up to room level. 'Come on you, two.'

She hauled them over to the couple who had just arrived. 'Conrad, Melinda. Don't you look spiffing.' She turned to Pat. 'Pat, this is Conrad Courtney. Connie, this may be our next District Attorney. And his better-looking sister, Eileen.'

Pat took Courtney's hand. The pale man was of an intermediate age where his white hair could still be called premature. He was married to a very plain but fashionably dressed woman. Pat took her hand without a clue as to an opening line. 'Melinda,' he heard himself saying, 'I think we met at Chapter Eleven one night late?'

Her face grew animated. 'It's always three a.m. and everybody's high on caffeine. You're the reason for this gathering of power?' Her voice had gone conspiratorial and her large eyes shifted sideways as if to be sure such devastating insights were not being overheard.

'The pro bono thing, yes,' Pat said. 'Not the DA idea. We have the best DA in the country.' He indicated Morgenthau across the room. 'I see no reason to try to replace him with a novice like me.'

Melinda's wide smile was a tribute to both her dentist and her own thorough dental care. It spoke of a privileged youth – Pat remembered that her father ran an oil company only slightly smaller than Madge Ludlum's Headol Corporation – and it spoke of dynasty and how to take care of it. It also, oddly enough, came on to him, a sexy flick of tongue at one corner.

'Why are you invited here?' Eileen demanded of Courtney. She had long ago found out that someone as petite and finely designed as she was could get away with the most amazing rudenesses if uttered with a smile.

'That's what I call cutting to the core.' The white-haired man began to emit a rosy glow, as if Eileen had stroked, rather than skewered, him. He had bright blue eyes and a smile as well cared for as his wife's. 'I'm here because Dan Ludlum is sucking up to me.'

'Ah!' Eileen laughed. 'You two have a secret?'

'Maybe,' Enid cut in. 'Maybe not. Keep tuned.'

Conrad Courtney's pale eyes narrowed and his face changed from a kindly fiftyish Daddy to what he was, a successful property tycoon. 'That's totally confidential, Enid.'

'I rarely deal in anything else.'

'No, I mean it.'

'Rely on me, Connie.'

He stopped short of repeating himself. Silence settled over them for a moment, long enough for them to hear Melinda Courtney produce a cackle of delight. 'I can't tell you how it pleases me to hear that,' she said, leaving them to wonder what Pat had told her.

'Young man!' Jack Pierce exclaimed.

Five heads turned towards him. He was staring at Pat Rossi. With his pale blond head neatly parted in the middle and the saturated blues and greens of his shirt and jacket, Pierce gave the impression of a visitor from a more daguerreotype era, even without displaying arm garters.

'Don't I know you?' he demanded in a fakely blustering voice, giving it the full Ivy League 'dern't I new yew?'

Pat seemed to grow slightly taller. 'Jack.' His voice had gone dead flat. 'I believe you know both these ladies?' He indicated Eileen and Enid.

The silence felt as if a cold billow of damp air had rolled in on them, not from the sea but from a graveyard. Why is reminiscence always dank? Pat would have bet that Enid, used to talking, would have been the first to break the moody silence. He would have lost.

'Get thee behind me,' Eileen said sweetly. And then, in the same reasonable tone: 'Jack, you're getting fat as a pig. Marriage must agree with you.'

'Past tense. I'm single again.'

'Not a moment too soon.' She turned to include Enid in this but Enid had left. She could be seen talking to Morgenthau at the far end of the room. Conrad Courtney excused himself and took Melinda to another corner of the party.

Jack started to address Eileen but she had by then attached herself to the Courtneys and moved off with them.

'Gee, Pat, was it something I said?'

His former roommate stared hard at him. 'You're like a smell.'

'Huh?'

'Sort of a vagrant fart.'

Jack looked hurt. 'I can understand Eileen or Enid being pissed off at me. I mean, marrying Cunty and all. But Conrad Courtney's one of my best customers. I have made him more profit over the last year – after taxes – than any of his goddamned office buildings.'

'Nobody loves a banker.'

'I know. We're arrogant.' Jack smiled his own forgiveness.

'Unfeeling.'

'Insensitive,' Jack agreed smugly.

'In short, real shits.'

The two young men eyed each other as if about to fall back on fisticuffs. Then Jack produced one of his tormented sighs. He touched Pat's forearm gently. 'How's your Dad? Is he here?'

Pat shook his head. 'How's yours?' he asked in the same tone he might have used to ask after the health of a part of the garden infested with ants.

Jack looked around them. 'Let's slope off into the sidelines, okay? I need a little advice about him.'

But Pat's head was shaking slowly from side to side even before the request was finished. 'I have to mix and mingle. Call me at the office.' He backed away from Jack's touch.

'This'll only take a sec–'

'Dan wants me pressing palms.' Pat nodded and walked off.

Standing next to his own portrait on the greenish wall, Dan Ludlum suddenly raised his voice. Probably quite consciously, he posed in such a way that the portrait doubled his visual impact.

He had been murmuring, like everyone else. His guests had quietly enjoyed almost an hour of Manhattan's most profitable mingling, networking, dealing and bartering of information. The complicated, secretive business of running the city was being conducted in half a dozen such gatherings, now winding down for the evening ahead.

Their participants had not only validated their own importance, but been seen to be important by their peers. Nothing is more powerful than the posture of precedence which only needs to be seen to be honoured. There is no more satisfied feeling than such an occasion, unless it also leads to actual monetary profit.

Now, however, Ludlum's voice took on a ringing clarion call, as of cavalry trumpets. Everyone politely, even deferentially, stopped talking. It was the coda, time to pay their dues.

'Ladies and gentlemen, thank you for your company on this occasion. I won't call it historic. But "pleasant" is a word that readily comes to mind. As you know, we . . .'

The boring end game was about to begin.

Twenty-Eight

This early evening hour drenched Manhattan's skyscrapers in moving shadows. The twilight was shot with horizontal spears of sunset over the flatlands of New Jersey.

The big man stood at the windows of his penthouse apartment on Central Park West and waited for his guests to arrive. They were his first guests. He had just moved in two days before, although, in actuality, he owned the entire building.

Through a dummy corporation, of course. It was one that owned a lot of Manhattan.

Not fat, his tall frame seemed generously fleshed because his head was quite small in comparison. His close-cropped dark hair only emphasised this contrast in mass. It gave him a bulk that was, like a lot of Manhattan, very much an illusion.

Minute by minute, as street lamps lighted, the city dusk seemed to change into one of those shape-shifting figures of shaman illusion, now a spiky patch of concrete thistle, now a misty bed, now a blanket over God knew what secrets, each one lancing upwards with a sharp burst of hot halogen light.

A lot of these underground secrets were lodged with the big man, one of Manhattan's greatest illusionists, Big Mimmo Caccia, not yet fifty, known to the press as King of the Airports. If he had been allowed to pick his own nickname it would have been King of Peace and Quiet. It was for those goals that he ruled this island.

There had been a time, when he had suffered his apprenticeship under the seriously pathological Vinnie Sgroi, that Mimmo despaired of ever being able to do the job. New York City and its tri-state area had always given organised crime a bad name.

Historic capos like Bonanno, Anastasia, Costello, Luciano, Genovese, Gallo, Gambino, Profaci, and affiliates like Lansky and Siegel had created a malodorous half-century which latter-day thugs like Gotti only further putrefied.

With Vinnie Sgroi, however, the purification began. Clinically insane, bloodthirsty, depraved, he went up against Big Mimmo's control of the airports and was chopped down in a La Guardia warehouse. Not, Mimmo mourned, because Vinnie had committed the lowest of crimes: killing an honest cop.

Well, he hadn't actually whacked Mike Rossi, but turning him into a hero had been even more stupid. Big Mimmo Caccia, perhaps because he came out of a younger milieu, aviation, nurtured a dream of respectability. It was now within his grasp.

Not because organised crime had grown respectable. But because society, the respectable core of it – government, business and the law, so well represented at the Ludlum gathering – had steadily grown more lawless.

There was no need, Mimmo often thought, for him to play the candy-ass role of 'honest crook'. He simply had to keep his nose moderately clean and let society fester. Soon they were matching him in criminality. Eventually they were being caught outdoing him in villainy. And he was kept busy scooping up the spoils.

He knew his associates had never made this observation, never enjoyed its profits. None had the same breadth of understanding he did. After all, Big Mimmo Caccia had a BA from Columbia and an MA from NYU ... in urban planning, of course.

His father had insisted on it. He intended his oversized son to handle municipal construction contracts, for which even a PhD was not enough. 'The Jews believe in lotsa education,' he would lecture Mimmo. 'Why not us?'

Largely because no one else was pursuing research at this level, Mimmo often felt he was the only witness to society's degradation. But he had actually been put on this line of thought by his father's fond reminiscences of the Prohibition era. 'Eh, Mim,' he would chuckle. '*Everybody* was illegal!'

Remembering this gem, Mimmo often found himself wondering how soon before America would reach and surpass the point where everyone was some kind of crook.

His doorbell produced an insistent cricket sound. He switched on the security television screen to see the doorman's face, with its toady smile, move aside to display two others.

One was Guido Smaldone, of Providence, Rhode Island, a know-nothing young bruiser of the old school. The second was Carmine Onofrio, a savvy ex-cop placed inside the Pierce organisation more than twenty years ago and now proving his weight in gold. Carmine pretended to share Mimmo's vision of respectability. Smaldone was still an unknown quantity.

After they had shaken hands, Big Mimmo Caccia suggested: 'I had them put in a west-facing garden. We'll have a drink out there. Kind of inaugurate it.'

He led the way to the terrace, pleased to be showing it for the first time. He himself had designed it. He himself had drawn the plans on his own drafting table. The site commanded views in three directions: of the park, of downtown Manhattan, and all of New Jersey, now slowly settling into the darkness of night.

Even without his height – Mimmo was six-four – he moved as a leader moves, massively, commandingly. He had been a fat child. It was only after he began running the airports that he took up serious weight loss and managed to wrestle himself down to a solid two hundred pounds. For a man who owned many restaurants, holding this line was never easy.

'You can smoke out here,' he announced. 'Inside's a no-smoking zone. Also, with all the traffic noise it's hard to bug a conversation out here. What's your pleasure? I have some of that lemony mineral water?'

'Fine for me,' Carmine said, always going with the boss.

'Howa bouta beer?' Smaldone wondered.

Big Mimmo stooped to an outdoor refrigerator and removed

several bottles. He uncapped and poured them. Then he produced a bowl of fruit.

'Organically grown.'

Smaldone blinked idly. Carmine looked impressed. 'You get them from the Costanzas in Connecticut?'

'Best in New England.' Big Mimmo settled himself in a white steel garden chair. 'To peace and quiet. Cin-cin.' They lifted their drinks. He concentrated his attention first on Smaldone. 'Congratulations. You got married in June, was it?'

Smaldone looked pleased at such attention from such a capo. Big Mimmo continued talking, as if it didn't really matter what Smaldone thought. 'But you nearly made it to the morgue first.'

Smaldone's face went dead for a moment. Then: 'You woulden b'lieve what Harry and Paul Pierce tried to run on me. Except the guy they set up for it wasn't no pro. Otherwise, curtains.'

'But you're looking healthy and well fucked.' Mimmo held up his hand. 'Excuse the vulgarity, Guido, but I never married. Yet. Having a pretty young wife on call could damage a man's health. Whereas a single guy has the right to sleep in peace if he doesn't bring anybody home for the night. Do I make sense?'

Smaldone's sallow face grew bright red. He nodded agreement and bit into a small Granny Smith apple whose pale green skin stood out in contrast to his blush. 'Mm! Tasty.'

Mimmo shifted to aim his body at Carmine Onofrio. 'Carmine, what went wrong?'

Onofrio's pug face looked rueful. He shrugged his wide, powerful shoulders. 'If you ask me . . .'

'I do.'

'There is a looney-tunes strain in the Pierce clan.' He held up one massive paw. 'Remember, I seen 'em through losses, big winnings, mistakes, smart moves. I always felt Paul Pierce was a genius. But we both know that geniuses are bugs.'

Big Mimmo nodded politely. 'I expect you must say that about me, too.'

Sheer fright washed over that flat-pounded face. 'I swear on my mother's grave, Mim, I never, ever – '

'Just ribbing you.' Mimmo sipped his flavoured fizz-water. 'Harry Pierce was wrong to demand a hit on Guido here? And Paul was wrong to sanction a contract?' He had a deceptively mild face but when he turned back to Smaldone, his eyes had a threatening glare.

'Just what did you do to get Harry so accazzare a te?'

Smaldone's young face screwed into an infant's grimace that heralds tears. 'It was a shipment went missing in Boston.'

'Snow?'

'And horse both. Call it a two-mill load. Harry Pierce said I swiped it. I tried to splain that a dick in Cambridge had diverted the stuff and was selling it up and down the coast.'

'A cop? Give me a name.'

'Herman Federman. Capt. Federman.'

Mimmo held up his hand to stall any further talk. He swung back to Carmine Onofrio. 'What gave Paul the idea this could be handled by an amateur?'

Onofrio produced another of his massive shrugs. 'They's a shortage of shooters up my way. Two guys are on the lam and one's in the slams. Instead of holding off till we got a pro Paul pulls this creep out of his left ear. And that's not all.'

He then proceeded to narrate, economically, the story of Gretchen Applebaum. Her husband, Herb, had been missing for weeks. Half out of her mind she had thought to apply directly to Paul Pierce for information. Pierce had worked her over dirty and left the clean-up to Carmine. 'So I made sure some of it stuck to young Jack Pierce.'

Big Mimmo Caccia nodded slowly. 'Smart, Carmine, smart.' And brilliantly disloyal, he added to himself.

It was odd the way his small head seemed to take on added gravity. 'Paul sounds psycho to me,' he said at last. 'The only other man who'd've done that to a woman would've been Vinnie Sgroi.'

'That's what I been sayin' for – '

'Not for wanting you zetzed,' Mimmo assured the now

cocky Smaldone. 'Guido, you may think you're in the clear on that missing shipment. To me you're still on probation.'

Mimmo picked up a large navel orange and contemplated it philosophically, as Hamlet with Yorick's skull. Roundness, he thought, is the primary shape of life, of the planet, the skulls that live upon it, the orbits traced through the galaxy, the rounds of birth and death.

Then he sank both thumbs, nail-sharp, into the orange's thick skin and in a few brute gestures stripped back the white pithy underside and broke the bare orange into segments.

'Carmine?' He held out two segments.

'Thanks, Mim.'

The big man hesitated and then, almost reluctantly, like a priest handing a host to an unconfessed sinner, gave two segments to Guido Smaldone. 'Young fella,' he said, 'you're alive because of an error in judgment, Paul Pierce's judgment. Keep that in mind and you may live to have grandchildren.'

The three men got to their feet, munching on the juicy segments.

'You know me,' Mimmo said as he ushered them to the door. 'Peace and quiet. I hate to solve anything the hard way when, with a little leverage, it can seem to do the job itself.'

He put them in the elevator. Back inside his apartment he dabbed a Kleenex at the dots of juice on his fingers. He walked to the wall of windows that faced Central Park.

Night had truly fallen. Pale pinpoints of fire lanced up from the carpet of the park, hinting at fires below. Big Mimmo yawned. Talking to retards like Smaldone took a lot out of him, although dealing with someone of smarmy intelligence, like Carmine, gave him the pip.

He yawned again. Out of the corner of one eye he saw movement in the apartment next to his. Two people stood in the window, not facing towards him. He had been meaning to review all leases to learn who his new neighbours were.

But there was never enough time for everything. Peace and quiet came first.

The couple shifted slightly and Mimmo's line of sight cleared. The new neighbour was the provocatively bright Enid

Bart. Big Mimmo decided he must be the last person in town to learn – but first-hand because neither of them had any clothes on – that she was romancing the next District Attorney of Manhattan.

As he finished his last segment of orange, he smiled. It was all well and good to operate on theories of society's degeneration. But success still needed pure dumb luck.

Twenty-Nine

It had taken Pat and Eileen weeks to find an armoured limousine company they could in good conscience hire to take their father for his medical check-up every six weeks.

'Complete protection?' a typical salesman would exclaim, as if they had asked for his scrotum. 'There will always be areas of a limo that give way. Windows for sure. Pour firepower into anything,' he would say in a brooding tone of doom, 'Fort Knox, anything, and eventually it'll give. Security? Just a brainy guess, we're looking at a ballpark figure of 70 per cent?'

'You're asking me to put my father in a vehicle where he has a 30 per cent chance of being killed?'

'Will he have an armed guard? Then we're looking at, say, 80 per cent safety.'

Finally, out of this morass of doubletalk, Fred Finch, a nephew who drove for a small limo company, suggested his firm '... because the head mechanic is my cousin and I know how much Kevlar shielding he uses. Uncle Michael will be safer with us.'

'And you'll be his driver?' Pat persisted.

'Promise.'

'And you'll use different routes each time?'

'Promise.'

'And be ready to change time and date on short notice?'

'Pat, we're so hungry for business I'll throw in free coffee and anise cookies.'

Fred would help Eileen transfer her father from wheelchair to limo and back. Now and then Michael Rossi's old pal helped, Gino Frenese, who'd been a Checker driver for decades.

'Gino has major arthritis,' Eileen complained to Pat. 'He needs as much help as Dad does.'

Pat gave her a grim smile. 'But he's made of the same stuff. Like Pop, he *would* fall on a grenade.'

'Is that all it takes?' Eileen asked. 'Gee, Pat, give me a try-out.'

This particular morning in March was an interim day, pregnant with change. The scuzz of winter, endless crusts of slush-born filth, had melted to grit and was being redistributed by thirty-mile-an-hour gusts.

But the sky! Bright, swimming-pool blue, sparkling with small, fast clouds moving like marathon runners across the city.

It would be the first time they tried an armoured limo trip. In their absence a crew of Uncle Barney Callahan's house cleaners was steam-scrubbing the rugs, waxing floors and washing all windows.

On the way up Third Avenue, Eileen sat in front with Fred Finch, a youngish, bald-headed man with a demure pigtail on the nape of his neck. 'It looks congested in the middle of 23rd Street,' Eileen pointed out.

The strategy was to stick to big, broad avenues and those arterial crosstown streets of the same width. But sometimes even major crosstowns got clogged.

'Right.' Fred backed out of 23rd Street and went north a few blocks. 'This looks clear.' A van muscled ahead of them as they turned into a narrower street.

In the back, Gino and Rossi were arguing about a cop they both remembered. Gino thought he had died. 'Alive,' Mike Rossi contradicted. 'Still alive. Mean bastards like him never die.'

'That must be the secret of your success,' Gino came back.

'I'm not mean,' the other demurred. 'I'm nasty. Look what I put my daughter and my buddies through.'

'You must be hell on the nurses, too.'

'I'm an easy thousand health insurance bucks. The clinic does all the tests. There's never anything wrong. Or, anyway, wronger. They collect their insurance loot and I go back home for another six weeks.'

'With me it's Medicare, but they never pay.'

Michael Rossi nodded sombrely. 'Notorious welshers. But I'm not old enough yet for Medicare, thank God.'

'When did the government ever do anything for us without a gun to its head?'

Rossi frowned at him. 'Not when Pat becomes the DA.'

Up ahead the van braked to a stop. Both sides of the street were crammed with parked cars. The van turned slantwise, completely blocking traffic.

Eileen whirled about and stared through the rear window. A second van had swerved diagonally and was blocking their rear.

'Dad, hit the floor.'

Gino eased his pal off the rear seat of the limo. Rossi huddled on the floor as Gino slid down on top of him like a frail blanket.

Fred hit a switch that locked all doors and windows with a sharp twanging click. He reached inside his blue serge uniform jacket and brought out a .45 automatic.

'You get down, too,' Eileen ordered.

'Look, I – '

'I can't lose my driver,' she explained. 'Get down.'

Fred bent sideways. His pigtail bristled in fear. He was working his radio-telephone, tapping the keypad.

She peered over the edge of the back seat, then over the windshield wiper. 'Nobody showing yet.'

In the middle of Manhattan, crowded midtown Manhattan, she got the suddenly feeling of being entirely alone. Nobody was watching. Nobody cared.

'Hello, 911?!' Fred asked. 'AAArdsley Limos. Hold-up on Twenty-Sixth Street between Third and Second. Two vans have our limo trapped.'

'Not hold-up,' Eileen yelped. 'Terrorist attack.'

She lifted her head to look down at her father. 'You two okay? You look like an old married pair.'

'What's happening upstairs?' Rossi demanded.

'Not a th–'

A steel-jacketed slug slammed through the rear window. With a rattling rush it exploded a shower of icy diamonds over all of them as it shattered the safety glass.

The slug slewed sideways as it headed for the windshield, piercing power drastically reduced, and bounced down onto the seat where Fred had been sitting.

Eileen reached for it and handed the squashed slug down to her father. 'There is no rear window. The next shots will be unimpeded.'

'Unimpeded. My little girl. What a vocabulary.'

She glanced out of the other windows. Nondescript buildings, devoid of humanity, loomed around her. No faces showed. No voices were heard, no shouts, no screams. Nobody was watching except people intent on murder.

Eileen reached down for the blue steel army Colt .45 Fred had been carrying. Her motion, the movement of her hand and fingers, seemed slowed-down, as if fear were a molasses they were stuck inside.

'My God, Fred, this gun is older than you and me put together.'

'Don't start shooting,' Rossi muttered from below the rear seat. 'Maybe this is just a scare job.'

'Maybe not.' She grasped the pistol in both hands and rested the barrel on the back of her seat. She shifted the safety catch open with her thumb.

Behind her, the windshield shattered as a steel-jacketed bullet from the front van crashed through.

The hail of tempered glass cubelets rattled like buckshot. Each one seemed to give off its own report, so slowed-down did everything seem.

Involuntarily, Eileen ducked out of sight. Her mouth had a brassy, electrical charge to it, like sucking a penny.

It was fear, she realised, and it also had the brutal vibration of an orgasm building up slowly but unstoppably.

'Here's the story,' she muttered, inching her way back to the visibility level. 'We are between two high-power game rifles, deer guns or whatever. Fred's called the fuzz. How long do you figure it'd take the street to wake up and start reacting?'

'These cowboys have five minutes. They've already blown a minute. That's why I think they're not for real.'

'Wrong,' Eileen said in a remote tone. She took a long, shuddering inhalation. She could feel her heart beginning to speed up.

'They have to kill to get out of the street,' she said, hearing how slowly she seemed to speak. 'This is a do-or-die set-up. Kill, ram us east till we reach Second, then take off. We're the cork in their bottle.'

Announcing the schemata of their death, her voice had a draggy, lacklustre note to it.

Fred sat back up behind the wheel. 'She's right. I'm gonna jam us in.'

He hauled the wheel into a leftward lock and rammed the limo into a parked car. Then he reversed with a right-hand lock and the long Cadillac was firmly trapped at nearly right angles to the street.

'Duck, Fred. Don't be a hero.'

'Easy, Fred,' Gino moaned. 'My arthritis.'

A silenced gun snapped like the bark of a chihuahua. The slug entered Fred's neck at the pigtail.

His head crunched forward into the steering wheel. Almost no blood trickled down his neck but began to pulse in great gouts from his mouth.

'What was that?' Rossi asked.

Eileen's voice was small, tight, trying to make a minuscule target. 'How do you unlock this damned door?'

'Don't,' her father cautioned.

'They can't see me. The limo's like a barricade.'

'Only against the rear van. To the front guy, you're a clear shot.'

She poked and twisted at various controls, then heard the door latch twang open.

'Eileen! Sit tight!'

'I'm fine.'

Small and crouched over, the Colt held in front of her, Eileen opened her door a few inches. No one fired.

She edged around the lower part of the door. The street ignored her. Manhattan didn't know she was alive. The thought curdled her mouth in a grim smile.

She could see into the front van. The hatchback rear door was open a crack.

It happened so quickly, she had no idea until it was over. The hatchback was closed. Then it opened three inches at the bottom.

All four shots were fired at almost the same time. Two incoming from the van, two rounds from her Colt.

It bucked and shook in Eileen's two small hands. She bit down hard on her lower lip.

The front gunman had been shooting at Fred's face. He hadn't expected fire from somewhere else.

'Christ!' Rossi shouted. 'What's up?'

She peered around the edge of the half-open car door. A thin trickle of blood ran down over the rear bumper of the van.

As she watched, she could feel her throat close and begin to spasm. Blood everywhere. She swallowed hard.

The trickle over the van bumper became a gush. A puddle formed on the asphalt street below.

She touched her lip and came away with a bead of her own blood, where she had bitten.

'Eileen?'

'Still here.'

'Damn it, Eileen.'

'I know. I'll fill you in later. Hold tight.'

She edged out onto the street, moving cat-like, the Colt twisting this way and that as if it had eyes.

Her breath was coming in short, angry spurts. Her heart had begun pounding against her ribs.

Hot oxygen turned her mouth's brassy taste stronger, as if eating its way into her flesh.

The questions were appalling. Would the driver of the front van be able to shoot? Could the shooter in the rear van see her legs under the car? Did Manhattan give a damn?

One thing she knew: the front van wasn't armoured and her limo was. Chances were the back van wasn't armoured, either.

She levelled the automatic. Crouched. Danced sideways. Squeezed off two shots at the windshield of the rear van. Danced back to cover.

The effect was amazing. The windshield erupted everywhere, a fountain of tiny green ice like rain from heaven.

The man behind the wheel threw his hands up over his face. Blood oozed through the fingers.

The man next to him, no windshield to hide him, awkwardly tried to shift the rifle. He moved as if under water.

Eileen danced sideways again. Careful aim. Hours. Days. The .45 slug entered his shoulder with such force it rocked the van sideways. Bits of bone and gristle exploded.

In the distance a siren moaned. And then another. And then a third. At last the city was paying attention.

Eileen slumped gratefully to the pavement. It felt cold beneath her. 'Dad! It's okay!' she gasped.

She closed her eyes and worked on her breathing, composing herself. Her ferocious heartbeat made her chest ache. Calmly now. Ease up.

'Eileen?' He sounded panicky.

'It's okay. Believe me,' she shouted.

When the cops arrived she had a role to play. How would it seem for the daughter of former Detective Sergeant Michael Rossi to look frightened out of her tiny mind?

Thirty

The greatest thing about Manhattan, Eileen told herself, was that you lived *inside* an info-network more rapid-acting than a threatened rattlesnake.

All science could promote was the multi-media information highway for yokels, where your own TV accessed virtual sex *and* auctions of zircon rings.

But actually living in Manhattan was like being one of those points of energy in the Mother Ship.

Way back in the 1970s, a movie called *Close Encounters of the Third Kind* showed the Mother Ship visiting Earth. It was a gigantic hive. Sizzling points of voltage hooked up, like bees in a real hive. Wired in series, they produced the mega-voltage that activated the Mother Ship.

Eileen had been a little girl then, but she never forgot the lift when being a small, nameless bee gave her interstellar power, reaching galaxies beyond the rim.

She felt it now as Manhattan's info-merchants converged on Beth Israel Hospital Downtown, where her father had been rushed for a check-up 'an hour after his original check-up,' Eileen told them.

'Miss Rossi! Miss Rossi! Can you – ?'

'It's Fred Finch you should memorialise. Frederick Burden Finch. He died protecting Michael Rossi.'

'Miss Rossi! How does it feel t– ?'

At the back of the knot of press and camera crews, she could see the slim frame of Captain Leroy Baxter, who commanded her father's old precinct.

'Miss Rossi! Your lower lip! Can you – ?'

'Miss Rossi! Can you show us the gun tha– ?'

Baxter was a machine politico of the new school, that is, a light-complexioned African American under the age of fifty who closely resembled John Gilbert of silent film fame. Unlike the old fatso precinct chiefs of the Irish-Italian era of Tammany, Baxter had not yet been caught in any act more corrupt than having his driver park in a no-parking zone.

'Miss Rossi! Eileen! Whose gun did – ?'

His presence here at Beth Israel, Eileen realised, was primarily to share her limelight but, after the arcs died away, to find out who the hell she thought she was, gunning down perps in midtown Manhattan.

Four men, two in each attacking van, had already been labelled perpetrators. None were known to the cops; they seemed casual out-of-town pickups. One was dead, two were wounded and the fourth was having screaming fits in a padded cell at Baxter's precinct. Apparently nobody had ever warned him that victims sometimes shoot back. Being a target had seriously unhinged him. As such, he had civil rights.

'Miss Rossi, can we pose you with the gun that – ?'

'Eileen? As the heroine daughter of a hero f– '

The central story was not what the men in the vans had done. In Manhattan assault with a deadly weapon was rather commonplace, after all. The novelty was what Eileen had done. In terms of news it went beyond being cute and petite and brave.

But in legal terms it also went beyond self-defence, as she well knew, because having your limo's front and back windows shot out was technically not yet punishable by anything as lasting as death.

'Eileen! Eileen!'

'How does this affect your brother's plans to run for – ?'

'Eileen! This way! Smile!'

The killing of Fred had to be Eileen's core defence. In a hurried talk with her brother as the press was shooed out, Eileen was made to understand that Fred's family might try for damages to an employee in a hazardous position.

'However, it was Fred's .45,' Pat summed up. 'He has a police permit. This implies advance understanding of the hazards. So a charge of unfair jeopardy won't hold up.' He gave his sister a long, thoughtful look. 'Where did you learn to shoot?'

'At Our Lady of the Perpetual Monoxide. The sisters used to take us to that shooting range in the village. Tira A Segno? They used t–'

'That's good enough.' He gave her a peck on the cheek. 'I think we can keep you out of jail.'

She frowned. 'I'm beginning to see how life works. The perps are victims. I'm the criminal.'

'Precisely. Watch Baxter like a hawk. Let him take as much credit as he wants. I mean, it was his squad cars got there so fast. Police heroism, lots of it. About the actual shootings, be vague. Refer everything to me.'

'He'll interview Dad first.'

'Pop's hardly a witness. He saw almost nothing.' Pat chewed on a thought for a long time. 'We can't keep the press away from Pop forever. But no interviews without me there. Okay?'

'Pat, we're skirting the real issue. Whose shooters were they? Who wanted Dad dead so badly as to hire unknowns to stage a foolproof takeout that had to include suicide?'

'First things first.' He looked vaguely guilty. 'First we have to protect our own butts.'

'God, you shysters are all alike.'

Former Detective Sergeant Michael Rossi looked grumpy. He lay propped up in his hospital bed, grousing about not being allowed to leave yet to commune once more with his far more interesting artificial intelligence software.

'It's the tests,' Pat explained. 'They'll be back from the lab any minute now and you can stop being so cantankerous.' He turned to Captain Baxter. 'Let's not stand on ceremony. He shakes with his left hand. Just pick it up and give it a squeeze. Rossi, meet Baxter.'

The police captain did as he was told, managing to convey a lot of sympathy as he smiled into the expressionless face of the hero-martyr. 'At last we meet,' he said.

'You're the new chief?' Rossi's pale green eyes opened wider, camera lens diaphragms seeking more light. 'I hear good things about you.'

'That's because I'm new. Later they'll start telling the truth.'

For some reason this seemed hilarious to both men, who chuckled for a while. Then Baxter released his hand. 'I'm not going to bug you any more. But I'd like to talk to your kids.'

'Yeah, sure. See you.' Rossi watched them leave the room. A nurse came in with some flowers and messages she placed on the adjoining bed. She checked the round Band-Aid patch on his left elbow vein where the blood had been tapped off for testing. 'You'll live,' she remarked.

'Ho, yes,' he said on a long exhalation of breath. 'These days it ain't easy to die quietly.'

'Thank God you have a gutsy daughter.'

'Ho, yes. Ho, yes. Ho, yes.'

'Sarcastic, are we?'

He gave her a long, level stare. 'Sounds to me like your old man doesn't appreciate your brave, selfless hard work ministering to the sick and dying. But what father ever truly appreciates a daughter?'

'Except to fry up his eggs in the morning.' The nurse turned on her heel and left the room.

'No rush, tomorrow's okay, I'll need a statement from you, Miss Rossi,' Captain Baxter said. 'I've taken personal charge of this case. It has a long history in our precinct. It's, what, over twenty years ago they did in your father's spine?'

'Captain,' Pat responded, 'the men who did that are dead. When we have IDs on these four neophyte killers, what will we know? Can we get a make on who paid them?'

Baxter's handsome, brooding face wrinkled at the chin as he made a gesture of dubiousness. 'The guy who went ape will tell us anything. He's not reliable. The wounded guys aren't in shape for interrogation right now.' He glanced sideways at Eileen. 'Those .45s make a hell of an exit wound.'

'But they're not in critical condition,' she almost begged.

'That's what the hospital tells us.' Baxter had been holding his dapper, semi-Tyrolean hat in his hand. Now he got to his feet, brandished the hat and bid them goodbye. He didn't wear the hat as he left, in case any photographers were still lurking about.

Eileen and Pat went back to their father's room. 'What's all this?' he asked, indicating bouquets of flowers and a handful of fax messages.

Eileen skimmed through them. 'They're not for you, you egomaniac. They're for your heroine daughter. Get this bouquet!' She brandished a great explosion of silvery-lavender roses. 'These are Sterling Silvers, Dad. Two dozen of them. You're looking at three hundred bucks!'

'You're worth a million of those bouquets.' His voice dropped to a growl. 'Who sent a three-C nosegay?'

She opened the envelope and withdrew a small business card with a scribbled message:

' "Good to know we still have brave women like you",' Eileen read. It was a strong, readable handwriting with no flourishes. She squinted down at the small print. 'John Domenico Caccia? Who?'

Pat took the card. 'Better known as Big Mimmo.'

Thirty-One

Normally, Dan Ludlum would drop into a colleague's office, Pat's for example, close the door and unload what was on his mind. This time he asked Pat to his office. The leggy Maria sat at a desk nearby with a spiral-bound steno book.

'You saw the *Times* this morning?'

Pat hesitated. He had expected to have to discuss the shoot-out. But in Manhattan yesterday's shoot-out is yesterday's dead fish.

Something else was on his boss's mind. Pat had got in the habit now and then of spending the night with Enid at her apartment. Although he was sure Enid read the newspapers some time during the day, as a child of TV she watched the tube.

'That skating rink thing?' he guessed.

'They're already calling them Satan's Punks. They killed the boy. The girl is hanging by a thread.'

'And they've got the three kids who did it?'

Dan Ludlum's face, with its big nose and powerful chin, seemed to draw together as if he were trying to touch one to the other. 'I have never seen such a slipshod frame-up. Those boys may be guilty of a hundred other crimes and probably are. They all have records. But they weren't even in the neighbourhood of Central Park when the attack took place.'

'Mayor Garvey has already tried and convicted them,' Pat pointed out.

Her pencil skating across her steno pad, Maria emitted a discreet snort. 'That's because we're coming into an election year,' Ludlum said. 'His cops have failed at everything but brutality. Send these kids to jail and he redeems himself.'

Pat was silent. He realised he was watching Maria's long legs, one swinging lightly over the other. He turned directly to face Ludlum. 'You're thinking of representing Satan's Punks?'

'Not thinking. I've been asked by one of the big civil rights groups. All three kids are black. One has a Puerto Rican father. All have solid alibis from people who place them elsewhere than the skating rink.'

'Any sex-crime on their records?'

'None. You see what I mean? Whoever attacked the skaters not only buggered the boy and the girl, but then went to the trouble of slicing them up and crapping all over the wounds. Several things he did with a knife are not even going to get in the newspapers, they're so perverse. And what's the Mayor's response: satanic killers.'

'Great headline,' Pat admitted.

'I want you to interview these kids. I'll have someone get authorisation from their parents. This case is a landmark. Whoever defends these kids will get a TV special all his own.'

'Is that supposed to lure me in?'

'Okay, FU2 needs the publicity.'

'Dan, if there's a gross injustice here, and it smells like there is, you don't have to ask me twice.'

'Attaboy.'

'And if there isn't?' Maria asked in that trombone voice of hers.

Pat mimed a gigantic flinch, as if unaware she was in the room. 'Did you hear something?' he asked his boss. 'Mice?'

But Ludlum was reading through some legal papers. It was all the notice he ever gave that a discussion had ended. Pat got to his feet and walked over to Maria.

'You have a run,' he whispered.

Her face looked panicky as she checked both legs. 'Liar.' She got up, took his arm and escorted him out of Ludlum's office. 'I think,' she whispered, 'you've got a case that will make more than a page in one of those ledgers of yours.'

'Who told you about my ledgers?'

'No one. I often rifle through your office when you're not

there. It's very sexy, spying on you. I get to know all your secret buttons. Those ledgers! God, what a record of injustice.'

'I'm going to have to put them in the safe from now on.'

'No, but I thought I might put them on CD-ROM for you. You must have damned near twenty of them.'

'Putting them on a disk would take you months.'

'I have free time. Working for Dan Ludlum is like being in the army: hurry up and wait.'

'You're serious?'

'Beats knitting and puts you even deeper in debt to me.'

'God, Maria, when are you calling in my IOU?'

'When you least expect it.'

Thirty-Two

The Reagan-Bush Eighties had been the scavenging era. In that decade no one any longer built corporations. They slashed corporations, gnawed off the bloody innards and left the gap-mouthed holders of junk bonds to mourn the corpse.

That was where Big Mimmo Caccia came in, just as these corporations were about to expire, their executives in jail, their assets in escrow. Highly respectable businessmen had dragged these firms into criminality. Now, as the century ended, Mimmo harvested near-cadavers.

Lately, like Dr Frankenstein, he was getting ready to electrify three bankrupt television production houses that had overexpanded, making commercials. They had fattened on insider scams and, what was far worse, been caught at it.

Mimmo bought warm cadavers, fixed bolts in their temples and created his own Boris Karloff: Peaceful Productions. It owned a dark theatre on 46th Street and a small office building on East 53rd. But its chief asset was Big Mimmo.

The week after the failed assassination he grabbed Victor Espada, just eased out of a producer's job at Lincoln Center.

'Victor, amigo, they have done *Carmen* in blackface. They have done it in modern dress. They have done it every way but in Spanish. I want to re-open the Peaceful Theatre on 46th Street with a Spanish-language Carmen.'

Espada's dark, deep-set eyes lit up. 'In New York? Where the mother tongue of half of us is Spanish?'

'You have a fast mind, amigo.'

'And I think there's a Spanish Zarzuela translation.' Victor added. He instantly drew up a tentative cast list from among

Mexican, Puerto Rican, Cuban, Argentine and Spanish opera singers. Espada had three Carmens in mind.

'No,' Big Mimmo said. 'For Carmen I want Serena Wainwright.'

'She's a mezzo. Carmen's a higher soprano.'

'Close enough. Or rescore it a third lower.'

'She's out of practice. She's not young.'

'Rehearse her. Youthen her up.'

'She isn't a Spanish-speaker.'

'Neither am I, amigo.'

Later, Jack Pierce backtracked over this ground, trying to learn how his mother had won out over dozens of mezzos perhaps no more qualified but surely more Carmen's age.

He suspected Mimmo of using her to get at Paul Pierce. It was hard to tell. She had never actually met the dark angel who bankrolled the now insanely successful *Spanish Carmen*.

'Tall, not overweight, but imposing?' Jack asked her.

'Never. He wasn't at the cast or angel parties.'

'You don't know, then, that he's big maf?'

There was a long pause between mother and son. Jack, her first born, had always been her favourite. It was possible to be open and candid with him. But not lately, not since his parents seemed to have gone entirely separate ways, physically apart, a true Catholic approximation of divorce.

Her life had done such acrobatics, her career sky-high, her marriage disappearing. Just how frank could she be with the son so beholden to his father? Paul had taught him everything and then given him the wherewithal to strike out on his own. It was a bit late to question the source of all this.

Serena made a small sighing sound, light as a whimper. 'Mafia money,' she said slowly, 'is the invisible guest at the wedding.'

She stared silently at Jack and reached forward abruptly to glide an unruly part in his hair from left to centre. Then she straightened his tie, needlessly. Jack Pierce's ties were always straight.

His thoughts were not. Nothing about his father was

straight. He had begun to believe that the power behind two decades of merciless physical dread, of open warfare like the 26th Street shootout, was Paul Pierce's diseased brain. Who but a maniac would persist in such persecution?

Jack let his interrogation drop. *Spanish Carmen* filled the Peaceful Theatre eight shows a week. There was a waiting list for cancellations. Theatre parties from as far away as San Juan and Teotihuacan booked a year in advance.

Serena kept a small suite in a hotel on Central Park South. Her view northward changed with the seasons, green, then autumnal, then bare and snowy, then green again. To the left, in the high 60s on Central Park West, she could see the art deco building she knew to be the home of Enid Bart.

At the age of fifty Serena had become a new woman, slimmer, more active, the darling of quick-talk shows like 'News is Made at Night'. Although known to be married, she was proffered marriage and/or fornication proposals as often as invitations to fashionable parties and dinners.

She hadn't seen Paul Pierce in many months but when she telephoned him she got Betty, who ran his office. What she learned was deeply disturbing. 'I'm not interested in mystery backers,' she told her oldest son now. 'I'm interested in your father. He seems to be breaking up.'

Jack swallowed nervously. 'Really?'

'Inside his head. There's always been a nutty streak in your father. You remember that time he made all of us take five different vitamin capsules at breakfast *and* dinner?'

She stroked his head. 'You remember when he beat up that Strickland boy who wanted to marry Paulie? He hurt him so badly it cost us millions to hush it up.'

She tried to fix Jack's glance, but he avoided contact. 'You know what I mean about your father. You've been avoiding him for a long time now. I have to admit: so have I.'

'Avoiding!' He made it sound angry but there was no punch behind his mini-explosion. 'I've built a bank that takes twenty-four-hour surveillance. Dad takes care of himself. You take care of yourself. Let me do the same.'

Serena's head, her black hair restyled in demented-spaghetti style for her permanent life as Carmen, shook from side to side, the hair jiggling wildly. 'That's no good, Jack. When someone in your family goes off the deep end, you don't hide behind your job.'

'Deep end?' Again the bluster sounded hollow. He finally let his glance meet hers. 'Okay,' he faked a smile. 'What's a little nervous breakdown among family?'

But her head kept shaking. 'Betty talks to me. We've been together many years now. Last weekend she stayed with me, here in the suite.' Serena pointed to a daybed convertible. 'Jack, please listen.'

Her voice failed her. She cleared her throat mightily, in the operatic, high-decibel manner. Then: 'Jack, it's no time for beating around the bush. That woman has welts all over her. Bites. She's been abused, tortured, defaced. She's – '

Jack turned away and almost ran to the windows. He glared at peaceful Central Park outside. He felt as if his mother had slapped his face. This past year he seemed to have lost his touch with women, even his own mother. He whirled on Serena.

'So you're leaving him?'

His mother's big eyes went even wider. 'What a crazy idea. I'm not leaving him. He's always had crazy sexual needs. I'm trying to get him some help. I'm trying to head off a scandal that will ruin him and everything he's worked to – '

'Don't worry about dear old Dad. He's Teflon. Nothing rubs off on him. He's got full-time cover-up, the best money can buy. You think Betty's his first victim?'

Her mouth opened in a shaky O. She seemed frozen in this gesture for the longest time. When she finally spoke her voice had dropped an octave well below Carmen's heroic tones.

'What do you know?'

'Too much.'

'I gave Betty some cash and sent her south for a vacation. I said I'd explain it to your father. I haven't the slightest idea of how to do that. Has he – ? Is it drugs?'

'Just mental.'

'Then what can we – ?'

'Neither of us has been up to the Landing in six months. Did you know he's cancelled all activities, lectures, concerts?' She nodded. 'He's laid off the staff, except for security people. If I get up there today will Betty be gone?'

'She went directly to a sister in Florida.'

'Does Dad have the address?'

'Jack? How – ?'

'This is a psychosis. I don't want any loose ends.'

'Dear God, you're going to help him, not murder him.'

Dealing at close range with the mentally disturbed heightens one's own disturbances. If he booked a copter for the trip to Athens Landing, the pilot would have to file a flight plan and Paul Pierce would be tipped off.

Completing his paranoic lapse, Jack took a local train to Summerville and the first cab whose driver's face was unknown to him. The cab jounced over country roads and up over the drawbridge to deposit him on the Landing. Then it left.

The gate guard hoisted himself lazily to his feet, a toothpick lodged between his lips. He recognised Jack and passed him through without anything more formal than a soft salute.

The deserted island seemed to close in around Jack as he walked toward his father's office. He suddenly knew what Eileen meant when she complained of living a life under surveillance. In its deserted state, Athens Landing had turned spooky. Eyes lurked everywhere.

In his paranoid mood, he decided Carmine Onofrio wasn't paying proper attention to guarding the Landing. Carmine, after all, was his father's first line of defence. If he went bad, Jack mused, Paul Pierce went bad.

But it went beyond that. Picking up persecution points as his mind churned. Jack quickly realised that his father's next line of defence was really Betty. She ran the Pierce empire from her network of data processing computers.

He drew near the small chalet where Paul Pierce played international executive, winner of shady Navy contracts and gold Neptune statues, where several years' worth of emergency food was stashed away. It suddenly dawned on Jack that before Carmine or Betty his father's main prop had always been Serena.

That meant he now had no back-up. Serena was enjoying a new life in Manhattan. Mother of three, she had cut them all loose – as indeed she should – and was now concentrated on her own career once again. And why not? She'd given up enough of it to build the marriage. Her turn was long overdue.

But Paul wasn't the only Pierce being isolated, Jack told himself. He stood outside the chalet-office and glanced up at the cupola, its tinted windows reflecting sunlight. The feeling of being watched was strong enough to touch, taste. He peered around him, trying to see its source. Then he decided he was merely going nuts, plain and simple.

That Eileen and Enid hadn't spoken to him since they stiffed him at the FU2 announcement party gave him a big head start on fantasies of being widely hated.

That was the main problem with being a banker: you had no one to hang out with but bankers. No human beings would want to associate intimately with you. But he depended on Enid to verify his own intelligence. If she thought he was smart, so would customers who saw him on her show. As for Eileen and Pat, he depended on them for ties to reality.

Christ, nobody at Pierce et Cie had said 'no' to him since the day he'd opened his doors.

Thinking back made his head ache. Made him wonder how many errors he'd committed because he'd cut himself off from human talk. Nobody had held a conversation with him about the state of his health, politics, a good chili joint, anything. The one time he called Pat for lunch he'd been busy. And no call-back.

The Pierces seemed to be targeted. Well, his own situation wasn't a disaster. It was only an ego-slap as long as the bank kept doing so well. All he needed was one or two more megabig customers to put a foolproof keel under Pierce et Cie.

But his father had a bigger problem. Somebody had isolated Paul Pierce in his craziness the way a lion-tamer backs a big cat into a cage. To avoid the trap, he'd obviously ducked out of Athens Landing. But where had he gone?

Jack's head ached with the intensity of his thinking, the sharp relief with which paranoia highlighted his father's fate. It didn't take that much more pain to guess the name of the lion-tamer who'd done the job.

Thirty-Three

Although he was tall, Big Mimmo had dainty fingers, in the same way that his head was smaller than expected. He fancied himself dextrous, somewhat in the manner of a lacemaker or a neurosurgeon, but on no evidence other than size.

For that reason, and for heightened privacy, he did the job himself, got into the apartment next door and deftly installed in each room a microphone-transmitter with one-year lithium battery. Although Enid Bart was rarely home except to sleep, Mimmo had collected a few tapes of telephone conversations and bedside rumbles with Pat Rossi. Dull stuff.

But he had great hopes for a tape of last night's party, in which some twenty guests shouted wittily at each other for four hours. This was the time Enid normally broadcast on week-nights. But Sunday night she played host to her networkers, movers and doers, enunciators, herald angels. Most Manhattan buildings had paper-thin walls. This older art deco structure, which masked most noises, last night failed utterly.

When the guests trooped home around three in the morning, Mimmo had sampled the tape. Like most raw conversation, it was an overlay of slurred words, fuzzy criss-crosses, repetition, long pauses and meaningless laughter. Someone kept trying to name all seven dwarfs. Someone else kept rehearsing a barbershop quartet for 'Whistle While You Work. Ronald Reagan is a Jerk'.

Considering this useless result, Mimmo was on the verge of removing the bugs. He considered moving somewhere else in the building next to quieter neighbours. He even imagined his quarry knew that eavesdropping was taking place and therefore produced conversation of stultifying boredom.

He had finally got to sleep around four a.m. The screams began around six.

'Up! Out of bed! He's going to run!' Enid yelled.

'Mpf.'

'Pat, get up.'

'Nmf.'

'Morgenthau's running for DA again!'

'Hmp.'

'Don't you und– ?'

'Good,' Pat managed to yell back. 'Do you know what time it is?'

'Six a.m.,' Mimmo growled. He sat up in bed and started thinking.

'Do you und– ?'

'Shut up!' Mimmo thundered. 'Lemme think!'

'Pat, did you hear something just then?'

At Bridges, the lunching members talked of nothing else but Morgenthau.

Jack Pierce sat at his 'best' table and pondered the way his life had come apart. He had finally swallowed his pride and telephoned Pat for a lunch date. He had got the dubious response of a secretary telling him the call would be returned.

It was, a week later, by her. She made a lunch date for two weeks later. A twenty-one-day stall was a rotten response from the man Jack still called his best friend. And now, with this morning's news, Jack imagined his best friend might even cancel the lunch. That is, have his girl cancel.

The only thing worse than having somebody's secretary stiff you was to have the dirty work done by an electronic answering machine. Jack peered around the room, hoping no one could read his bitter, self-pitying thoughts.

Not that anyone was interested in him. These were fellow members, familiar faces, people he did business with or had gone to school with or something, some goddamned connection. But were they interested in him? He might as well not exist.

Being ignored was lately the main thread of his life. The

pattern of it had become disconnected, defying the laws of cause and effect. To begin with, his father seemed to have disappeared off the face of the earth.

His mother had no clues. She'd phoned Betty, in her Florida hideout, who knew even less. Messages left for Carmine went unanswered. Paul Pierce's bedroom dresser showed he'd abstracted most of his socks and shorts, as if for a trip. But little other clothing, as far as Jack could tell.

Troubles came not singly but in legions. While Jack was at Athens Landing, there had been a currency crisis in Europe. Pierce et Cie clients were often put into Swiss funds, the few that a secret agreement between Switzerland and the United States didn't forbid to American investors.

Denominated in Deutschmarks, Swiss francs and guilders, these funds had overnight lost 12 per cent of their value. And tonight, of all nights, Jack was invited to a dinner that could make Pierce et Cie so powerful it would never again worry about such matters as market ups and downs.

He sipped his pinot grigio and decided the kitchen was taking too long to prepare a plain dish he'd originally suggested to the chef, a room temperature pasta with tonnato sauce. Originally used on veal, the creamy tuna velouté now covered rigatoni.

Jack caught his waiter's glance and gave him a rapid series of finger-snapping motions.

Actually, he warned himself, he shouldn't have let Gaynor Marcus con him into a family dinner. Business presentations should be made in an office or a restaurant. Without women.

But the Marcus clan, gregarious Jews who often married outside their faith, resembled the Pierce clan too much for comfort. They were close, in constant touch. They lived out of each other's pockets, both spiritually and financially.

They saw nothing wrong with talking to a banker at a Monday night pick-up potluck dinner that included wives, sisters and daughters, a gathering which, Gaynor had warned him, usually deteriorated after the meal into bridge or poker.

At fifty, Gaynor was perhaps most equal in a family of equals. Patriarch, no. CEO, yes. Chief Executive Officer of a network of family enterprises whose annual banking volume exceeded five billion, about what Jack's bank now handled per year.

'How's Pierce et Cie doing after the devaluation?' Jack imagined Gaynor wanting to know. 'Did you outguess it?'

It was possible to lie, but Jack feared the Marcus clout. A lie could be found out. So the honest answer had to be: 'Matter of fact we lost our depositors a cool 12 per cent. That's only six million bucks down the drain.'

And then there was Myra, Gaynor's daughter.

Damn the kitchen! He'd been waiting at least fifteen minutes for a simple cold-pasta dish.

Jack found his waiter's eye again and jabbed his index finger at his wristwatch. The man nodded furiously and sped out towards the kitchen.

There was absolutely nothing in Gaynor Marcus's preliminary discussions with Jack that indicated anything more than curiosity about what Pierce et Cie could do for the Marcus clan. 'I've heard interesting things about you,' was as far as Gaynor would venture.

But the dinner invitation spoke of a state of mind already conditioned to look favourably on Jack. It also had a faint resonance of son-in-law-dom.

Gaynor had not asked any giveaway question like 'I heard you were divorced.' His silence was the tip-off.

He had asked no marital question of a man whose six-month marriage to Hasco Re-Investment had drawn all sorts of sly smiles. He'd asked nothing because he'd already checked. Gaynor was already fitting him into a bridegroom's morning coat.

Jack finished his wine. He glanced around the room again at people gabbing happily, laughing, touching, poking, passing food to be sampled. And he sat alone and hungry. Slowly, unheedingly, he ran his fingers through his blond hair and messed up the centre parting.

He had arrived at one o'clock. It was now one-thirty. He could feel his face burning with anger. He got to his feet and walked directly to the cashier's desk. 'Larry, the manager, please.'

'Yes, Mr Pierce. Any problem?' the girl asked.

'How about a thirty-minute wait for a cold pasta that still hasn't arrived?'

'Oh! Gosh! I'm terribly – '

'Jack!' Dan Ludlum's voice boomed behind him.

Jack turned, anger flushing his cheeks, and found himself looking at Dan and Pat Rossi, both grinning. 'You eaten yet?' Ludlum demanded.

'I – Matter of fact – '

'Jack,' Pat said. 'Your hair! Dear me! You look low. You look down. You look starved.' He grabbed Jack's right arm, Ludlum his left, and marched him back to another 'best' table. Bridges was crammed with them.

'By the way, Jack,' Pat murmured. 'Give me a cheque for a thousand. You owe it to the doctor of a friend.'

Thirty-Four

The armature of Manhattan is Fifth Avenue, the backbone on which the whole body hangs. For that job, the longer, zigzag diagonal of Broadway doesn't work.

Since it was up Fifth Avenue that the city first grew northwards, it is to Fifth Avenue that many of Manhattan's elder structures cling. Once one rises north of Dan Ludlum's lair, the financial district and the major courtrooms, everything becomes individual buildings.

It's the Woolworth, Flatiron and Empire State Buildings, the Library lions, St Patrick's, the Plaza Hotel and Central Park. There Fifth soars past leafy parkland, where lies the vast Metropolitan Museum itself.

Across from the museum are buildings of the nineteenth-century's fat years, one-family mansions like Marcus House. Gaynor himself had a triplex with his third wife, Kitty, and, from his first marriage, daughter Myra. A white elephant of a ballroom monopolised a whole floor but was rarely used.

Myra's mother, Eleanor, lived in a large flat on the fifth floor with a clarinettist named Shep, which is why Myra lived with her father. Her Uncle Ted, Gaynor's kid brother, occupied a duplex with three small sons whose mother had run away last year.

Eleanor handled intra-familial catering. Her top-floor apartment had a huge glass-roofed conservatory. Tonight Jack Pierce counted six Marcuses.

Gaynor hadn't placed Myra next to Jack. It didn't matter since she did the serving, homespun style, which brought her bosom over Jack's shoulder quite often. She was a buxom girl, dark haired and incorrigibly smiley, attractive but no dress sense or small talk.

Jack was used to extremely fashionable scarecrows like Cunty with a great line in last week's parties. He was also accustomed, in her intelligence and her erotic fantasies, to Eileen, his co-conspirator in life.

After dinner Myra served him a brandy and sat down beside him. He made some minor quip. 'Tee-hee,' she said.

Her dark eyes had an almost hormonal shine to them, as if she had this very evening come into childbearing nubility. 'What did you say?' he asked.

'Tee-hee?' She looked entirely unrepentant. 'Was that the wrong thing to say?'

Jack took her hand and turned it palm up. 'Mm.'

'Can you really read palms?'

Jack's lips pursed in thought. 'Many men have loved you.'

'Yes, they have.' The smile faded from her face. She turned her hand over to grasp his. 'Are you my true friend, Jack?'

Her warm hand squeezed his with great fervour. 'My mother Eleanor says I'm a very simple person. I need truth and honesty in men. My mother Kitty says I should be taking Prozac.'

'And what does your father say?'

'He says if I'm not married by the time I'm twenty-five he'll go mad. Tee-hee.' She was smiling warmly again.

'Why does he say that?'

'My Zadie's bequest comes due.' Her dark face went sad again. 'It's meaningless. He used to give me electric trains when I wanted dolls. It's Wright-Bellanca he's giving me.'

The brandy in Jack's glass shivered. 'The aircraft people?'

'They're mostly in rockets and satellites now. Yech.'

Jack sipped the cognac as if it might be poisoned, then took a large gulp. 'Wright-Bellanca's immense, Myra. My father has a company that produces engines for them.'

'Boring.' She let go his hand. 'I keep forgetting you're a banker.' Her dark eyes scanned his face for a long moment. 'I didn't mean it. I'm sorry, Jack, please forgive me.' She brushed his centre parting apart, exactly as his mother did.

He made a clown's mouth. 'Tee-hee.'

The poker game ended early because none of the women wanted to play. Brother Ted, Uncle Simms, Cousin Bertrand with the faintly French accent, all treated each other with such casual grace – 'I'm out of cash. Ante me for a thousand' – that they operated as no other branch of the human race understood.

By midnight Gaynor and Jack were alone under the vast glassed-in roof. From time to time they could hear snatches of singing in the kitchen where Eleanor and Myra were cleaning up and probably smiling a lot.

'Eleanor doesn't have a maid?' Jack asked.

Gaynor pulled a long face. He had been very athletic in his thirties and was now trying to hold off a growing waistline.

'She's a very simple person. She believes life is also simple. I'm afraid this mistake has rubbed off on Myra.'

'Myra's a lovely girl. I really like her.'

'I, too.' He got up and went to one of the glazed parts of the roof that overlooked Fifth Avenue. 'Look at this.'

They stood there, insulated from the random midnight traffic, the bus noises and occasional horns. The cut-up hulk of the Metropolitan loomed below and beyond. A glass wall on its north side, which by day illuminated an Egyptian hall, seemed to phosphoresce from the eerie night lighting within.

'Spooky,' Jack said.

Without warning, Gaynor said: 'Near as I can work it out, Pierce et Cie handles a five billion volume. Which means that if we banked through you, we'd double your volume.'

'Is that an offer?'

Gaynor produced a choked laugh. 'I haven't finished the research. You make a Swiss bank look gabby by comparison.'

'That's what we have to offer,' Jack said. 'Discretion and a few bits of sleight-of-hand the IRS can't seem to crack yet.'

Gaynor nodded. 'I imagine you're a good enough conjuror to get around this latest devaluation.'

Jack's heart slowed. Part of Myra's simplicity had been handed down from her father. He might be as cautious as the

188

next tycoon but if he liked you he became very up-front. This was his home-made test for honesty.

'As a matter of fact,' Jack said in a rueful tone, 'like the rest, we got hurt.'

'Badly? Citibank took a ten-point beating, I hear.'

'Citibank has domestic consumer volume that never gets near Euro currency. But Pierce et Cie is different.'

'Tell me.'

'Last week we bottomed at a 12 per cent loss.' Jack's face looked appropriately grave. 'I've been patching the hull. The leaks are stopped. We're back to Citibank's figure, ten per cent. And we'll improve. But, meanwhile... not pleasant.'

He watched Gaynor to see if the lie had been accepted. Bottomed out, indeed. They were still haemorrhaging. 'A month or two?' Gaynor asked. 'You'll be back where you were?'

Jack nodded. 'We're spreading into more Tiger funds in the Far East. It won't be long before we're in hyper-drive again.'

Gaynor turned away from the window to face his guest. 'We have a board meeting next week. I'm going to suggest that we give Pierce et Cie a trial run: six months? A year?'

'Jack. Dad.' It was Myra. She had been wearing a dull draped pistachio dress for dinner. She seemed to have removed it and donned a red-and-white-and-blue wraparound apron that gave her a French maid look, mostly legs and breast. Jack's groin quickened.

On the front of the apron was embroidered: 'World's Greatest Chef', with depictions of lamb chops, a wedding cake and a fish on a platter. Jack had a sudden, clear insight: Myra had done the tacky embroidery herself. Her whole family seemed just as transparent.

She put a tray down on a nearby coffee table. 'It's decaf,' she said. 'Eleanor made those Florentine pastries. Good night.'

Thirty-Five

No detention pen is ever pretty. The one for juveniles accused of sex crimes was the most recently built, with the coarse cinder-block brutality that goes with a low budget. Anyone shoved against it immediately begins to bleed.

Under a seven-foot reinforced concrete ceiling that squashed down every occupant, devoid of windows and, therefore, rank with urine, semen and the acrid stench of roach-killer, the pen this morning held only three boys.

Collectively they had already been dubbed Satan's Punks. Individually, Pat Rossi noted as he scanned his clipboard, they were Rebert Custodial Miller, seventeen, Arch Halliwell, fifteen, and José Remedios, also fifteen.

Before entering the pen, Pat had left his watch, wallet and pocket cash in a manila envelope with a police sergeant. All he carried inside was a ballpoint pen and his clipboard.

He had never before been called on to defend someone accused not merely of murder but of sexual crimes. He entered the pen and stood with his back to the door as the sergeant slammed and locked it behind him.

One overhead fluorescent fixture glared down on them. They had been pictured as killers without conscience, murderers by whim. He was locked in with them.

'Morning.'

Three bunk beds that folded up out of the way supported the three boys. The tallest, Rebert, seemed to lounge seductively, rather like Madame Récamier. Out of a perfectly deadpan face he said: 'Suck this, copper.'

'I'm Pat Rossi, your lawyer.'

'Show us y'asshole, lawyah. Let's get – ' Rebert's taunting

voice went saccharine, 'a sphinctah diametah. You too slack you don't git no cock at all.'

'Your cocks have already got you in shit,' Pat remarked. 'Keep on using your cock instead of your brain you'll end up flushed down Charley's craphole with the rest of the turds.'

'Hoho!' Rebert shouted. He wriggled eagerly. 'Whadda we got here? A talking asshole lawyah.'

'You're Rebert, the mouth that walks like a man?'

'And these two chickees,' Rebert went on, 'I keep on hand to vacuum up my juice. One sucks me front, the other in back.'

Pat began taking notes, simply to gain any kind of ascendency. Rebert Custodial Miller was tall, with the big shoulders and narrow torso of an athlete. His colour was dark brown with a sebacious shine that made him seem blacker.

If he had let his eyes alone – not squinting fiercely or shifting his glance about in roguish come-ons – he would certainly have had a look of intelligence, a welcome face in a sub-stratum of society where studied ignorance was the fad. He was slowly pulling his penis out into the open.

'Jism time, Archie. On your knees.'

'That's a felony,' Pat Rossi remarked. 'Contributing to the delinquency of a minor. You have a choice: behave and we'll make progress. Act up and I leave. I don't care, either way.'

Rebert caressed his long, slack penis for a thoughtful moment. 'But you come back tomorrow. You got time to waste on three fucked-up niggah gangstahs.' His penis hardened at the thought and began to curve upward.

'The State of New York, City of New York, County of New York has all the time in the world, Rebert. Put your dolly away and let's get to work.'

'Jism time!' Pat screamed.

He was thrashing about in bed, not yet awake. 'Pat, calm down.' Enid had her arm around his shoulders. His body felt clammy. She snapped on the bedlamp. 'Calm down.'

He blinked for a moment. 'Those kids. They're succubi.' He twisted around until he and Enid were breast to breast.

'It's only a week of talking to them and already they've spooked me.'

'Not you.'

He hugged her fiercely. Her body felt warm and dry and safe. 'Nothing they tell you is real. Nothing you see with your eyes is real. They are organisms of our society, unique to us. Nothing about them connects to the human race except the snakepit in which they grew up.'

'Please, Pat. Your heart is beating like a pile-driver. You can't let a pack of ignorant, degenerate – '

'They're not ignorant. Their leader is quite bright. They're not degenerates *unless* you admit that our society, which created them, is degenerate.'

'Get off the case.'

'Not on your life.'

'Get off the case or they'll kill you the way they killed that skater. Kill you and shit all over you.' She could feel her own heart start to pound with anger and fear for him.

'There's too much at stake, Enid. Every day I get new evidence that they simply weren't there. They didn't do it. Meanwhile, someone walks free . . . to do it again.'

'That's the job of the police.'

'The police who put them in the frame? Get real, Enid. Once a cop sets a frame, it's set in concrete.'

'And meanwhile you have to associate with such filth that it gives you nightmares?'

They lay there for a long time in silence. When she finally spoke again, Enid had a thoughtful tone, searching. 'Pat? Does it do anything to your case if . . . I don't know how to express this. I mean, we already have trial re-enactments all over the TV dial. They're vulgar trash but terribly popular, real crimes, real trials. Why can't they be done – not as trash but as a sort of citizen's classroom in the law – as pre-trials? Why can't we have actors present the case. Actor-cops. Actor-criminals. Actor-lawyers.'

Thinking this was a joke, Pat picked up the thread of her idea: '. . . actor-judge and bailiff. Actor-psychiatrists. And if we get a guilty verdict, actor-jailers. Or if the ban on the death-penalty gets lifted, actor-executioners, right?'

'You can be cruel when you want to.'

'I can if what you're attacking is due process. Enid, as nasty as these three kids are, they are entitled to justice. Justice is administered, haltingly, by the police and the courts. Not by fucking vulgar TV trash!'

'I have touched your prime nerve,' she murmured. 'The justice/injustice button.'

'Should be yours, too. Should be everybody's.'

'Pat, if we can't dramatise, what about nightly updates as the DA and the defence create their cases? Do you think Morgenthau would – ?'

'He and my clients are entitled to secrecy.' Pat gave a helpless laugh. 'I guess TV people don't admit that the English language has such a word.'

'I'll tell you what I won't admit.' She withdrew her arm from around him and sat up in bed. 'I won't admit that the government is the sole custodian of justice. I won't admit that government alone has the right to play Papa. "We know best, children. And secrecy is best." That can't be supported. Papa and his due process have fucked us up once too often.'

'Good morning, my man! You want it down the throat or up the shithole?'

Pat Rossi heard the door slam shut and lock behind him. 'Rebert, why are you making yourself out such a hard-on dude when you weren't even in the area that night? You three had nothing to do with the skaters. You stole another guy's crime. He's the real gangstah. You're fakes.'

Rebert, stripped to his underpants and curled sideways in an enticing slouch, made a sucking movement with his lips. 'Don't get me riled, lawyah. I got a beautiful butt. I was gonna let you suck it. In lieu of a fee. You get me angry, I give it to José first.'

Pat glanced about the smelly room. Scattered sheets from tabloid newspapers littered the concrete floor. He realised how keenly his clients were enjoying their own publicity. In their case the tabloids skated as close to the edge of family-newspaper content as possible.

'Strange, inhuman sexual practices, sado-masochistic forms of domination, unholy appetites savagely sated,' these were some of the milder hints supplied by perpetually, profession-ally shocked journalists. The letters columns, stirred vigor-ously, were filled by now with the kind of hatred that fizzes so righteously it begins to make no sense. 'Boiled in oil, thrown to wild beasts, drawn and quartered, heads impaled on stakes,' were some of the readers' calmer suggestions.

The case was providing, for the press and its readers, a glut of salacious wish-fulfilment. Any jury catering to its own need for dirty sexual satisfaction would have to bring in a verdict of guilty and a recommendation for staking onto an anthill under the noonday sun.

Pat's best strategy, therefore, was delay, until long after people began asking 'Satan's who?' Perhaps by then Manhat-tan would be deep into the mayoral campaign and Garvey would let the cops find the real murderer. Or the real McCoy might strike again.

'Let me tell you what the next move is,' Pat said out loud.

'No, lawyah, the next move is we gangbang you till we rip you a new asshole.'

'The next move is I shut off the press. I get an injunction forbidding any more interviews. You stink in here for months till Manhattan forgets you ever existed.'

For some reason nobody had a smart answer. Rebert, who did most of the talking, seemed to expire on his cot, all flat and waxy. Little Archy looked stricken. 'Y'cain do that.'

'Watch me. Easiest thing in the world. It protects your civil rights. No more publicity.'

'Man?' José's girlish voice was the highest, as yet unchanged by age. 'Man? Ain' this a free country? A free press?'

'My problem is you three are enjoying every minute of this. You're in the limelight. Everybody knows you.'

'We's somebody, lawyah.' Rebert dragged himself into a sitting position. 'We ain' scum, animals, garbage. We's Satan's Punks. It's a good feeling, lawyah.'

'Even though you're innocent.'

'That makes the joke even bettah, lawyah. You woulden understan.'

'I understand there's somebody out there sicker than you and he's laughing at you because he's getting ready to kill a few more people.' Pat watched the idea expand in Rebert's eyes. It was almost as if he finally got the truth of his situation. 'And when he does,' Pat said, 'you three are nailed as cheapo fakes. You're amateurs, on borrowed time.'

'Sez you, suckhole, sez you.'

But the boy's voice had gone flat and disappointed. For the first time Pat felt he'd opened Rebert's skull and let some sunlight in.

Thirty-Six

History has always failed us on details. All we are told is that Ben Franklin narrowly escaped electrocution that thundery night in Philadelphia. And what can we make of Bell's dim 'Come here, Mr Watson, I want you'?

Eileen's mind confronted such thoughts as she prepared to stage-manage an historic event. She moved two chairs closer to her father's sofa.

The two men due to arrive soon were not guests. They were witnesses, one to keep the other honest. Timmy Groark, of the DA's office, would testify later, if need be, that the other witness had indeed been shown the heart of the matter.

The other witness was Captain Leroy Baxter. That was the moment of history. He was being shown Vinnie Sgroi.

Not his long-rotted corpse, still carrying a vicious spray of assault-rifle bullets. The entire Vincenzo Sgroi had been re-assembled, cross-referenced, graphed, plotted and put back together three-dimensionally so that he existed in what computer savants called 'virtual reality'.

He could have been resurrected more easily as words or formulae. But Michael Rossi understood that the buyers for his latter-day Lazarus would, first, be police and, only second, academics or computer buffs.

So he had created Vinnie as a real-time multiple-access video.

The mobster almost walked the streets of Manhattan. Name a date and you would 'see' him keep his appointments, make his deals, collect his loot, re-invest it, pressure his associates, share out his profits and grow visibly more powerful.

It ranked with the invention of the telephone, which also produced a virtual reality that 'heard' someone else. It ranked, Eileen felt, with Franklin's foolhardy kite and the magical energy that, two hundred years later, ran the world and all its info-highways.

'What part will you show them?' she asked her father.

'Whatever their tiny hearts desire.'

Former Detective Sergeant Michael Rossi's voice trembled with eagerness. He had even submitted to having his hair combed and a rather nice tie knotted in place. Except for the fierce green flame of his eyes and the tremor of expectation in his voice, he was dressed as a rather passive onlooker, not the man who had raised Vinnie Sgroi and his entire world back to the living again.

'Will that be sexy enough to interest Baxter?' she wondered. 'He lives and dies for publicity. He looks very political, does the captain, very senatorial, even presidential. He may have decided that this is the year of the light-complected black. It may well be.'

'Depends how big a fight he wants to start. Vinnie had lines into every large East coast multinational corporation.'

'Is that news?'

'Don't be blasé, Eileen. If Baxter has big eyes, he has to tackle big scams.'

Eileen glanced around the living room. She had known it from infancy, learned to crawl and walk and dance its length. During her childhood and Pat's it had been crowded, messy with abandoned clothing and school gear, books, scribbled papers, a level just below pig-sty, but biologically more or less clean.

Now that her brother rarely came home to sleep, she had redecorated, painted, wall-papered, thrown out twenty years of tired, ancient dressers and rickety folding chairs. The bathroom had been retiled. Windows had been double-glazed against the roar of Second Avenue. The place looked vastly more inviting than it ever had before, a fitting stage upon which this electronic bombshell would be detonated.

Odd that ever since the failed massacre, life had become

easier at Rancho Rossi. Pat was making a lot more money, of course. But Baxter had committed his precinct to giving them twenty-four-hour surveillance. Through brute force he'd shamed the clinic into sending a nurse and doctor to Rossi, rather than risking Rossi to them every six weeks.

Eileen smiled slightly, not so much a sign of content as the tired smile of one who can, for the first time since infancy, relax her guard.

'Enough chitchat,' Rossi said after his two witnesses had been seated and given very pale whiskey highballs. 'I asked you here to meet Vinnie Sgroi, and I wasn't ribbing you.'

His left hand fingerwalked its way to the remote-control keypad and began tapping instructions to the computer, using the large 32-inch screen of his TV set. One of those looping, tube-saver patterns danced across the screen for a moment. Then the impossible began.

Later, after Groark and Baxter had time to reminisce, they found that both of them had expected some sort of sleight-of-hand. Nothing dishonest, just very sketchy and only a notch above having a duty sergeant read from his clipboard.

But, as it dawned before their eyes, neither of them were prepared for what they saw. Slowly, unwillingly, as if being summoned from a great distance – quite true, as it happened – a man wearing a pale tan Panama hat strode towards the viewers. He had big, greedy eyes and very high cheekbones over skin debauched by acne.

'Hey!' Timmy Groark's tough, tubby body sat forward like a bulldog being shown fresh-cut sirloin. 'Where'd you get that footage, Mike?'

'It's not footage. It's virtual reality.'

'Virginal what?'

'Wait. Is that Sgroi?' Baxter asked. His café-au-lait colouring gave him the look of a well-to-do vacationer with extra hours in the sun. His normally aloof manner, part college dean, part Sherlock Holmes, fell away. A deep line of concentration creased his forehead

'It's Sgroi,' Timmy growled. 'Look at the bastard.'

'Hi, Vin,' Rossi told the TV image.

'Rossi, is that you?'

The illusion was chilling. Vinnie was in semi-closeup. His face and lip movements seemed perfectly synched to his words. But he seemed somehow blind, groping for an altered reality. His hungry eyes searched for his interrogator who would always, it seemed, be invisible, a god incredibly *ex-machina*.

Baxter actually growled and almost got up from his chair, as if to grab at the electronic image. Rossi lifted his finger in a silent calming gesture.

'Vin, sorry to bring you back from Hell. Some guys here want to talk to you.'

'Hey, copper, thanks for nothing.'

A sense of shock abruptly forced both witnesses into speech, goaded by the impossibility of the scene. Both Timmy and the police captain began to bark angry questions. They looked like hounds spotting the fox.

'Mike,' Baxter said, 'there's no hesitation. You ask. He answers. But they're *your* questions. Let me try him.'

'You figure these are set-ups?'

'I didn't say that, I'm – '

'Go ahead. Ask.'

'Ask anything?'

'Ask everything.'

'Vincenzo Sgroi,' the captain began. He paused, but only momentarily at a loss for words, still a bit ashamed to be seen interrogating a cathode-ray tube. 'On the afternoon of 4 March 1970, describe your location.'

'Describe my location,' the simulated image repeated, '4 March, 1970.' The greedy mouth fell slack for a long moment. Then: '4 March, 1970, three p.m., 32nd floor, Chrysler Building, De Bartolo and Skates, Property Management.'

The face went slack again. 'Vinnie, it's show and tell,' Rossi prompted. 'Let's show.'

Instantly the image on the screen, half way between photography and animation, changed to a street scene. A dark

Lincoln Continental drew to the kerb and the driver, hastily donning his cap, got out to open the rear door.

Out stepped Sgroi. He and his chauffeur looked from side to side. A third man joined them from inside the limo, looking fiercely for inappropriate passers-by. Then Sgroi crossed a sidewalk into the Lexington Avenue art deco enamel and aluminium entrance of the Chrysler Building. His bodyguard followed him in.

'Cut the show biz, Mike,' Timmy Groark muttered. 'This is serious.'

Rossi touched the remote control and the bodyguard disappeared from the screen. Alone now, Sgroi got out of an elevator and walked a long corridor toward a door marked 'De Bartolo and Skates'.

'Once I start these sequences, they have to play in their own time,' Rossi said apologetically. 'I can edit them but not much.'

They watched Sgroi enter the office. The receptionist ushered him into a large conference room where several other men were already sitting. 'Larry, Sam, Vito,' the Sgroi image shook hands all around.

'Last names, Vinnie,' Rossi called out.

'Larry De Bartolo. Sam Schreiber, alias Skates. Vito Battipedi, alias Feets.'

'Freeze frame!' Captain Baxter shouted. 'I can't take it!'

The TV image went motionless. 'Mike,' the police captain complained, 'you expect me to believe this is a virtual reconstruction, from history. But you can cut in and make it expand with details like last names?'

'They're important. De Bartolo was Vinnie's legit front, not a made mafioso. Dead now. Skates couldn't be made because he was a Jew. But Feets was the real thing. Still is.'

'It's like you own them,' Baxter complained. 'Like they're your puppets.'

'I can show them doing anything,' Rossi agreed.

'Even telling lies?' Baxter persisted.

'Sure. This is my software. But what would be the point of me using it to tell lies? The whole idea is to show the truth.'

'Whose truth?' Baxter demanded.

'Look.' Timmy Groark's harsh voice sounded strangely conciliatory. 'Either we take Mike Rossi on faith, or we get up and leave right now.'

Baxter grinned. 'Miss Rossi, can I have a glass of water? I'm thirsty, but I'm not leaving.'

'Action!'

Vinnie Sgroi sat down between Sam and Vito. 'I got the cash,' he announced.

'Eighty mill?'

'Forty mill cash, forty mill Class B American Steel, non-voting, due 1982.'

'Son of a gun. Nice work.' Battipedi shuffled some beribboned folders. 'Sign all four copies. It's in the Smythson-Jellinek name.'

In silence Rossi, Groark, Captain Baxter and Eileen watched Sgroi sign four times, mechanical-repetitive movements. In a strange way, this obviously robotic act fine-tuned everyone's understanding of what they were watching. Not a playlet of humans but a titanic think-tank of data given human shape.

From the way their glances focused on the screen Eileen realised they now 'bought' the reconstruction. They knew they were watching a hand-doctored reality, but it had become a convincing one.

'American Steel loves you?' De Bartolo asked.

'They love not having to bargain with a CIO-AFL steel union. My stiffs do what I tell 'em.' Sgroi handed over the signed contracts.

'What's the building?' Groark demanded to know, as if he had Vinnie in a cell and was already sweating him. 'What'd you just buy, you lousy crumbum?'

The image of Sgroi paused and once again assumed the slack lower lip. Then it jerked back to life. 'Just off the northeast corner of 42nd Street and Second Ave. Torn down a year later.'

'Amazing,' Baxter said in a low, fervent voice. 'Damned amazing.' He glared at the screen. 'Vinnie, remember Phil Marcus? Tell us how he ended up?'

The Phil Marcus story had been a staple of Sunday magazine sections for years. Once head of the Marcus clan and a major Manhattan bank affiliated with one of the Vatican money laundries, Phil disappeared on a weekend in 1974. So did seventy-three million dollars in bearer bonds.

The image on the screen became a closeup. The scene in the property management office faded away. Sgroi, who had never removed his tan Panama straw during all this – a refinement Rossi had no time to reprogram – stared boldly at the screen. His eyes bugged agressively. 'Phil Marcus.' He repeated his stalling technique while the software searched itself.

'Phil Marcus. Gabriel Philip Marcus. Not terminated.' The words were spat out almost contemptuously.

'He's alive?' Baxter pounced. 'Where?'

'He didn't say that,' Rossi interrupted. 'He doesn't know. He's stalling.'

'Jesus,' Baxter complained, 'keeping up with this is like running a marathon.'

'Time for a rest.' Rossi tapped his keypad and the TV screen went back to its looping tube-saver patterns.

'Chief,' he went on, 'I can't fill in where I don't know. There are gigabytes of information on my CD-ROMs. I'd guess trillions of bytes about millions of things that my AI chews on. But since it can't say Marcus is alive or dead, I can't call up an answer for you.'

The two active cops, Groark and Baxter, exchanged glances, guarded at first, then questioning. Some sort of telepathic signalling was going on. Finally, almost together, each nodded very slightly.

Baxter sat back and crossed his legs. He frowned and sipped his glass of water. 'Detective Sergeant Michael Rossi, formerly NYPD,' he said in a rather solemn tone, 'I came here expecting tricks. But you can recreate a whole era of corruption, of tracking crime so highly placed it's almost untouchable. That's some trick. You're getting what could be a couple of dozen high-level indictments from your guinea pig, Sgroi.

If we had your software, we could put it to work on other matters. On Phil Marcus?'

Rossi turned to Eileen 'I told you this whole scheme was a money-maker. What should I charge the NYPD?'

'Whatever you charge, it's not enough,' Baxter told him. 'But because it's priceless, you're going to donate it free of charge.'

All three men, police of various backgrounds and experience, burst out laughing. 'Don't tempt me,' Rossi said.

Someone rang the front doorbell. It was a mark of how keyed up they all were that each of them reacted openly, whirling around to stare or barking a wordless exclamation. 'What the hell?' Rossi demanded.

Eileen went to one of the newer additions to the upgraded Rancho Rossi, a television-speakerphone. 'Yes?' she asked, pressing a button that switched on TV.

All of them could see the face of Jack Pierce, staring hard into the camera, his eyes wide and rimmed with dark skin. 'Sorry,' Eileen carolled cheerily, 'we don't want any.'

'Christ, Eileen.' His voice was harsh. A near-sob pulsed through his breathing. 'Open up, please.'

She turned to glance at her father and then at the other men. None of them had collected his thoughts. 'What's the problem, Jack?' she asked.

'The bank.'

'What?'

'Pierce et Cie. The run started this morning. We're ruined.'

'Send him away,' Rossi growled.

'Jack, I – '

'Please, Eileen. I'm begging you. This is the worst d-day in . . .' The sobs came softly at first. His face slid away from the TV screen. He was scratching at the door. Even without the speakerphone they could hear his sobs.

Eileen gave the men a helpless look, shot open the bolts and swung open the door. Tears streaming down his face, Jack Pierce half crawled, half fell into the front hall.

'Mike,' Captain Baxter remarked, 'I have to hand it to you. You're the king of virtual reality.'

Thirty-Seven

Out behind Rancho Rossi sat a tiny concrete yard where Eileen kept two black plastic trash cans. She perched on the edge of one while Jack Pierce, his chin on his knees, sat on the back door steps that led to the kitchen.

It might seem to a passer-by that even in that cramped space she was keeping her distance from him. But, as they shifted position, it became clear that he wanted as much separation as she did. He had the guilty look of someone with an infection who was trying not to pass it on.

Inside the house, Michael Rossi was taking his witnesses through a second séance with the spirit of Vinnie Sgroi. Jack had been hustled outside so fast he hadn't suspected anything much was happening except a gabfest among coppers.

'I'm truly sorry to bust in on you like this.'

Jack had been rubbing at his face with his handkerchief. He was still in a highly disturbed state and it was possible for Eileen to see that he hadn't actually shaved or washed his face whenever he'd risen this morning. Tears and dirt had sadly soiled his large linen handkerchief.

'Five a.m.,' Jack said. 'Basel called. It was eleven a.m. there. The run had started.'

'When you say "run" . . . ?'

'People coming into the bank. People calling in. Faxing in. Messengering. Telexing. Forming lines that go out to the street. Advertising it to the world. All of them wanting to withdraw as much cash from their account as possible.'

'But why?'

In all the various ways she had seen Jack, awake, asleep, randy, exhausted, whining, bragging, she had never seen him so catatonic. He sat perfectly still. It was as if his inner electricity had been shorted out. His face, only vaguely messed by a day's growth of blond beard, looked older, heavier. His hair seemed cast in lead.

'We have regulations about how much you can withdraw at a moment's notice. That put off total disaster by a day. But once our American customers joined the run at nine this morning, our goose was cooked.'

'That doesn't explain why.'

'And the clerical work! We don't have a staff out there at counters. We're not really a walk-in consumer bank. We're just so swamped w-w-with . . .'

His voice broke. With his head resting on his knees he made himself smaller, hiding his face as the tears started to squeeze down his cheeks again.

'Jack. Tell me why.'

One eye opened and stared coldly at her. 'Does it matter? We're ruined. What blood we put off spilling today will be sucked dry tomorrow.'

'You're avoiding telling me. Is that it?'

Suddenly he sat up straight, rigid with anger, no longer still. 'I don't fucking know!' he howled. 'I didn't come here for a third degree, Eileen.'

'Just for a shoulder to cry on?'

'No.' He paused. 'Yes, I guess so.'

'I read the gossip columns, Jack. What's wrong with Myra Marcus's shoulder?'

'None of this would've happened,' he muttered, just on the edge of being heard, 'if I hadn't started chasing the Marcus account. Everything was fine till then.'

'Not what I heard.'

He stared up at her. She watched his first, arrogant glare go to pieces. He sniffed hard and wiped his nose. His look turned to a begging one, slowly freezing into a catatonic state again.

'Currency exchange losses,' she said. 'Worse than the other banks suffered. And Pierce et Cie couldn't stop the slide because nobody knew how. Right?'

'Something like that.'

'Something like having top management – you all by yourself – with no experience of the ugly downside when things go bust. My father put it in a nutshell. "He's a fair-weather sailor. He can't handle hitting a squall." '

'You two discuss me?'

'As little as possible.'

He tried to smile but the result was ghastly. 'I'm flattered,' he managed to say. 'I'm flattered that anybody in this town gives a rat's ass what happens to me.'

'Let's not overreact, Jack. We'd discuss you like we'd discuss troops being ambushed in Sarajevo or Mogadishu.'

'As if I'm a disaster.'

'Right. Tell me about Myra.'

'Myra.' He sniffed very hard and his glance slid sideways to check on her face. 'She's a very simple girl. She's got a Jewish father. But she has an Irish Catholic mother. Like you.'

'God, that's a worse genetic mix than Italian-Irish.'

'She's very simple. She cooks and sews. She likes serving the dinner. She's . . .' He gave up.

'Sounds like my day, boring.'

'Christ, Eileen, when she's twenty-five she inherits Wright-Bellanca.'

'Ah. That's not me.'

'I can't figure out how he did it, or why. Her father, Gaynor Marcus. Somehow he's behind this run on Pierce et Cie. I don't know why or how. It's like – '

Suddenly he was crying again. Eileen frowned down at him. 'Cut it out, Jack. When did you ever cry over money?'

'It's like a truck knocked me over in the street. And now it's trying to run me down . . . flat.'

'What a way to treat a future son-in-law.' She shook her head. 'Has he shifted his account to your bank?'

'He was about to when this run started.'

'What do your colleagues think?'

'What colleagues? A cousin or two?'

'All your age? What does your father say?'

The silence that fell over them was like rain, shutting out normal life. 'Jack?'

'My dad? I haven't told him. It's just happened.'

'But he'll certainly hear of it before tomorrow. What are you stalling for?'

'Yeah. Well. You always had a better relationship with your dad than I did with mine.'

'Jack. You're talking bullshit. He was your chief backer. He has to be consulted.'

'Yeah?' His voice started to rise. 'Consult him? That it?' He seemed to fill his lungs and scream. 'First I have to find him, you dummy! He's disappeared!'

He leaped to his feet, his mouth wrenched sideways. He looked aghast at what he'd shouted. He dropped to his knees and hugged her legs, stroking them over and over. 'I'm sorry! God, I'm sorry. I'm going crazy, Eileen.'

He began kissing her legs. His day-old beard made a scratchy, shushing sound on her stockings. 'Oh, God, Eileen, I'm so sorry. You're my only friend in the whole world, you and Pat. You're the only people who care if I live or die, you two.'

His tears were dampening her legs. Unconsciously her fingers had buried themselves in his thick blond hair, messing it slowly about, stroking him with one hand as he was stroking her.

The kitchen door opened very slowly.

Timmy Groark stood in the entrance, obviously about to say something. Instead he made a what's-this? gesture with his thumb, indicating the kneeling man. Eileen put her finger to her lips. As silently as he'd appeared, Groark retreated and closed the door.

'Who was that?' Jack almost shrieked.

'Friend of ours.'

'How much did he hear?'

'Calm down, Jack. All he heard was the great Jack Pierce, on his knees, apologising at the top of his voice for being the arrogant, shameless, careless, *stupid* rich bastard he is.'

'Careless? Stupid?'

'Anybody who gets a bank handed to him and fucks it up

like a free lunch, can be called careless, wouldn't you say? But anybody who, in the process, has also lost his father? He's just plain, downright stupid.'

Thirty-Eight

At night, through his one office window, Pat Rossi could see the sparkling bridges that crossed the East River to link the spaceship of Manhattan to Brooklyn and Queens.

He could see the upthrust of the Empire State Building with King Kong's mooring tower topping it off. To the right shone art deco slashes of light atop the Chrysler Building and the oddly sloping solar-cell roof of Citibank.

But tonight he wasn't watching. He was studying a shabby pile of documents. The extremely slim school records of his three Satanic punks were there. So were their far fatter police records and, in the case of Rebert Custodial Miller, his dossier from two reformatories.

Through one of his father's pals, Pat had got illicit copies of the police interrogation, not the ones he would later receive, but the truth before everything was sanitised.

There was absolutely no reason for the FBI to have been called into a local case. But because so much publicity was involved the FBI quickly produced its own review. He had it.

One corner of his desk was devoted to hospital reports on the girl skater's condition. Secondary infections, fecal matter rubbed into deep slashes, had finally been neutralised.

It was no wonder, Pat thought, that he was still here at ten p.m. when the rest of FU2 was taken over by cleaning ladies. But, since Enid, he'd become a night-owl whether he liked it or not.

He stared at the documents. The more he studied them the clearer it was that Dan Ludlum had been right: it wasn't even a *good* frame-up. It was the police giving Mayor Garvey a quick fix to brag about at the polls.

But yesterday, in one of Manhattan's weekly gossip newspapers, there had been a satirical editorial calling for the real killer – in the name of civil order and political calm – to give himself up.

Pat supposed this was really the way to protect the three boys entrusted to him. It was more difficult to find hard evidence clearing them than to poke vicious fun at the frame-up. When the time came to empanel a jury – and he would demand a jury – no one would believe a word of the police version.

To do this he had to make a monkey of due process. The first step would be to get Enid Bart interested. At the moment she loathed both the defendants and her spotless public defender being associated with such human garbage.

Pat's telephone produced a high, demanding chirp. 'Hello.'

'Darling, dear God you're working late.'

'I was just thinking of you,' he said.

'You're sweet. There's an emergency here. So naturally I thought of my most photogenic talking head.'

'What's the topic?'

'That's the problem. It took a month to put together a papal nuncio and two protestant ministers on the latest encyclical's effect on New York Catholics. The nuncio cancelled five minutes ago. So we have no topic.'

'But you still have Protestants?'

'I'm about to cancel Protestants, too.'

'What kind of Protestants?'

She laughed. 'Teaching Protestants.'

'So they have contact with kids?'

'Why do you ask?'

'If you want me to help, change the topic to something like "Young Murderers" and I'm yours.'

'Not that infected trio of perverts?'

'Ever-younger offenders. Children whose most heinous crime used to be smoking ciggies out in the alley, now slash, rape and kill.'

'Feh.'

'I never met a topic closer to the headlines,' he persisted.

'Pat, I have some responsibility to my viewers not to send them to bed with images of human degradation.'

'Dear me. What town do they live in that degradation bothers them?'

'No cynicism. Help me.'

'Okay: how's this? My punks may be satanic but they are innocent of this horrendous crime. Someone else is and, by God we'd better find him.'

On Enid's end of the line someone was barking at her in a voice too raspy to be understood. 'Oh, shut up,' she said. 'What?' The voice rasped on.

Pat could make out, finally, that at this late hour they were having no luck cancelling the two ministers, probably somewhere en route. Such are the trivia that reshape history.

'Pat? Tell me some way to elevate this sordid topic with a dash of religion.'

'I'll have it by the time I get to the studio.'

'Bless you. Twelve-thirty. Look pretty.'

Only one minister got there, an ex-nurse who ran a church school up in the Bronx. By the time Enid opened the discussion the Reverend Sarah Selleck was asking to be called Sally.

'Parents send us their kids,' she explained. 'That means parental interest. It's the difference between life and death.'

'We've been trying all week,' Pat responded, 'to locate someone who will authorise us to defend any or all of the boys. No parent or guardian has come forward yet.'

'Nor will they,' Sally snapped, 'as long as they're afraid the cops will beat the bejesus out of them.'

Instantly the programme went into lift-off. The telephone lines lit up. Callers were screened by two young women who tried to get rid of cranks without losing callers who were merely colourful.

'Pro-kids 4, anti-cops 8,' read a scribbled note handed to Enid. Then a second note: 'Dan Ludlum Line 13.'

Enid punched up the Ludlum call on her phone. 'Do you

wish to address our immense audience?' she asked. 'Or are you just calling to tell me I look smashing tonight?'

'Is it the dear nearness of Pat Rossi?'

'I always look great when a discussion hits takeoff speed in the first second. Why'd you call?'

'Next Thursday night, at the St Regis, we're doing a big fund-raiser for Democratic candidates. The keynote speaker will be Conrad Courtney III.' Ludlum paused for effect.

Then: 'He will announce his campaign to become the Democratic candidate for mayor of the City of New York.'

'Bravo Connie Courtney. He's about the only candidate who could stay out of jail till Election Day.'

'And the only one,' Ludlum reminded her, 'with enough of his own cash to make the running.'

'But not much political smarts.'

'All he needs is a smart campaign manager who can also stay out of jail,' Ludlum mused. 'Somebody, oh, you know, handsome and already a public defender. Somebody handsome and street-smart where Connie has too much of a society image. Somebody handsome who refuses to run against Morgenthau.'

'Gee, Dan, who could that be?'

'He'd go on a six-month leave, with pay, from FU2. Connie's budgeted a hundred-thousand fee plus expenses. I want him to make the announcement when he makes his own. You have a week to talk him into it.'

'What's in it for me?'

'I will place my body and soul beneath the heel of your foot, together with my everlasting devotion.'

From time to time the studio cameras cut to a three-shot in which, while the debaters talked, Enid could be seen on the telephone. She had long ago learned to hold the instrument in such a way that it masked her mouth against lip-readers.

'Dan Ludlum, my devoted slave. But I thought I already had that.'

'Well, it can't hurt to get it renegotiated. We both know how Pat feels about justice and injustice. This is his chance to enroll the next mayor in his crusade. Say yes.'

Pat was arguing with a caller from Pennsylvania who was advocating for juvenile offenders' enforced brainwashing or the gas chamber. Choose one.

She watched the way his face seemed to light up from within as, line by line, he explained what democracy was. And what it wasn't. She could picture the compromises he would have to face in a mayoral campaign, the contrasts between his world and Courtney's.

'Dan? It may be the end of a glorious love affair.'

'You always have me to fall back on.'

'What? The sixth Mrs Dan Ludlum?'

'Who said anything about matrimony?'

She glanced at Pat, fielding yet another caller. He looked so young, so earnest, so . . . gorgeous. What would he be like six months from now? How would he feel about the woman who talked him into trading his soul for an election victory?

Of course, in Manhattan six months was a long time. How would she feel about him by then? Her deep sigh came over the phone to Ludlum. 'Well?' he demanded.

'Well, okay. Yes.'

'Bless you.'

Funny, she thought, it felt more like a curse.

Thirty-Nine

There are two kinds of fund-raising dinners in Manhattan. One is held in a good hotel at a token per-plate donation of $100 to cover what the hotel charges. Its guests are the true insiders of a political party. When they are asked for contributions, the sums are modest.

The other is staged in drop-dead glitz at $1000 to $3000 a plate. The guests at this dinner know absolutely nothing about politics. They will pay dearly for their education.

Although they'd already booked the St Regis Hotel, the Democratic Party honchos hadn't yet decided the nature of the party at which Conrad Courtney III was scheduled to announce his mayoral bid. At the same event Dan Ludlum hoped to be able to announce Pat Rossi as campaign manager.

'I'm going.' Former Detective Sergeant Michael Rossi told his family. 'I don't care if I look like a rag doll, I'm going to be there on the goddamned dais.'

'With your elfin daughter beside you? Feeding you dogfood bits?'

'No, he's right,' Pat argued. 'He belongs there.'

'So we're deeply in debt without even having tasted the rubber chicken. Marvellous.'

'I know, Eileen,' her father agreed. 'But how often do I ask for anything?'

His children glanced at each other, but said not a word. Not one word. That didn't prevent Eileen from some sideways work with the poignard. 'In what capacity do you deserve to be on the dais?' she asked sweetly. 'Sire of P. Rossi, Tammany's chief pretty face? Or in your own right as Tsar of Computer Reality?'

Her father had the good grace to blush, not much, more symbolic than telltale. 'No,' he responded. 'As Father of the Fastest Female Mouth South of Fourteenth Street.'

'Our Lady,' Pat chimed in, 'of the On-Again-Off-Again Boyfriend. Patron Saint of Busted Bankers.'

'Martyr,' she added, 'to Two Gadarene Swine Who Think They're Funny.'

'Did you get one of these?' Serena Wainwright Pierce asked. She was sitting in her dressing-room this Wednesday evening, slowly making up for yet another sold-out performance of *Spanish Carmen*.

Thanks to a crazed hair permanent and a lamp-produced tan, she had very little need of make-up these days. People rushed up to her on the street and began chatting in Spanish. Now in her second year as the fiery cigarette girl, she had also taken on hyper-active body movements and facial expressions that closely resembled those of a Latino teenager, not the mother of three adult offspring.

One of whom clearly needed cheering up. She had never seen Jack so depressed. He studied the stiff card-stock invitation to the Courtney dinner. 'Dan Ludlum's handiwork.' His voice had a hollow ring to it. He nodded and produced one of his up-from-the-heels sighs. He glanced at his watch. 'I have an evening meeting at the bank.'

'Didn't you shut it down?'

'We took a stop-trading injunction. But it's only for thirty days. Then we have to face the music.' He paused, as if unwilling, then shook his head shamefacedly. 'Actually I'm meeting Eileen for dinner.'

Serena dabbed a bit of dark foundation base on a small sponge and touched up her tan. 'Is she,' she asked tartly, 'your new banking consultant?'

'You surely know I've been seeing Eileen off and on for years now.'

'What a romantic way of putting it.'

'Lay off, Mom.'

She teased her eyebrows out and up with a mascara brush.

'Jack, when was the last time you saw your father? Did he look all right?'

'The last time.' He gave a fair imitation of trying to remember. 'Couple of weeks ago. Looked okay.'

'That's it? Looked okay?'

Jack shifted uncomfortably. This was what came of lying to one who clearly had a right to the truth. 'He asked how you were.'

Serena let the brush drop from her fingers to the glass-topped dressing table. 'Don't make up stage business for your father. He's not a "how is she?" person. It's not a Paul Pierce line. To check on my health all he has to do is read the drama pages. Where is he, Jack?'

'He's up in Connecticut.'

'That tells me nothing.'

'I'm not sure where,' Jack retrieved. 'I'll phone Carmine Onofrio. He'll know.'

'Carmine who?'

'He's head of security at the Landing.'

'That's another thing.' She pulled open a drawer and fished about in it. 'This was forwarded to me by the Post Office.'

Jack took the folded letter. It was a second request from the State of Connecticut for payment – with penalty – of taxes on the jointly owned property known as Athens Landing. Miming nonchalance, he tucked the letter in his inside breast pocket. 'No problem.'

'Glad to hear it. Pierce et Cie can still provide that kind of money? Can it even buy Eileen dinner?'

He looked glum. 'If we don't have drinks.'

She poked around in her purse and brought out a hundred-dollar bill. 'I think Eileen's worth a decent meal.' She shoved the money across to him. 'Just stop lying to me about your father.'

His face darkened. 'He's d-disappeared,' he faltered.

'Did you notify the police?'

'Are you crazy? Dad would disinherit any child of his who took anything to the cops.'

Her eyes fixed on his for so long, suddenly darted sideways. 'Do you think he's in danger?'

'I think he blew town on his own.'

Her great, mascaraed eyes swivelled to another part of the floor. 'Then . . .' She paused. 'Then . . . I don't know what to say. Yes. Yes, I do. Propose marriage to Eileen. Fast!'

He could feel the sobs lying just below his heart, waiting to rocket out of him. 'I'm marrying Myra Marcus,' he blurted.

'Gaynor's daughter?' He nodded miserably. 'Who dresses like my cleaning lady?' He nodded again. 'To save the bank?' He nodded once more. 'Is that what you're telling Eileen at dinner?'

'Afraid so.'

'Jack? Next time you see Dan Ludlum, ask him how a mother can get a divorce from her son? It can't be too hard.'

Eavesdropping the apartment next door, Big Mimmo now had a fairly reliable chart of when Enid Bart came or went. Willy-nilly, he had a similar chart for Pat Rossi, although his itinerary was not as certain.

In any event, the apartment was normally empty until early morning. Mimmo had invited half a dozen associates for seven p.m. Two bowls of organically grown fruit sat on the long cocktail table. There were no ashtrays. Anyone who had to smoke stepped outside on the terrace to do so.

On the table stood thick amber-tinted plastic tumblers, a large ice bucket and three blue glass seltzer bottles, the kind that Manhattanites knew from their youth. A man came with a crate of bottles topped by bright chrome levers. He would take back empties.

It wasn't much different these days. Mimmo owned both of the companies selling seltzer door-to-door. They delivered a crate, iced, every Monday and Thursday.

'Alfie,' the big man said in a low purr, 'what was the meaning of that raid on the freight hangars at Newark?'

'DEA thugs. They gave us forty-eight hours' warning to clear out the warehouse. Then they busted in like heroes, planted some scag and found it. We're back in action already.'

'Thanks, Alfie.' Mimmo's eyes narrowed. 'Whose scag?'
'Not mine.'
'Find out whose. I have to know which of my guys is playing footsie with those gonifs at DEA.' He swung sideways, shot a jet of charged water into a glass and popped in three ice cubes.

'Guido,' he said, handing the glass to a hulking young man across the table from him. 'Guido, what did the doctor tell you last week?'

'Doctor?'

'Guido, you saw a Dr Eliot Marmelstein up in New Haven. What did he have to tell you?'

The young man grew pale but remained calm enough. 'I'm healthy as a pig, he says.'

'Is that how you'd describe a guy who tested HIV positive?'

'Wha'? Me?'

'One of my labs rang the alarm. You get your blood tested for anything here in the North-east and you have to deal with my labs. How many Guido Smaldones do you think there are in New Haven?'

'Mim, I swear I – '

'Basta. I don't want to spoil the mood.' He turned to the short, pug-faced man near the door to the terrace. 'Carmine, this is sort of a celebration for you and Guido. You have cleaned up the whole Pierce problem. Am I right?'

'One hundred per cent. I hate t' brag but there ain't a Pierce left to piss on. Hey, and it all started when they put out a hit on Guido here.'

'That's what I call a job well done.' The big man fizzed seltzer into a glass, added ice and handed it to Carmine Onofrio. 'To you, Carmine, the smartest of them all.' They lifted their glasses, touched them and drank. 'My profound thanks.'

Carmine sipped. His plastic tumbler shot out of his hand as he grabbed at his throat. Both hands clawed at the pain.

A black ripple of cyanide sputum oozed smokily down from one corner of his mouth. He choked, spun sideways and died in mid-vomit. The stench of bitter almonds filled the room.

'A good, fast death. Guido, my HIV associate, find a place

for Carmine in Connecticut soil.' Big Mimmo gestured with his thumb. Guido Smaldone and a colleague dragged Carmine's small but muscular body from the room. 'Alfie, get a broom and clean up the rug. Open a window. That smell.'

It wasn't lost on any of them, Guido especially, that in removing Carmine Onofrio they were wasting a good man *because* he had done a good job.

Not just a good man, but one whose entire career celebrated old country tradition. Up against the new style of Big Mimmo Caccia? No contest.

It wasn't lost on them but none of them had any answer to the problem of staying alive in the new regime.

'I don't know these people,' Pat Rossi complained. 'I don't know their friends. Their way of life. Their neighbourhoods on Upper Fifth and Madison and Park. I'm exactly the wrong guy for a top-hat-and-tails candidate.'

His words, at half past three in the morning, activated Big Mimmo's eavesdropping system and, almost at once, wakened the big man.

He sat up in bed, listening intently. Was he, at last going to get something useful out of all this?

'But what you do know,' Enid Bart said, 'is the New York electorate.'

'See? Right there you're off track. There are at least three electorates.'

'See?' she countered. 'You already know that.'

'You have what the Brits call the Chattering Classes. Professionals. Teachers. People in finance and communication. Eggheads. Poseurs. Social climbers. That's one electorate.'

A confused rustling and creaking interrupted him. Mimmo realised they were undressing for bed.

'The second is white working class beer-guts out in Brooklyn, Queens, the Bronx and Staten Island. They will always vote Republican if you give them a dese-an-dose candidate like Mayor Garvey. They will never vote for a Democrat who graduated from Yale and is worth almost as much as his oil-heiress wife.'

The bedsprings produced luxurious mewing and groaning. 'Right there,' Enid told him. 'Harder.'

'And the third electorate is black and Latino. It never agrees on anything. Ever. Most of its leaders are charlatans. But that hardly distinguishes them from white leaders, does it?'

'Shut up. Use both hands.'

'Are you listening?'

Mimmo grinned in the dark. No, he thought, but I am.

Forty

As the century moved into its last five years, the ruling icon became the couple.

For those who mimicked the Clintons' White House partnership the concept was twin-rule, from changing diapers to, above all, joint earnings.

This applied equally to the inner life of politics. Where once the rules were made by paunchy male pigs in their seventies, soaked in the fug of cigars and whiskey, now open-air, sunlit public meetings, lawn sales and church garden socials were the stage for the Kingdom of Couples.

Conrad Courtney III planned to announce his candidacy for the mayoralty on Friday, the second of April. The night before, he and his wife, Melinda, held a small dinner for Dan and Madge Ludlum and the bachelor Pat Rossi, allowed access when coupled with Enid Bart.

Pat would have preferred to bring Eileen. But in the new politics coupling was meant to double resources, bringing together disparate power centres. To couple brother and sister smelled both of incest and genetic carelessness.

'Tonight is about eating dinner,' Melinda Courtney murmured significantly to each guest, 'the way the Boston Tea Party was about serving tea.' Nobody seemed to understand.

'I'm a control freak,' Conrad Courtney added, close to her side as couples should be, almost no air between them. 'Everything has to be in place before I make my next move.'

'And your next move,' Dan Ludlum pointed out, 'is to lock Pat Rossi into place.'

Pat was running late. The youngest of his punks, José Remedios, had tried to hang himself in the middle of the night by suspending his jockstrap-like underwear briefs from the ceiling fluorescent fixture, looping them under his chin and stepping off an upended trashbasket into space.

This immediately brought down the fixture, blew all fuses and set buzzers to yapping like dogs. Every guard came running. José lived, a celeb once more.

Pat arrived for dinner an hour late. 'Give up on them,' Ludlum said. 'Turn those punks over to an assistant.'

'He can't,' Enid interrupted. 'Nobody but Pat could ever humanise them enough to make people wonder if they were actually innocent.'

'But he'll have to drop them,' Melinda pointed out, 'once the campaign goes into high gear.'

'To say nothing of how it looks for Pat to, um, consort with such people on the one hand and manage my campaign on the other.' Conrad Courtney's pale good looks, under a photogenic thatch of white hair, assumed a pose of dignified confusion, all-white moral affront tempered by official Democratic Party sympathy for the underdog.

'No,' Dan Ludlum corrected him. 'It's Pat's underclass link that gives your campaign street cred.'

Sitting on a small chrome-steel bench next to Enid, Pat Rossi realised from the way his mentors and hosts were talking so freely and volubly above his head, that their one-hour wait had got them nicely boozed up.

He turned to Enid to murmur something along that line and saw, from her alert, eager posture and the quick shifting focus of her glance, that she considered herself one of those in the control centre, the cockpit of this moon-shot. He was about to point this out – that she was violating the ground rules of couplehood – when the Courtney butler came in and announced dinner.

They rose quickly and filed out of the large, square living room. It overlooked the Metropolitan Museum at the third-floor level, a roomy triplex apartment one house south of the Marcus mansion.

This was each of the Courtney's third marriage. Each had,

along the way, acquired both children of their own loins and painting or sculpture of the loins of artists whose work was to be seen across the street, or at the Guggenheim or, more often, off Fifth Avenue on 53rd Street at the Museum of Modern Art.

As a direct result, all walls were painted a neutral off-white. Ceiling tracks of spotlights bathed everything in self-importance, even light switches and door knobs. One looked about for a small card giving name, maker and date. 'Double pole, single throw 120v. on-off switch. Shaped brass, phenolic resin. UL Approved. Original Provenance, Scalfaro Construction Corporation. Manufacture, Leviton Electric Co., New York, 1977.'

Nowhere, not even their separate bedrooms, gave much evidence of human occupation. So when tonight's guests filed into the dining hall, with its differently angled view of the Met, each got the not unpleasant feeling that he or she was on dramatic display, an unique objet d'art, expensive and worth studying closely.

The butler and one maid, both in uniform, served a high-tech, low-fat dinner that began with baked buffalo mozzarella chips sprinkled with fresh basil leaves and drizzled with jalapeño steeped walnut oil, balsamic vinegar on the side. The main course was a bottom fish of no discernible breeding macerated to imitate crab flakes, then patted together as a cake and microwaved. This came in a delicate puddle of unadulterated octopus ink with tough bismati rice baked into a golf-ball timbale.

'The frozen yoghurt,' Melinda announced, 'rates three calories a serving. Enjoy.' It tasted enough like plain old chocolate ice-cream so that every speck of it disappeared within moments.

'I'm sorry about the octopus ink,' she went on. 'It does stain your teeth a bit.' For some reason this started them laughing.

Pat glanced around the table and watched a lot of expensive dental work flashing blackly like clown's make-up. He would never, he supposed, understand these people if he lived to be a hundred.

They had spent a lot of the dinner commenting on the dinner which was, Pat realised, deliberately designed to monopolise conversation. But once the truly delicious dessert was finished, Ludlum and Courtney launched into politics.

'I see no reason,' Ludlum said, 'for Pat to do anything but stand up and take a bow. It's you they want to hear, Connie.'

'Yes, and he has his speech. We sweated over it all this week,' Melinda put in.

'Short?' Ludlum asked.

'Half an hour.'

'Could you ball it down to a paragraph?' Madge Ludlum wanted to know. Not from Texas but born a southerner, Madge also balled eggs. She glanced at Enid. 'People lak thangs balled down.'

'They do indeed.' Enid turned to her host. 'Connie?'

'Oh. Well.' He blew his aristocratically slim cheeks out and sucked them in. 'Nothing a Democrat would object to. Jobs. Civil rights. Care of the old and the ill.'

'Taxes?' Pat Rossi spoke up. 'Property, sales, income?'

'Nothing concrete. I don't want to have to eat my promises later.'

'Crime? Violence in the streets? Schools? Jails?'

'I touch on them all.'

'You see,' Pat went on more slowly, trying not to sound like a courtroom cross-examiner, 'the reason I haven't actually said yes to your handsome proposal is that I'm not sure any candidate can do anything about New York City as we now run it.'

'You have indeed said yes!' Dan Ludlum barked.

'No,' Pat said. 'I haven't agreed because there is no point at all in fighting an expensive election just to repeat past errors.'

'Pat,' Enid moaned. 'We have been through all – '

'Pat,' Madge cooed, 'yoah such a nahs puhsn – '

'Pat,' Melinda demanded edgily, 'you simply cannot at this late – '

'Let the poor guy speak,' Courtney said, laughing. 'Better he turns me down now than at tomorrow night's dinner.'

Dan Ludlum said nothing. His dangerous face, all nose and chin, seemed to crimp in the middle like a huge lobster claw trying to clamp down on prey.

'I'm not here to turn anybody down,' Pat said then. 'I'm here to propose the only way I think we can win. If we commit to it, I am totally committed to running the campaign.'

'Say it,' Ludlum said through tightly clenched teeth.

'You know,' Pat went on, 'being admitted to Enid's inner circle gives me access to some amazing people. Historians. Statisticians. Social scientists. I asked a tough question: why do we get less and less service for an ever larger tax bill?'

'Ha!' Ludlum's voice suddenly sounded triumphant.

'Why, I asked them, is the basic social contract of our democracy shot full of holes? You know what I mean: you pay your taxes and we build good schools and roads, punish criminals, defeat our enemies abroad, teach our kids and make sure our old folks live decent lives. We have reneged on each and every item of the contract, while still collecting more and more taxes under false pretences.'

'Solve that,' Courtney said, beaming broadly, 'and you can be king of anywhere. Have you solved it?'

The butler and maid moved swiftly along the refectory table, reminding Pat of physicians in an operating room. With precise, economic movements, they removed plates and set coffee cups. (A high-tech, low-fat meal never produces crumbs.) Now the pungent aroma of dark, dark coffee filled the room as they poured, murmuring 'black or white?' in the time-honoured British tradition.

Pat stopped talking, entranced at the precision of their movements. Not a drop spilled. No awkward delays. Three kinds of sweetener. Cream or milk. Small, delicate white cups, slightly larger than a demitasse, with Wedgwood swirled fluting. He always enjoyed proficiency in anything.

'Not solved it,' he began again as the butler and maid left, 'but found a way to mitigate it. To cut it by a third, or so Enid's statistician pals tell me.'

'Aha!' Ludlum repeated, a bloodhound tracking spoor, finding evidence that his protégé was, indeed, competent.

'One of the things we've let happen,' Pat continued, 'especially under Reagan, was to give organised crime its own place at the table, its own corner of the establishment. It's become the high-risk, high-profit sector of American business. Largely because it pays almost no taxes, unless you consider tithing to corrupt cops a tax.'

'Hold it,' Courtney told him. 'You can't be mayor of New York if you get the cops down on you.'

'But if you show the voter how he can get the maf tapeworm out of his gut, you *will* be mayor.'

There was a longish pause as the couples considered this from their separate viewpoints. Enid was the first to speak. 'But that's a Catch 22,' she complained. 'If you show how to do it, you're honour bound t–'

'Our first job would be to spell it out in dollars and cents. You know, "if organised crime paid its taxes, you'd pay 27 per cent less on yours." That sort of –'

'How?' Ludlum rasped. 'How do you make the mafia pay taxes?'

'My father told me the story of Al Capone,' Pat said. 'He had people murdered. He bought and sold cities and their politicians. He paid for massacres. He corrupted lives. He engineered vast injustices. He broke every rule of decency or law and he walked free. It was not paying his income tax that sent him to Alcatraz.'

'A technicality.'

'You can murder and the world says, "well, it didn't touch me." But cheat on your taxes and the world hollers "hey! I'm paying more because he cheats." Taxation is the mafia's Achilles heel. It's a very sexy political issue.'

'Is it?' Courtney wondered. 'Frankly, I'd never given it a thought.'

'It's the only issue that cuts across the classes.'

'Is it?' Melinda asked. 'Dear me.'

Pat sipped his coffee. 'Two kinds of people will vote Democratic. You have the communications people, including advertising, educators, young professionals before they're rich, technical people. They don't come up against organised crime very much. But they do pay taxes. The second kind of voter is blue collar or unemployed or retired. Taxes are important but his whole life is choked up against the mafia's rear end. The common denominator between these two voters, for two different reasons, is the mafia.'

'He's rot!' Madge exclaimed.

'What?' her husband barked.

'He's right,' Enid interpreted.

'Is he?' Melinda wanted to know. 'I'm such a novice in these matters. I mean, one lives in Manhattan, in the heart of things, and tries, well, not to notice crime.'

'He's not talking about street crime,' her husband explained. 'He's talking about business crime.'

'Both,' Pat assured him. 'The junkie who mugs you on your doorstep is collecting the price of a fix imported by the maf. The dealers funnel back that cash, laundered, to their bosses in construction, transport, entertainment, food, finance. It's all one.'

'I don't know,' Melinda said in a thoughtful tone. 'I sit here listening to Pat Rossi. He's young and full of beans and so good-looking. I just know he's right.'

There was a general, female, murmur of agreement, but Melinda wasn't finished. 'Trouble is, Connie's supposed to say those things. And Connie is a whole other image, middle-aged and rich. Never mind he earned most of it himself. People only remember he inherited his father's fortune.'

'You left out good-looking,' her husband murmured. 'I mean, in a middle-aged way.' He twinkled at her.

'You look at Connie,' Ludlum opined, 'and you see a man who has successfully met a payroll most of his adult life.'

'Means nothing to young folks,' Madge disagreed.

'But from his lips,' Enid suggested, 'you get the Pat Rossi truths young people believe.'

'Do we?' Melinda wondered. 'Will we? Pat hasn't said yes, you know.'

'It's the candidate who has to say yes,' Pat explained. 'He has to tell me, yes, I buy the anti-mafia position as our keystone. We will have other big issues. But they will rest on the idea that if New York wants to breathe free it has to chop off organised crime at the kneecaps.'

Conrad Courtney's normally pleasant face grew grave. Pat had the unhappy thought: he's pretending to think. He's a man for whom the mafia is semi-mythical, bad ginzos with pinky rings. He's getting ready to go along with this street-smart Italo-American just to give himself credibility.

'Pat,' Courtney said, 'how can I say no to what's right?'

'It's not easy. You will get drawn into no-win debates. For example: decriminalising drugs, a very popular idea for depriving the maf of cash flow.'

Courtney produced his rich-uncle grin, indulgent and generous. 'Nothing worth fighting for comes easy.'

Dan Ludlum made a groaning noise. 'Ay-men.'

Melinda Courtney gave her husband a sharp look. 'So, the answer's . . . yes?'

'Yes.'

'Yes?' Madge asked her husband.

'Yes,' Ludlum said.

'Yes?' Enid asked Pat.

'Yes,' he concluded. He thought of the long, hard road to get Courtney elected. He found himself thinking of his list of specific injustices, the one Maria Jenner had now put on a CD-ROM disk. He pictured talking Courtney into addressing some of these crimes once he became mayor.

His face lost its positive look, but he kept it from seeming negative. The first, he thought, of a long line of compromises. He stretched toward Courtney and they shook hands for a long, long time.

Forty-One

Announcing one's itch to become mayor is not as common in Manhattan as it might be in other cities. There are so many bizarre hurdles of financing and political approval that an expensive media blitz is only an opening wedge to attract New Yorkers' attention.

By the week after the announcement at the St Regis dinner, the press had all run editorial comments and potted biographies of Conrad Courtney III.

Women's pages had all reported on Melinda Courtney's activities in charity and the arts, usually with a chart showing which art was promised to what museum.

Business pages all surveyed in some depth Courtney's Manhattan property holdings and what oil money Melinda could expect as her father's sole heir.

Amid this impressive media blitz, however, the New York County Democratic Committee, also known as Tammany, said nothing at all. Its silence was not yet ominous, only premature. For the Tammany sachems to announce, they had first to know what was in it for them.

Pat Rossi returned late to his office to find Maria Jenner standing at his window, staring out at Manhattan's dusk and filling the room with cigarette smoke.

'You were with those awful boys, weren't you?'

Pat sat down at his desk and automatically emptied the ashtray of crimson-smeared butts. 'The oldest one, Rebert? He's had offers from two publishers to write his life story. I told him his life story wouldn't even make a cigarette paper.'

Her trombone voice hit a disdainful bass note. 'Who would read anything about him?'

'One publisher is offering an advance of a hundred grand. A ghost is ready to do the writing. Rebert wants me to vet the contract. I told him to get an agent.'

'He trusts you?'

'Not just trust. Lust. Rebert says he lusts after my butt. I get all the elegant clients.'

'What's wrong? I lust after your butt, too.' She turned around to face him in the darkened room. Her perfume billowed in around him like searching fingers. 'Young Patrick, you're always wondering when I intend to call due your IOU?'

'I tremble.'

'Anybody who lives with Enid Bart already has good nerves.'

'I don't live with her.'

'Not till after three a.m. anyway. That leaves a lot of extra time out of twenty-four hours.'

She took a long, deep breath which seemed to expand her breasts to a degree that Pat decided could be called sinister. She seemed to absorb any space between them. 'Dan Ludlum's assigned you a huge office suite in Courtney campaign headquarters on Sixth Avenue. You have a corner with views in two directions.'

'I lose my window here? Never!'

'He's assigned me to help you get started. We'll share adjoining rooms. Dan couldn't handle it if I had an affair with someone here in the office. I mean, actually, physically here. But I don't let him dictate who I see on my own.' She had surrounded him now, breast to face. 'And you, young Patrick, are now my own.'

'Your appeal to menopausal women,' Eileen mused, 'is something I can't understand.' They stood in the kitchen, where they could hear their father snoring lightly in the next room.

'Maria menopausal?' He handed over a silvery CD-ROM disk. 'She spent forever programming this.' Pat was silent for a while, chewing as usual on a thought. Then: 'I'm not terribly happy Maria's been seconded to me. She is honour bound to report back to Dan. I wanted you to be my strong right hand.'

Eileen looked glum. 'In all this tumult,' she mused, 'you haven't been keeping track of Michael Rossi. At the request of Captain Baxter he is producing a new video called "The Life, Death and Digital Resurrection of Phil Marcus".'

'And you're . . . ?'

'. . . his talent scout, researcher, programmer, writer, producer, cook, art director, nurse and constant companion.'

Pat was silent again, thinking. 'Why Phil Marcus? He's an operator in the Boesky-Milken mode. He leads not much further than himself. If Captain Baxter wants someone really useful he ought to pay Pop to re-create Big Mimmo Caccia.'

'Ah! Big Mim! My Chevalier of the Sterling Roses!' She gave him a mischievous look. 'I hear he's a bachelor.'

'Funny you should say that,' former Detective Sergeant Michael Rossi said from the other room. As usual, when considered asleep, he had merely been eavesdropping.

'It's only funny if I marry him,' Eileen pointed out.

'No, funny is I offered to do Caccia next. I already worked up a document. You know, "Scarlet Pimpernel Meets Zorro"? Nobody knows who he is but he's the hero? Well, everybody knows Mim. He just gave the Guggenheim an auxiliary building. He gave Cardinal Mahaffey a million for the CYO.'

'But he's the villain,' Pat finished for him.

'That's why I offered him to Baxter. Police work is all about getting the case closed. The Marcus case has been open on his books for so long it stinks like a fish. So, when I gave him his choice, that's what he picked.'

The three Rossis considered this for quite a long moment, as if emulating Pat's chewing pose. 'So I won't marry Mim,' Eileen offered.

Mike Rossi contemplated the silvery CD-ROM disk Pat had brought home. 'Does this have all the stuff you used to keep in ledger books?'

His son nodded. They had finished dinner and Eileen had escaped to visit a girlfriend. Mike Rossi had been expounding on how, without Eileen, he would be a year behind his computer projects. 'She has a real flair for it.'

'At least it keeps her mind off Jack Pierce.'

'You two never patched it up?'

'We three. That little melodrama you told me Jack staged the other afternoon, crying on hands and knees. It hasn't patched up anything. As for Pierce et Cie, life goes on. They have wangled a thirty-day moratorium before filing for a Chapter Eleven bankruptcy ruling. And a big white knight investor is expected to ride in and rescue them.'

'Jack's old man is having a fit.'

'He's missing. Jack told Eileen Paul Pierce hasn't been seen for months.'

'No good.' Mike Rossi brooded for a long moment. 'You know this South American thing, where "disappear" is a verb as in "they disappeared my father"? Well, Baxter tells me his precinct alone is handling three times as many as last year. People just go off the face of the earth, lots of them big names. It's like a new virus.'

'How's your Phil Marcus disappearance project?'

His father's face contorted faintly in anger. 'I told you I wanted to do Caccia. Marcus is a waste of time, a dead end. Caccia is where the money is. I can't get Baxter to agree. It's as if Caccia's paying him to keep me off the subject of Caccia.'

'Maybe that's it.' Pat's face took on the same look of choked fury. 'After all, Baxter will argue, he can only go after one rat at a time.'

'That would be the biggest injustice of all.'

Neither of them spoke for a long moment. Pat lifted a half-full glass of Diet Coke to his father's lips. 'Swallow.'

'Paddy, if Baxter is on Caccia's payroll, I've been wasting my time. And I don't have any to waste.'

'Swallow anyway. I want to throw the glass in the sink.'

Mike Rossi let some of the drink enter his mouth. 'The things I do for my kids.' He turned his face away, spurning any more of the drink. 'I didn't waste *all* my time. I had Eileen do copy disks for you. Paddy me bhoy, you now own a first edition of Operation Vinnie. I want you to feel free to lift any part of it for Courtney's anti-maf campaign.'

'I hope I can keep him honest. He said yes too easily.'

'Right.' Mike Rossi squinted at him, sizing him up to receive some extremely heavy load. 'Let's put Baxter and Caccia on the back burner. I want you to put Courtney in the frying pan. What's the mob to him? He's above and beyond such matters, like most aristocrats.' He paused. Then:

'Pat, you weren't too bad in history, right? Did they teach you the Opium Wars?'

'No.'

'It's British history. Married to little Eileen Callahan, I have an Irish view of British history. I look at two whole generations of British aristocrats and nobility who made their money dealing drugs. From Chinese opium, bought on the cheap and sold worldwide.'

He stopped to gauge his son's reaction. 'Behind any aristocratic clan, anywhere in the world, dig deep enough and you find crime. No aristo crime. No duelling pistols. Just down and dirty double-dealing.'

'You're implying that Courtney . . .'

'Implying, hell. When I hand over the Vinnie Project I'm giving you an insurance policy. You'll find Courtney's name, and a dozen other property guys, totally blackmailable. Just calmly tell him you've got him by the nuts. If he welshes you'll twist them off and have them for lunch. Okay?'

Pat surveyed the mean look on his father's face. He grinned into the teeth of it. 'God, don't ever let me run afoul of you, Killer.'

On his knees still, Jack Pierce nuzzled between Eileen's thighs, making a soft snorting sound like a pig nosing truffles. She clamped his head tightly. 'Jack, my only excuse for this shameful liaison is that nobody in the world does that better than you.'

'Tell me how you know that.'

'Because since we stopped seeing each other, nobody in the world has gone down on me. I hope Myra appreciates your talent. My poor old dad thinks I'm visiting a girlfriend.'

'I told you she's a Catholic? She will not allow a man to –

this is her word – penetrate her until he's married to her. But giving and getting head, that's okay.'

'You're always Satan, always tempting.'

'I like that. It's Myra doing the tempting.'

'And it's you scarfing up home-made pussy a mile a minute.'

'Miss Rossi!' He looked up at her, licking his lower lip. 'Please confine your outbursts to the usual moans of sheer, perverse, adulterous ecstasy.'

When his father actually did get to sleep it was almost midnight. Pat Rossi walked out on the front doorstep of the Rossi home. It was a clear, soft April night. Through the toxic mix of Manhattan atmosphere – roach killer, monoxide, dog turds and some air – the moon had risen over the eastern horizon, just past half full; gibbous, Pat recalled the term. He leaned against the iron railing and watched Second Avenue traffic edging southwards, honking even at midnight, truck brakes hissing, headlights raking across his retinas.

Bucolic scene, he thought, for a kid born and raised here. And April always had a haunting scent of spring, even at the bottom of this canyon. Without any warning, a strange feeling of well-being sneaked over him. Followed by an outrageous sense of self-pride.

Well, why not? New York rarely voted for a society candidate unless convinced he was so rich he would never be caught with his hand in the till. What was that old image out of Salvation Army days? Caught wid his duke in the tambourine.

A smile crossed his face. He'd do anything at this point to get a break from pro bono. His punks had done that to him. If they'd been guilty, vicious pervert killers, that would simply have been, for him, a nasty job but someone had to do it.

But they were, after all, weak human cubs fixated by orgasm, babies still hypnotised by faeces, tiny egos swollen with society's shocked publicity. All too human. Now that he had cast such doubts on their involvement in the crime, he'd engineered a standoff.

He stared at the uptown sky. From this angle, as from his office, major peaks still glowed, the Empire State and the Chrysler to the north, the Trade Center twin towers to the south-west. Even now, with office space a drug on the market, Manhattan was still building, still scraping the sky.

Even now, as bankrupt as a Bowery bum, as shot through with corruption as a river-to-river whorehouse, it was still Baghdad on the Hudson, Gotham City. The only place to be.

This was how Jack Pierce must have felt when, fresh out of Harvard Law, he'd put together the roaring success of Pierce et Cie. How he must have felt. The invitations. The women. The access to networking. It would have dizzied anybody else but Jack. One day, soon, it would begin to dazzle Pat Rossi because the seduction had already begun. Onward to fornication.

He was about to tackle this lady head-on. With Courtney's bottomless pocket and Pop's insurance policy, there was nothing to stop this campaign from victory.

He felt a sharp surge of adrenaline. It was a scene out of a late-night TV movie. Some working-class hero like Dane Clark or John Garfield would look up at Manhattan's jewelled skyline, shake his fist at it and shout: 'You're all mine! This town belongs to me!'

What a town! He hadn't yet turned thirty. But Manhattan had laid herself open to him and invited romance. He took a deep, sooty lungful and laughed as he mimicked out loud Conrad Courtney's words when he introduced him at the St Regis dinner last week:

'... that real son of Manhattan, that street-smart defender of justice who knows what it's like to be on the short end of injustice, crusading Patrick Michael Rossi!'

This town, he thought, giddy with hormone, belongs to me!

Forty-Two

And so began the election summer.

It didn't obey the natural season. Nor did it follow the social summer, which begins with a holiday at the end of May and ends with Labor Day at the start of September.

The election summer had actually begun at the St Regis dinner the night after April Fool's Day. It would end on the first Tuesday in November when New York went to the polls to choose the man who was to govern the ungovernable.

Early in May, to a faint grinding of teeth, the Republican Party announced that Mayor Gary Garvey, who doggedly claimed to have brought peace to the violent streets of New York, would run for a second four-year term, 'to finish the job'.

This should have been followed by a countering announcement from Tammany. Its chieftains had been conferring endlessly with Pat Rossi, negotiating for Courtney.

But, before they could cut a deal, citizens replied to the Mayor with LA-style drive-by street shootouts on four consecutive nights, ostensibly between rival gangs in the South Bronx, to produce twelve dead bystanders, including three children.

To cries of outrage that the Mayor of Peace was still the same old corrupt 'Gravy' Garvey he'd always been, the Democrats then announced that their candidate would indeed be the honest Conrad Courtney III. He immediately picked up the nickname of Courtly.

Impatient commentators had complained that this would be a lacklustre election year. Obviously neither major party was madly in love with its nominated candidate, but in both parties no one else of fire or charisma or funding had appeared.

This lack of enthusiasm seemed also to have infected major fat-cat contributors. The press, which can only create news out of a noisy, expensive free-for-all, reported that in a ho-hum year contributors were sitting on their wallets.

That was before Arnie Glass appeared.

There wasn't much to know about him except that he had been fired from an upstate radio station for a phone-in programme on sexual problems. Arnie had suggested callers might perfect their 'masturbation techniques and learn that your best friends are your fingers.' A nut, but a Republican nut.

After he returned to join Manhattan's vast horde of the unemployed, he had begun working for his local Republican club writing leaflets and speeches. But once he appeared on 'News is Made at Night' his job changed. A ho-hum election perked up.

His one-liners began to be quoted around town. 'Courtly Courtney is so clean when his rent collectors deliver money to him, his butler launders it in Chanel Number Five.'

'Melinda Courtly's word-class collection of hundred-dollar bills is being re-done by Pablo Picasso. He's giving Ben Franklin three eyes.'

'Courtly's got a simple anti-crime plan: pay off muggers by writing a cheque. Then stop payment. Sounds simple to him. But what doesn't?'

Not that they were funny, but they matched New Yorkers' qvetchy kind of humour. Enid Bart got on the phone to Courtney Headquarters, asked for Pat Rossi and got Maria Jenner.

'He's out in Staten Island this morning, Enid.'

'Did you catch "News is Made at Night"? Have you heard this Arnie Glass?'

Maria's voice seemed to go down an octave. 'At that hour I am in bed, doing other things. But I'll pass this on to Pat.'

'I want to book him opposite Glass.'

'Pat isn't a comic.'

'Neither is Glass. He's a dedicated right-wing supporter of

Garvey and dirty-mouthed enemy of Courtney. By now he's made himself the voice of the GOP.'

'Hot news for masturbators. I'll tell Pat.'

With five days left before Pierce et Cie would either have to reopen its doors and face a final crippling run on deposits, or file for the shelter of a Chapter Eleven bankruptcy, the news suddenly got much better.

It was too big to be carried in one section alone of the *Times*. Gaynor Marcus's announcement that he was buying a 49 per cent share in the bank took the top right-hand corner of the Business News section.

The announcement of the marriage of Myra Miriam Marcus to John Abercrombie Pierce at a nuptial mass in St Patrick's Cathedral 1 June took up three columns in the Sunday paper, accompanied by a photograph of the couple.

Gossip is rarely buried in marriage announcements. But this one, by omission, kept from the world the groom's first marriage in a civil ceremony to a Protestant. Thus he needed no annulment to marry Myra, just proof that his earlier marriage and divorce were entirely secular.

Pat, Eileen and their father all got engraved invitations, RSVP. Only Pat accepted. He arrived very late as the reception was ending.

That noon Satan's Punks had been released from detention. Mayor Garvey called an angry press conference along the usual 'they are now free to kill again' lines.

But instead of killing anybody, the three boys went with Pat to their publisher's office on Lower Park Avenue. Rebert Custodial Miller signed a contract to turn their story into a book, a two-part TV special, a Sunday magazine section feature and a comic book.

Afterwards, over on Seventh Avenue, they signed contracts for a line of casual sweatshirts and jackets called Satan's Punk Threads.

'Glad you could make it,' Jack exclaimed, pumping Pat's hand. 'Say hello to my bride. Myra, it's my closest friend. Maybe my only friend, Pat Rossi.'

She threw her arms around his neck and kissed him moistly on each cheek. 'Did you send those superb Sterling roses?' Her lipstick had smeared earlier in the day and no one had seen fit to warn her. Nor had she checked her mirror.

'On my salary?' Pat smiled at her. 'Myra, give me your handkerchief.' He took it and managed to control the blowsy swagger of her lower lip. 'Now give me a kiss.'

'Tee-hee!' Myra planted one on his lips. 'I love you, Pat. I just met you and I'm crazy about you.'

Pat shrugged modestly. 'Now I wish I had sent the Sterlings.' He banged Jack on the forearm and wandered off into another immense room of the hotel suite across from St Patrick's. He spotted Big Mimmo instantly.

He was surrounded by men, all of whom looked smaller, shorter, less vivid than he did. When Mimmo saw him, he seemed to part the knot of hangers-on like Moses at the Red Sea. But Pat didn't approach him.

'Do you ever send any other flowers than Sterling roses?'

'But I only send flowers,' Mimmo demurred, 'to exceptional ladies.'

That night, sharply at midnight, Enid Bart's cameras recorded her introduction of Pat Rossi to Arnie Glass. Later, a video of this moment sold for $19.99.

'Buona sera, amico,' Arnie drawled. He was a weedy, loosely hung fellow in his late twenties, chinless but not weak-looking. The camera lens backed up for a two-shot.

'Sei gezündt, Arnele,' Pat responded, holding out his hand. 'Was machst du?'

'Rossi is a Jewish handle?'

Pat gave him a beaming smile. 'Just being Courtly, old man. They tell me you want to drape that deadbeat, Gravy Garvey, around Manhattan's neck once more.'

'I want protection, Rossi. I want a mayor with balls.'

'That'd be welcome news to Garvey, too.'

Arnie turned to Enid Bart. 'You told me he was good looking. You never said he had a mouth like a razorblade.'

'You're not exactly ugly yourself, Arnie,' Enid parried.

'Hey, doll, I got a face like a cat's ass.' He swung around and shoved his face in Pat's. 'See what I mean, Patsy?'

Rossi peered intently into Arnie's mouth. 'Oops, there's still some left you didn't get out.'

They never became friends, just deadly Manhattan street enemies who appreciated a sense of humour. But between them, appearing together over the hot summer every Friday night and often not signing off till four a.m. because the incoming phone calls wouldn't let them, Arnie Glass and Pat Rossi managed to insult both political parties in new, scabrous and, on Arnie's side, barely broadcastable language.

By August the campaign issues between Garvey and Courtney had been explained, contradicted, re-stated and re-attacked while Enid's viewership mounted steadily into the dog days of late summer.

Detailed polls of the station's viewership plotted the changes taking place. In June viewers had been more inclined toward the rough-hewn Garvey. By August they were favouring the gentlemanly Courtney two-to-one.

'Shit,' Arnie muttered, off camera, as he and Pat read through the poll results. 'Look at these Neilsens. We should be doing this for big bucks.'

'I am. What do the Republicans pay you? Bupkes?'

'Will you for Christ's sake stop ribbing me in Yiddish? It kills my image with the Yidlach.'

At about two a.m. Arnie had launched into one of his why-would-you-vote-for-a-society-schmuckola-like-Courtley? diatribes.

'At a Trinity Church garden fund-raiser Courtly and Melinda held for the faithful it was twenty bucks a plate for Episcopalian chicken salad. If you want to know what New York will feed on if Courtly's elected, here's the recipe:

'Shred a lettuce. Add watered-down mayo and some grapes sliced in half. Serve.'

Not averse to playing straight man, Pat said: 'You left out the chicken.'

'If anybody voted for Courtly, it'd be some turkey.'

'Leave it to you to ham it up.'

'Malechamuvis.'

'Schlomozolnitzer.'

In the background of this Hebrew-Yiddish slanging match, one of Enid's young assistants brought her a sheet of paper Pat could recognise as having been torn from a teletype printer, either AP or Reuters. He let Arnie continue foaming at the mouth while he watched Enid's face go chalk white.

Finally she looked up and her gaze went directly to him. She placed her finger on her throat and drew a horizontal, neck-cutting line. 'What?' he burst out involuntarily.

'What?' Arnie demanded.

Calmly Enid watched the camera zoom in on her. She held the piece of paper up to view. 'Gentlemen. Ladies. Viewers all over town. All you sleepless fans of "News is Made at Night". This is an Associated Press story that states...'

She quickly re-read the paragraph. 'It states that our television station has been bought by a foundation called Citizens for Christ, as of close of business today, that is, yesterday. "News is Made at Night" will have the Reverend Michael Bob Ribbs of Demopolis, Alabama, as anchor person.'

'Oy,' Arnie Glass moaned. 'Oy veh'ts mir.'

The Arnie-Pat team got viewers rabid enough to keep telephone lines busy. But now the girls at the switchboard felt a sudden earthquake-like upsurge. Lights flared, blinked, buzzed. The whole panel was alight. People from as far away as Pennsylvania and Massachusetts were protesting. Manhattanites' stunned voices kept repeating: 'Don't let 'em do it.'

But it was already done. At nine in the morning, Pat accompanied Enid to the small offices of the holding company that owned the broadcast channel and held the Federal Communications Commission license. A secretary arrived at ten, by which time several reporters were also waiting for answers.

The secretary held up a sheet of paper. 'I found this in our fax machine,' she said. 'It's from my boss. He's down in Alabama. He says nobody, including him, will be back in New York to answer questions. He says you should telephone

Citizens for Christ and ask for Reverend Ribbs.' She stopped and quoted a telephone number, repeating it twice.

'That's it?' Enid Bart demanded. 'A popular programme for and about Manhattan is going to be run from Demopolis, Alabama?'

The girl made a don't-ask-me face. 'Moreover,' Pat Rossi added, 'the programme gets axed once it shows a terrific lead for Conrad Courtney?' He got to his feet to survey the half dozen press people. 'Any of you have background on Citizens for Christ?'

The *Times* man nodded. 'It's a clone of other pentecostal money-makers. You know: send in your ten dollar bill today and we'll pray your kid off his crutches in no time flat.'

'No political bias?'

The woman from *Variety* smiled. 'Pat Rossi, stop pretending you were born yesterday.'

She had been tapping out a number on the keypad of her cellular telephone. 'Good mawnin',' she said in a cheery, suddenly southern voice. 'Zit powsible to speak to the Reverend Michael Bob Ribbs? This is *Variety*, cawlin' from N'Yawk City?'

She switched her telephone to speaker. Everyone could hear the voice at the other end saying: '. . . jes hold on, Sister.'

'Mawnin',' an older voice began. 'I guess you folks want to know about us buying the TV channel?'

'Brother Michael Bob,' the *Variety* woman asked him. 'We're so *im*pressed? A Manhattan TV channel is a mighty expensive proposition.'

'Hit shorely is.' He cackled a moment. 'But the good Lord provides in his infinite wisdom.'

'Meaning?'

'Meaning an anonymous contribution of ten million dollars to buy the channel and take over all its programming. We already do that for fourteen UHF channels coast-to-coast, plus Dallas and Fairport, New York, and Honey Grove, Pennsylvania. We have a video library of over a hundred hours of our own sermons and prayer appeals so we can start up immediately with our own material.'

'And "News is Made at Night"?'

'I'll do that remote from here.'

'But the phone-ins?'

'Afraid we can't afford them.'

'So your anonymous benefactor has limits. How anonymous is anonymous, Brother Michael Bob?'

'After we bought the channel and license for cash there was still two million left for operating expenses. It buys a lot of righteous TV time and absolutely no publicity at all about which of God's children saw fit to share his worldly wealth with his fellow Christians.'

'Then you've talked with him?'

The telephone line abruptly died. It was replaced by a dial tone. 'Thank you for sharing,' the woman reporter said. She glanced at Pat. 'Your move, Counsellor. But if Citizens for Christ doesn't want to tell you, you can't make them.'

'Anyway,' the *Times* man added cheerfully, 'With the Neilsen ratings you people have been pulling, an offer from another channel is only a matter of time.'

'It's the Neilsens,' Enid said in a mournful tone, 'that attracted this secret buyer. It's the Neilsens that made our old owners grab at a cash offer. There's such a thing as being too Goddamned successful.'

'Oops,' the *Variety* lady said, 'Brother Michael Bob wants clean mouths as well as clean minds. You get your brain vacuumed, Sister Enid, and vote for Brother Gravy Garvey. Therein lies salvation.'

'Pat,' Enid asked, 'before I burst into tears, say something?'

He chewed on this for some time. 'I might,' he said then, 'once I find out who had pockets deep enough to shell out ten million just to shut you up.'

Forty-Three

The *Times* man was right, after all. Once he did a feature article about Enid's plight, it took less than a month to find a new TV channel for an after-midnight show now called 'Never Too Late' with Enid Bart.

By then the election was less than a month away. In the interim, Arnie Glass had also got a show, on a UHF channel where after-midnight hours were devoted to pay porn.

'Give Yourself a Great Big Hand' was the name Arnie had devised for a no-pay format that trolled for phone-ins by promoting the masturbatory stuff that would follow.

After thirty minutes of Arnie free, everyone was ready to pay for anything. He tried for guests like Pat Rossi but had to settle for the porn-flick actors and actresses who would be seen later for pay. Never forgetting his allegiance to the Republicans, Arnie would tease from his guests some of the weirder political statements of the election campaign.

'I adore a mayor with balls,' Velva la French put it. 'Mayor Garvey really stokes my pubes.'

'That's the election in a nutshell,' Arnie agreed. 'New York is not going to jump in bed with some society eunuch. It's getting down on Mayor G., back in the saddle again.'

In his third week he got to Rebert Custodial Miller, whose bookings were handled by his publisher's publicity people. It was a close call, promoting a guest with such a mouth, but the publisher was an old-line firm with authors on its backlist that constituted a cram course in Amer. Lit. If an author of theirs freely employed all the forbidden four-letter words of TV, it must be okay.

'You had Courtly's manager as your mouthpiece, huh?'

244

'You are referring to that sweet-as-shit piece of suck called Pat Rossi?'

The next morning Arnie got warned by the station's management. Then his sales manager took him aside.

'You understand the front office has to play shocked. But pay no attention. Arnie. Keep on freaking the people.'

'Never Too Late' had a two-hour format with a classier look to it and a back-up production staff that produced a transcript for sale. Enid celebrated this upgrading by having most of her long dark blonde hair converted into a three-quarters-of-an-inch bleached crew cut, somewhat like her old producer, the female Pat.

Where Enid had once looked deep, intense and titillating to know, she now resembled a cute body with breasts. Viewers took a bit of education before they reaffirmed their allegiance.

'From now until Election Eve,' Enid told them, 'we promise not to stray from the mayoral contest. Once New York has a new leader, we promise to keep him under our microscope. To those who want to hear newsy chat of morning-after birth control or lesbian marriage or incest-abuse we promise we'll get around to *everything* eventually.'

When she offered to host a face-to-face debate between the candidates, Conrad Courtney agreed. At air time Mayor Garvey didn't show, but sent the voluble and aggressive Congressman Dominic Tessio instead.

'Oh, no,' Pat hooted on camera. 'No Gravy, no more Mr Courtly Courtney.' He helped Courtney up and away, murmuring, as if only to him but clearly heard by viewers, 'Sir, you don't have to be pictured next to this man. His reputation is too risky.'

Then he sat down and himself risked facing the tainted congressman. 'How did you and Gravy figure you'd get away with this?'

'With what? The Mayor's delayed coming in from Queens. He'll be here any minute.'

Pat chuckled dismissively. 'What delayed him? A shoot-out? Under his regime, street crime has risen 5 per cent a year over the past four years. That's an increase of 20 per cent during his term in office.'

'That's bushwah.' Tessio had a brush haircut that seemed to have the ability to bristle. He also had the valuable trait of being able to look enraged. His hair trembled with it. 'That's unsubstantiated bushwah.'

Pat seemed to pause, flummoxed. He looked about the studio, as if for help. He assumed, as did his viewers, that Mayor Garvey had simply ducked out, whatever his excuse. Pat had counted on confronting the mayor directly with statistics developed by one of Enid's pals, illustrating the one key plank in the Courtney campaign that was to be sprung as a surprise.

Was this going to be his best shot at springing it? Timing was everything. If he waited for a confrontation with Garvey he might never get it. But if he hung in here like a bulldog with his teeth locked, he might force Garvey's hand.

A lot hung on getting the timing right. In expectation of facing Garvey tonight, an expensive advertising campaign had been scheduled to kick off tomorrow on all network stations and several key UHF ones. To delay, even for only a few days, would diminish the impact. Which was clearly why the mayor was stiffing him.

'Congressman Tessio, it seems the milieu of crime has come up.' Pat's right hand delved inside his left breast pocket.

Tessio registered alarm. 'What miloo? What's a miloo? A society word for background? What's in your pocket? A piece?'

Pat's fingers seemed to be searching for . . . what? A gun? The suspense built rapidly. One camera zoomed into a tight close-up of the gesture, making it seem menacing.

'Because Conrad Courtney has a surprise for New York City criminals,' Pat went on in an abruptly grave tone. 'We wanted to keep it a surprise. In the war against crime, we need every help we can get.'

He got to his feet and conferred with Courtney, his hand still hidden in his pocket. Then he looked up at the camera.

'The decision is to go for it.' He pulled out something bulky. It wasn't a gun. It was a TV cassette.

'Tomorrow, this commercial,' he brandished the cassette, 'will air all over the New York City TV area. But "Never Too Late" is getting a scoop.'

He handed the cassette to Enid.

While one can still buy a video of the first Arnie-Pat joust for $19.99, a recording of this next moment is priceless. As it goes for the jugular, it looks like this:

EXTERIOR, DARKENED ALLEY. DRUG PUSHER SELLING PACKETS TO YOUNG BOYS AND GIRLS. HE ZOOMS OFF ON HARLEY-DAVIDSON ROADHOG CYCLE.

NARRATOR: (VOICE OVER) Five hundred bucks. Chicken feed.

ROADHOG PARKED AT KERB OF SHINY OFFICE BUILDING. CAMERA PANS UP TO HIGH WINDOW, ZOOMS IN TO INTERIOR SHOT.

PUSHER HANDS CASH TO RESPECTABLE BUSINESSMAN WHO ADDS PACKET TO OPEN ATTACHÉ CASE ALREADY BURSTING WITH CASH.

NARRATOR: Fifty thousand bucks. Still chicken feed.

ROADSIDE QUEENS RESTAURANT. JAGUAR ARRIVES, THEN CADILLAC, THEN ROLLS. THREE BUSINESSMEN, EACH CARRYING SEVERAL ATTACHÉ CASES, ENTER RESTAURANT.

NARRATOR: Couple of million? Watch it at work.

SMALLER AUTOS ZOOM AROUND TOWN AT SUPER-FAST CARTOON SPEEDS MAKING DELIVERIES TO A SUPERMARKET, A CONSTRUCTION FIRM, A TRUCKING CONCERN, A WALL STREET BROKERAGE.

NARRATOR: Unlimited cash flow, none of it taxed. Unlimited buying power, tax-free.

ONE AUTO PARKS BEHIND POLICE STATION. BUSINESSMAN STUFFS MONEY IN HIS POCKETS AND WALKS INSIDE STATION.

NARRATOR: (VOICE OVER) Who pays the mafia's taxes? You do!

(SCREEN SHOWS PLAIN TYPE MESSAGE. NARRATOR READS:) If we forced the mafia to pay what it owes, you and I could save 27 per cent of our income and sales taxes. For the average New Yorker, that's over $5000 a year! *Get the mafia out of your pocket. Vote Courtney.*

When the TV image returned live to the studio, Congressman Tessio was busily dialling a telephone number. He turned away from the camera and engaged in a short, angry conversation. When he hung up and faced the camera again, there was a cat-eats-canary smile on his normally grim face.

'That was Mayor Garvey. He's in the Midtown tunnel. His car will be here in four minutes.'

'If he can get a portable phone to work in a tunnel, more power to him.'

Pat Rossi sank back in his chair and made sure there was no smirk on his face. His ploy had worked. The mayor had had no intention of a one-on-one with Courtney. Pat had smoked out Garvey in the nick of time.

He got up and ceremoniously ushered Conrad Courtney back to his original seat before the cameras. 'Bingo,' he murmured handing him a thin pack of file cards on which all the statistics had been typed. 'Now: go get him.'

Forty-Four

When Carmine Onofrio died – quickly as far as observers could see but surely not fast enough for Carmine himself – it was for doing his job. No one who watched him die could miss the moral: if you know too much, you too must die.

Troublingly for a good Catholic, Carmine died unconfessed with a lie on his lips. He had just sworn that the Pierces were all dead: 'There ain't a Pierce left to piss on.'

He had actually spent the last months of his life trying to find Paul Pierce, using his security staff and net of electronic sensors and TV cameras. Ironically, he passed Paul Pierce several times a week as he crossed the Landing. It had become a desolate place. Weeds had begun sprouting.

The attic of Pierce's ski-chalet office, shingled in cedar shakes, had small windows on all four sides. They had been glazed with tinted glass to mitigate heat from the sun. Peering out through them, Pierce was all but invisible.

There had always been a separate, parallel communications system as back-up if his normal phone/fax circuits failed. He knew enough electronics to radio-lock into the telephone number of an upstate tobacco agribusiness. With his standby system cloned to the farm's phone, he led anyone monitoring such traffic a wild-goose chase.

On this circuit he recruited Jim Booth and Carl Hajik. Both had worked for him, Booth as a gardener, Hajik as a handyman. Both had been fired for concealing prior police records of armed assault and suspicion of murder.

Now Pierce was not only willing to overlook this but give them new criminal work that paid outrageous bonuses. One job had been the 26th Street shootout, featuring two vans and four unaffiliated hired hands. Freelance incompetents.

The way it turned out should have been a warning to Paul Pierce that he had maladroit help. But a man marooned in his own attic and quite tired of opening cans of tuna to eat with crackers, cannot be choosy.

Months of isolation, while the work of your lifetime is dismantled, does something to your mind. Writhing in the toils of menopausal mistakes, forbidden tastes, Paul Pierce had already lost what judgment he had.

It had been a shrewd jungle judgment, almost supernaturally able to smell out weaknesses in others, claw open their gut and gnaw out their life blood. The only part of that shrewdness left to him was his understanding of Big Mimmo Caccia.

He was the new. Thirty years ago Pierce, taking over from his father and uncles, had been the new. His daring had leaped chasms. Think of it! Heading up the old Persico holdings as a tenured professor at Yale. Such bravado!

And now, he saw, it was Caccia who dared and won. Capitalising on society's ever lower standards, ever greater criminality, Big Mimmo was the shape and cutting edge of the twenty-first century.

But not yet. First, Pierce thought, he has me to deal with. He has to cough up the Pierce empire he is starting to gobble. I have to slice his throat. Hack through to the backbone. And put his severed head where the world can see it.

Overextended on the shaky support of two fools who believed themselves clever, Paul Pierce should have begun looking for sounder help. What he needed was an outside man who was truly clever. What he needed was his son Jack.

At the moment, he couldn't touch Jack. Big Mimmo had seen to that. Paul understood why Mimmo's ambition was to own a powerful bank without any banking authority knowing. He had obviously been manoeuvring Gaynor Marcus for some time now to serve as the catspaw to hijacking Pierce et Cie.

On his own, Gaynor was far too bright to buy up a bank in

serious trouble. Even marrying off his difficult daughter didn't justify such expensive sacrifice. Obviously Mimmo had powerful blackmail leverage over the Marcus clan, probably the missing Phil Marcus, black sheep of a far-flung flock.

Mimmo craved the bank precisely for the reasons Paul Pierce had created it: American cunning and Swiss connections. In the immortal words of Brecht, 'what is robbing a bank compared to owning a bank?'

In the bloodbath one Pierce was left untouched, alive and well. Jack lived because Mimmo needed him as a figurehead. Did Paul want his son alive? Hmm.

Forty-Five

One of the givens of life is that however long the journey, however tortuous the road, however anticipated the climax, everything finally ends.

Even mayoral election campaigns. The last speeches are made, favours called due, loyalties betrayed, scandals exposed. Newspapers, associations and unions make public their preference. Opinion polls weigh in. In less than a week...

For the incumbent, Mayor Garvey, the cost of a campaign is footed by untraceable public funds fattened by private firms who benefited most from Garvey's term.

His opponent, though well-to-do, did not grow rich by staking his own money on elections. Conrad Courtney III's millions in campaign debts must also be paid.

Thus it was that Conrad and Melinda Courtney designated the Saturday before Election Tuesday as their greatest fundraising dinner. They had their own guest list and that of Tammany but made a point of calling the event 'non-partisan'.

That enabled Dan Ludlum to add key show biz names to guarantee press coverage. Enid Bart could then produce Manhattan TV and theatre people without having them commit to a specific party. The idea was weird, but had serious advantages.

Normally there is no such thing as a non-partisan fundraiser. But thanks to Pat Rossi, a Courtney victory was clearly in the air. People, regardless of party, wanted to be associated with a winner. In truth, they wanted the personal publicity without having to declare their party. That opportunity was worth a lot to them.

On that basis a long-time Republican like Gaynor Marcus volunteered something more than money: the Marcus mansion, not all five floors but the triplex in which he and Kitty lived. It contained the original ballroom its first owner had installed in 1877, space for a hundred key guests.

An invitation quickly became much more than nonpartisan. It became priceless, a ticket people would kill for.

'What?' Pat Rossi asked. He had been checking guest lists with Maria Jenner. 'He's invited Big Mimmo Caccia?'

She recrossed her legs, filling Pat's office with her own aromatic musk. 'I find him in this list, too.' She showed Pat the small group which had each contributed half a million dollars to Courtney. 'And on this,' she added, showing him Garvey's Republican list of high rollers.

'Okay,' Pat agreed. 'He bought his way in. But then why does he need Gaynor Marcus to invite him? Can't he just forge an invitation?'

'Ask your best friend, Gaynor's son-in-law.'

Pat got a mulish look. 'He's too busy playing banker. The moment he married Myra the run on Pierce et Cie ended. And once again people are fighting to hand over their money.'

Maria lit a cigarette and blew smoke at him, not a lot, just enough to let him know who she was. 'Some hanky-panky?' she asked, her voice going to bassoon level. 'Between the Marcuses and the Caccias? Something the New York State Superintendent of Banking,' she hit a tuba note, 'would like to know about?'

'No Marcus would be that stupid. Big Mimmo isn't allowed to own a bank, even in Hell.' He stared at her. 'What have you heard?'

'Nothing.'

He stared harder at the woman who, until recently, had been privy to every secret Dan Ludlum possessed. He tried to give his father's Number One Steel-Eyed Interrogator Glare.

'If you're right, and Courtney wins, he's faced with turning two of his major contributors over to the DA's office.'

'If I'm right,' she corrected him, 'it means whoever the new mayor is, Big Mimmo owns him.'

'He doesn't own Court–' He stopped, got up and went to the water cooler. Over its ten-gallon clear plastic carboy hung wall shelves.

Pat had always believed in the Edgar Allan Poe school of hiding important things. A group of four three-and-a-half-inch computer disks with a rubber band around them sat on the shelf next to some styrofoam cups, a bottle of aspirin, a box of Band-Aids and small tube of antiseptic ointment.

'I should have spent more time with these disks. They're a gift from Pop.'

Marie nodded. 'I checked out the section on our next mayor.' Her brunette hair, cropped short, had a sheen to it as she smoothed one side down. 'Young Patrick, do I need to tell you what it means to be a property developer in this town?'

'So Courtney's done business with Mimmo before?' He looked glumly at the disks in his hand. 'Why didn't you tip me off long ago?'

'When you work for Dan Ludlum, you learn to speak when you're spoken to. I'm not a crusader. When I find a nest of dragons I don't run screaming to the nearest white knight.'

'I guess I'm grateful you remembered it at all.'

'Young Patrick, I'm entitled to forgetfulness. Give or take a few years, I'm old enough to be your mother.'

'Favourite aunt.'

She leaned forward long enough to give him a leisurely kiss. 'Fairy godmother?' she inquired.

'Nah, forget it.' Former Detective Sergeant Michael Rossi made a gesture with his lips as of a baby rejecting its bottle. 'I did the dais bit at that St Regis dinner. It's boring.'

Eileen produced an audible sigh of relief. 'I was hoping you wouldn't want to go. This dinner is too unstructured for a guy in a wheelchair. You might end up in the soup tureen.'

'Considering the guest list, I might end up making a citizen's arrest.'

'If you're thinking of collaring some perp, let me put a name at the top of your list.'

'Jack Pierce?' His pale green eyes went dark. 'Is there some way the Rossis can buy back our intro to that bastard?'

She fell silent. At some Courtney affair or another she had finally met Myra Pierce and realised what a tragedy lived there, for Myra, not Jack.

All he had to put up with was a nature-girl-child-bride who was basically a decent person. While Myra had to find out that her worst fears had come true. Someone had married her entirely and only for her money, or her family's.

Eileen had had it out with Jack that same night, one of those fiercely quiet interchanges in the corner of a noisy party. 'You are a total shit,' she murmured, smiling. 'How mad about money do you have to be to ruin that girl's life?'

He'd writhed, twisting his arms sideways. 'That's not it at all. It isn't money. I mean, yes, maybe. It's saving the bank. I suppose that's money. But . . . but it's not money.'

She managed to keep from hitting him, turned on one heel and marched off.

'Then I'm not going either,' she told her father now.

'Hold it, Eileen. We'll get somebody.'

'On a Saturday night? I'm staying home and going to bed early and that's it, Detective Sergeant Rossi. Get it?'

The telephone rang. 'Hello, Eileen? It's Leroy Baxter. Your Dad called me this afternoon?'

'Captain Baxter, he's right here. Hold on.'

'Hey, Chief, thanks for calling back. Is that big Saturday night Courtney shindig in the precinct?' He paused and laughed. 'The guest list, Lee. If ever I saw an explosive mixture this is it. People worth kidnapping. People some nut might want to attack. All of 'em worth robbing. It's a perp's dream.'

He listened for a long moment, his eyes finding Eileen and giving her a non-commital wink. Finally: 'I'm sorry the Courtneys are against uniformed guards. You know, us old-time cops always feel that the uniform alone stops a lot of creeps in their tracks.'

255

He was silent again. Then: 'You don't have to tell me it's a whole nother world. Sorry I bothered you. You're doing all you can. Take care, Lee.'

After he switched off he sat in silence for a while. Then he gave his daughter a second wink. 'I did what I had to do. It seems the Courtneys don't like a heavy security presence. Baxter is not going to make the possibly next mayor mad at him.'

'What kind of security will there be?'

'Few plainclothes guys. Some hired Keystones as waiters and bartenders. Maybe six or eight. On three floors.' He paused and moistened his lips. 'Unarmed.'

Eileen nodded. 'I knew I was doing the right thing, staying home. I wish Pat didn't have to be there.'

Jack had left the bank around four-thirty. He walked south from the 60s on Park Avenue, looking in store windows. The late October weather was crisp, invigorating. It also felt good to have saved Pierce et Cie, merely by selling his body.

It felt even better that volume had suddenly expanded with solid loans and commercial accounts, not consumer types who could be stampeded into a run on the bank.

As for the run, everything had crept back to normal. Gaynor Marcus was not interested in hands-on operation. He left that to Jack.

South of 57th Street, he stopped in front of a florist's shop he couldn't remember seeing before, Florappeal. It had probably been there for ever. But this afternoon its windows were crowded with the kind of velvety silver-violet roses someone had given Myra at the wedding reception.

It took Jack a moment to see that a man inside the shop was beckoning to him, a tall fellow, vaguely familiar. Abruptly he realised who it was. He had a choice: snub Big Mimmo Caccia or give him a piece of his mind. Which?

But Mim came out onto the street, dainty hand outstretched. He grasped Jack's hand and shook it with familiar pressure. 'This is one of my shops,' he said with some pride.

'I'm ordering bouquets for the Courtney dinner. Come on in, Jack.'

'I – '

'Come on. We're not enemies any more.'

'Is that – ?'

'It might've had some difference with your father...' Mimmo's small head seemed suddenly like a cartoonist's joke of bad drawing. How could anything from that brain be of value, Jack wondered.

'Uh, my father?'

'But that was just business.'

The past tense of his statement had an ominous ring. For Jack, brought up just outside the inner circle of mafia leadership, it also had a lethal meaning. All take-outs were a matter, purely, of business.

For a long moment, Jack could find nothing to say. Contradictory feelings shifted about inside him. He hated this man. This man was very tight with Gaynor Marcus. Gaynor owned half of Pierce et Cie.

They were inside the florist's, breathing air heavy with scent and thick with humidity. 'That's right,' Mimmo said, as if that small brain had just realised it. 'Your head office is only a few blocks north of here, isn't it?'

He turned to the florist, targeting him with his big body. 'Vit, Florappeal ought to supply Pierce et Cie with a daily window display. Something nice. Not the Sterlings. They're *too* elegant. Something neighbourly. Carnations? They dress up the place. And that clovey smell is always nice.'

He opened his wallet and laid some hundred dollar bills on the counter. 'A new arrangement every morning. The first week's on me.'

He turned back to Jack. 'You'll get used to my style,' he said then. 'You'll enjoy doing business with me.'

The garage on East 23rd Street was meant for small trucks. Three delivery vans bore the Florappeal logo on their sides, a design in which the 'o' was a huge daisy with white petals and a yellow centre.

Paul Pierce had choreographed everything except the dialogue. Jim Booth, native born, was the front man. He entered the garage's messy little office while Carl Hajik, a Croat immigrant, stood in the shadows to back him up.

Booth had a tall Clint Eastwood body, lacking only Eastwood's looks. He reached for keys hung on a wall rack while the garage attendant looked up from his tabloid newspaper. 'What's it, Jack?'

'Florappeal van. Late deliveries.'

'Uh.' The attendant got to his feet. 'Says which?'

'The keys, buddy.'

'Hey, do I know you, Jack?'

Hajik, squat and muscular, brought the iron bar down on the back of the man's head with such force that the metal rang, loud and clear, like a church bell. The attendant dropped to the floor. Blood formed a puddle on the floor.

'Okay, Carl. Fun's fun. Let's blow.'

Jim Booth gathered all three sets of keys. He squared his shoulders and walked tall to the vans. When he found the keys that fitted the first van he dropped the others. He and Hajik jumped in, started up and roared out of the garage.

'Pretty slick,' Hajik crowed.

'That's us, Carl-baby. A pair of slick operators.'

'For fifty grand apiece.' Hajik had a slight squint that made Booth wonder where he was actually looking. 'I think we smarter than Pierce, you know?'

'We smarter than God, Carl-baby. Pierce gonna find out the price has jumped to a hundred grand each. Am I thinking or am I thinking?'

Hajik giggled contentedly. At 57th Street, Booth turned the van west and paused beside a dark blue two-door Escort. Hajik opened the car's trunk and removed a bundle wrapped in a baby blanket. He put it in the back of the van.

'Check the damned things?' Booth asked. He did an Eastwood grimace. 'The guy who sold them is nobody I know.'

Hajik turned around and unwrapped the small pink blanket. He looked down at three semi-automatics called Tec–9s, the street name for the Intratec .9 mm machine pistol.

Manufactured in Florida by patriotic anti-Castro Cubans, they added to the already oversupplied assault weapon market a .9 mm Luger knockoff with a stubby stock for steadiness and a pierced-shroud flash shield to keep muzzle heat from burning the shooter.

Notoriously inaccurate, they were consequently loaded with fat dum-dum slugs that opened wide on impact and ripped great holes through the body. This made accurate aim unnecessary, as well as impossible. Each Tec–9 nestled on the little pink bed complete with long sixteen-round magazines clipped in and three extra magazines for good luck.

'Little babies. Nice,' Hajik muttered. He hefted the magazines. 'Heavy as hell.'

'You're looking at a thousand bucks.'

Hajik giggled again. 'Hey, you, I'm smart. I'm looking at two hunrid tousand bucks.'

Catering staff had been arriving all afternoon at the Marcus triplex. Their numbers were complete about the time the Met across the street let the last of its visitors out and locked up for an early-closing night.

Vans had begun unloading at the Marcus sidestreet entrance: food still hot from catering kitchens, liquor, wines, soft drinks, ice. Produce vans brought salad vegetables. Bakery vans brought small, firm, nutty granary rolls.

A van arrived with place settings, not the full range with accompanying flatware and glasses, but the plates and forks necessary for a buffet dinner most people would eat on their laps. Vans swarmed everywhere, the worker bees of a hive like Manhattan where gridlock is part of life.

At both ends of the great oval ballroom, bars were established next to long tables where the buffet would be laid out. A small band, guitar, drums and muted cornet, was setting up. More vans brought clear Plexiglas folding chairs. Waiters, some of them private detectives, were opening and placing the chairs around the great hall.

Van drivers anarchically set their own traffic patterns. Some shoved to the front. Some followed dutifully. Some hung back. The Florappeal van with its big daisy was nowhere to be seen.

At the front entrance of the Marcus mansion, on Fifth Avenue, the huge bronze doors – originally from a Mantegna baptistry – had been fastened wide open. November was only a few days away but the weather was crisp, not yet chill. Pat Rossi stood inside rearranging a sheaf of papers on his clipboard. The invitation was for seven-thirty p.m. to make sure people began arriving by eight.

A cellular phone, tucked in his jacket pocket, started chirping. He pulled out its antenna. 'Rossi.'

'Rossi,' Eileen responded.

'I'm glad you talked Pop into staying home.'

'Bored with big events. What's the RSVP total?'

'We'll overshoot our goal of one hundred guests. In terms of funds we figure to hit a million, a million-two. The big question is, will there be dancing? I have promised the first dance to Maria.'

'Does Enid know that?'

'Enid is a party animal.'

'And what kind of animal is Pat Rossi?'

'Your quarter has run out. Please deposit twenty-five cents for the next three minutes.' He made a clicking noise.

'Big Brother?' She hesitated. 'Do me a favour? Please take care of yourself? Please, Big Brother?'

'What? Sure. Sure. So long.'

As he pushed the phone antenna out of sight, Pat Rossi found himself wondering about the telepathy between them. A strange shiver shot across his shoulder blades. He made a face. Damn the Irish and damn their feyness.

By eight-thirty people had begun the normal inter-clan sniffing, touching and kissing rituals by which they certified their right to be there and begin networking.

Being American, laughter was a major recognition tool, everything from appreciative chuckles to jackass brays. But, needing to warm up, they tended to cluster first among their own. Chita Rivera chatted at length with Lauren Bacall,

Donna Karan with Calvin Klein, Peter Jennings with Walter Cronkite.

By nine-fifteen people had begun to strike off elsewhere in the great room. Enough champagne and spiritous drinks had been downed to raise the sound level. John Cleese, tall, tended to move about with Mickey Rooney, short. Former New York mayors clustered near the entrance. Strolling alliances were formed, enhancing one's chances of knowing people.

Pat had had an immense TV set up in one corner of the ballroom as a kind of delegate from the real world outside. From time to time, as local TV stations went on the air with news, the programme was piped into the ballroom to give a purely social occasion the sound of political seriousness.

People gathered at the tube like flocks of hungry birds, then scattered as if elsewhere someone was broadcasting handsful of seed.

A great chandelier hung high above the centre of the ballroom, its dozens of electric lights multiplied by hanging crystal prisms that flashed refracted spectra across floor and walls.

The music trio had been joined by Eleanor Marcus's live-in lover, Shep, quite drunk but still able to noodle away at the clarinet when not chatting with Bobby Short or Barbara Carroll. He wore a funny paper hat around which he had pinned elderly Clinton/Gore buttons.

As if background music was necessary to their personae – as it was in their acts – the film and rock contingent clustered near the band. Cher and Streep signed autographs. Non-celebs, invited for the size of their bank accounts, occasionally asked the band for a certain song.

Melinda Courtney finished a long conversation with a handsome black rap singer she considered a favourite of hers, but whose name she'd forgotten. She picked up one of the band's microphones and said:

'Dear Friends, our hearts are overflowing with your love. May I ask you now to choose one of the two buffets – either to the far left or the far right – and join us in what we hope will be a victory dinner for us all.'

Everyone applauded but made no move. It would take

another complete wave of drink-bearing waiters before they would be ready to be seen eating. Behind Melinda, on the TV screen, a news programme dissolved to Arnie Glass interviewing Rebert Custodial Miller, either alive or on tape.

'Reeb-babe,' he said, 'it's shitty you can't vote till you hit eighteen. If you could...?'

'Youth is tarred of sucking old ass. We gonna force all you old guys to suck us.'

'Old? Me old?'

When Jim Booth drove the Florappeal van to the shop just south of 57th Street, the manager was closing. He stared at Booth. 'Those blooms went out this afternoon. They're already delivered.'

'That a fact?' The Eastwood grimace looked deadly. 'That isn't the only mistake you made tonight, scumbag.'

Booth brought his toe up hard into the man's crotch. He watched him scream and fall. Then Booth and Hajik swept up armfuls of mixed bouquets and loaded them into the van.

Almost as an afterthought, an easy adieu, they slit the manager's throat, snapped off the shop lights, and in the darkness grabbed a pad of delivery invoices and escaped in the van.

'Smart,' Hajik complimented Booth. His slightly crossed eye shone brightly. 'You got us a legit delivery thingie, huh?'

He was breathing heavily, as if killing made him breathless. To have escalated this fast from a grievous wounding at the garage to a sure death in the florist's was, somehow, as oxygen-depleting for the killer as the killed.

Booth sped up Park Avenue. His own breathing had begun to speed up, too. At 85th Street he swung left and, at Fifth Avenue left again. The Marcus corner was deserted. Where there had been dozens of vans there now were none. No one stood at the doors in expectation.

Booth turned left a third time and rolled up to the side-street entrance. He braked to a halt. One of the entry spotlights shone down on the decorative daisy logo. In the sudden silence Booth could hear his breath whistle in his pinched nostrils.

'Nothing to it,' he said, exhaling mightily. He began filling out the invoice with a pencil.

'For two smart cookies like us, the rest is just a tea party.'

Forty-Six

They were simple men, both of them, with the deadly American 'no-problem' confidence that keeps you from seeing yourself as you really are. But they had their dream.

The dream worked along simple lines. You had a boss. He paid you to do what he wanted. You did it well. You became a boss. The dream took you all the way from nobody to big shot.

You had Paul Pierce, showing you photos of a tall guy with a small head. Telling you where to buy the Tec–9s. Warning you that on auto they had a kick that spoiled your aim.

The rest of the dream came from TV and tabloids. Rock stars. Sitcom clowns. Soap opera queens. TV confessors.

But Jesus Christ, nobody had warned them there was a real dream when they entered that ballroom. Celebs everywhere! Gorgeous women! Faces they knew! They panicked.

Moving on automatic pilot the bouquets got them almost to the centre of the ballroom. Then –

Just as they arrived under the chandelier –

Just as Melinda Courtney came forward to accept –

Just as Hajik unwrapped his pink baby blanket –

The photos Paul Pierce had showed them. Rehearsed them. Drilled into them. Where *was* the guy?

Big guy. Small head. Where the fuck was he?

Spray anyway. You're bound to get him.

Panic pulled the triggers. Both Tec–9s opened up at waist level. The muzzles jumped sky-high and shattered the chandelier. Hajik yanked the barrel lower.

Someone's head exploded brains all over the floor. The stench of cordite was a sexy, nitric perfume.

Hajik emptied more of his sixteen-round magazine into Melinda. Her husband with white hair sprang forward.

Hajik sprayed his last four slugs, then unclipped. He squinted crosseyed as he reloaded. He could do this all night. None of these dumb assholes had guns.

He caught a fat black TV celeb crawling for shelter under a dead man with a beard. He sent a slug whistling up her big behind. The muzzle shroud of his Tec–9 was smoking.

Hey! The dream was fun.

Booth, more obedient, finished three big guys with small heads. He dropped a young waiter carrying an open bottle of champagne. It creamed out over crawling bodies, turning blood to pink foam.

When the screaming got on Booth's nerves, the dream ended. Backing out of the room he cut Hajik in two, gut blown open in a shower of bluish intestines reeking sewer gas.

Cradling his Tec–9, Booth dashed down the stairs, out to the van, off into the night. He tried to remember how to get uptown onto the parkways to Connecticut. Uptown was . . . ?

Dumb Carl: no money. Smart Jim: all the money.

He squared his shoulders, pulled them back in the manner of a horseman and hurtled tall through the night, trying to recapture the dream.

Forty-Seven

Sunday, a day of mourning.

One hundred and fifty people, guests and staff, had been in the Marcus ballroom at the moment of the massacre. Considering the firepower of the weapons and the killing power of dum-dum ammo, it was a miracle only eleven people were dead.

These were celebrities, for whom the descriptive word became 'beloved'. St Patrick's and several of the larger Protestant churches held special noonday masses. Nearly forty people had been seriously wounded. Many more had suffered superficial damage.

'Scratches,' Dan Ludlum said. Madge gave him aspirin tablets and a scotch. 'Just scratches. Not like poor Pat Rossi.'

Jack Pierce was, of course, entirely untouched. At eight a.m. he and Myra had come to reassure his mother at her Central Park South apartment. 'Then I'm off to . . .' His voice died.

'To Lenox Hill Hospital,' Myra supplied, 'to see what's happened to Pat.'

'You don't know?' Serena demanded.

'All sorts of busybodies take charge,' Myra said matter-of-factly. 'They come out when they smell blood. Tee-hee! Oh, Serena! The blood! The poor wounded people. Some of them will take forever to heal. Much better to have died.'

Serena stared hard at her daughter-in-law. Her telephone rang. 'Serena, Dan Ludlum.' A faint tremor shook his voice. 'I called Jack and he's not there. Is he . . . all right?'

'He's here, Dan. How are you?'

'Scratches. Just scratches. Can I . . .?'

Serena handed the phone over to Jack. 'Dan? You okay?'

'Scratches. Just scratches.'

'Dan, I have to see you. About that massacre.'

'Captain Baxter's letting me into Lenox Hill. It's under armed guard. Ishmael will pick you up at your mother's in half an hour. Be there.'

Those at the party were among the last to know the casualty list. Thus the great number of telephone calls. But nobody called the Courtney triplex.

Anyone standing when the dum-dum bullets began to spray could hardly forget how Melinda Courtney died, still smiling. Pat Rossi had shoved Courtney down on the floor and dropped beside him. That moment came the last four rounds of Hajik's burst.

Forensics determined later that as the two victims dropped there had been a diagonal downsweep of four dum-dums caused by the weapon's recoil in amateur hands. Two had hit Courtney, stomach, then groin. Two had hit Rossi, thigh, then shin.

They had just finished pinning and stitching him. Pain-killers did no good. It was impossible to sleep. He kept seeing himself as his father had been, crippled for ever.

'Just tell me: will I be able to walk?'

Eileen had managed to reassure him and talk him to sleep. She sat in an armchair by his bed. A uniformed cop opened the door and wiggled a finger at her.

Outside, in the hall, stood Ludlum and, beside him, Jack Pierce. 'Those whom the gods love die young,' Eileen murmured. 'You two will live for ever.'

'How is he?'

'Sleeping. And you're not going to wake him.'

'No, no, no.' Ludlum fell silent. Neither he nor Jack had yet managed to establish eye-contact with Eileen. 'No, just wondering, I mean, you know.'

In the silence that followed she read Ludlum's subtext. 'Oh, you're wondering . . .? How soon he'll be up and around? Active? Earning his keep?'

'Not at all,' Ludlum said, meaning 'yes'.

For some reason this made Eileen turn on Jack. 'He's the ventriloquist? You're his dummy? Say something, Jack.'

'I'm just happy he's alive.'

She nodded grimly. 'Good phrase. Say something else.'

'How's your Dad taking it?'

'Excellent response. You always did give good small talk.'

'I've got a lot on my mind. The two hit guys.' Jack glanced at Ludlum, then back at Eileen. 'I know who they are.' His face looked pinched with suppressed anguish. He took a shaky breath. 'I guess I'd better find Baxter and tell him.'

'I guess you should've told him last night,' Eileen snapped. 'Who are they?'

'I don't know their names. I remember them at Athens Landing, years ago. They were gardeners. Fired or something.'

'But, Jack, your father...' Eileen stopped. Her face went pale. 'All these years of persecution. Jack, tell me I'm wrong. What was my dad to him? What possible reason...?'

He stared helplessly. 'Christ, Eileen, I don't know.'

Eileen signalled to the uniformed cop. 'Please get Captain Baxter? In a hurry.'

Dan Ludlum reached for Eileen's tiny hands and took them in his. They seemed to disappear within his horny flesh. 'I'm on my way downtown,' he said in an earnest tone. 'It's an emergency meet of Tammany, the New York County Democratic Committee. It's unprecedented.'

He sighed heavily. 'There is protocol for the death of a mayor. We know who steps forward to replace him. But there is no protocol when a candidate is murdered two days before an election.'

Captain Baxter appeared. He gave them a politician's smile, not too broad before knowing why. 'What's the rush, Eileen?'

'Jack Pierce has something to tell you.'

Baxter's tan Sherlock Holmes face turned towards Jack. 'I'm listening.'

The biggest problem was jurisdiction. Obviously you couldn't leave it to the Summerville, Connecticut, police. And you certainly couldn't come riding in rough-shod with a New York City SWAT team, sharpshooters and all.

Mass murder by government killers we sheepishly accept. If we protest they could easily kill us, too. Private mass murder we want avenged. The Connecticut governor stepped in. Experienced Manhattan assault cops were melded with state troopers in their Smokey The Bear hats.

The situation then escalated, mistake by mistake, so that even without FBI masterminds a kind of New England replica of the Waco, Texas, disaster was created.

Nobody had told them, for instance, that the island had been empty for some months now. They had heard it was a sect situation, nuts waiting for Armageddon.

Apparently the leaders of this sect were barricaded in a two-storey ski chalet in the woods with target rifles of great accuracy and choppers using murderous dum-dum slugs. If the cops rushed the building, they would run great risk from these maniacs with their superior position.

The decision was to smoke them out with tear gas.

At this Tammany meeting there were no couples, married or otherwise. It was an all-male, all middle-aged gathering of local politicos, a terribly self-important congregation. Even Dan Ludlum, with all his clout as a fund-raiser, was asked to wait in an anteroom.

'You understand, Dan, we all lost beloved friends last night. We're all in deep mourning.' The meeting had begun at nine a.m. At eleven, Ludlum's friend stuck his head outside. 'Okay, Dan, five minutes.'

He walked into a boardroom dominated by a long conference table that could seat twenty people. Empty coffee cups perfumed the air, along with cigar smoke. The Tammany sachems looked tired, cross and sweaty. Dan had heard shouting off and on. Now they sat in silence, glaring at him.

He stood straight, one hand in his trouser pocket. He knew all of them. He had saved more than a few from jail. But, though messed about, their dignity was intact.

'You have reached *no* conclusion. Am I right?'

'Five minutes,' one of the men snapped.

Dan said: 'This meeting shouldn't be for damage control. We should be here to figure out how we can still beat Garvey.'

'Okay, Dan, four minutes.'

'One man . . . Pat Rossi.'

The meeting's decorum blew up, men shouting. 'Gentlemen, before he managed our beloved Conrad Courtney's campaign, Pat Rossi was already a name. If you polled the electorate, you'd get as high a recognition for Pat as for Connie.'

'It's too late to substitute a candidate,' Dan's friend pointed out. 'Connie went the full route, including the primaries. You can't just put up a name at the last moment.'

Arguing broke out again. 'Just a second,' Dan rumbled in an awe-provoking voice. 'Isn't this the New York County Democratic Committee? Isn't it here that you could nominate Mickey Mouse if you so pleased, and he *would be the official candidate*?'

'Dan, the ballots are all printed. The voting machines are all programmed.'

'Excuse me,' Ludlum's voice rang out, 'isn't this the sovereign body that decides what goes on those ballots? Don't tell me soulless sheets of paper have usurped your power?'

Suddenly, among the growls of rejection, he could hear one or two growls of anger that the power of Tammany was being weakened 'by some walk-in killers'. 'Is that who we take orders from?' one politico shouted.

Dan stepped back from the table. The rest he could now leave to them.

Forty-Eight

There is precious little news on a Sunday. Tammany's bombshell dominated the late TV programmes and early Monday newspapers with few rivals for attention.

Over and over again, because there was no other footage to accompany the news, viewers watched the scene at Lenox Hill Hospital. By wheelchair, former Detective Sergeant Michael Rossi was trundled into the room where his son, bandages and all, lay propped up in bed.

State Supreme Court Justice Jeremy Jonathan Bergen, who represented Tammany's most legal face, stood by the bedside between the two Rossis. 'Champion son of a champion father,' Judge Bergen intoned, 'in this dark hour of darker criminal deeds, sacrificing the lives of beloved, brave men and women, only you, Patrick Michael Rossi, can guide us.'

He took a deep, feeling breath. 'Our ship of state must not be held captive by pirates of evil. In the name and august authority of the New York County Democratic Committee, I hereby transfer, bestow and convey upon you the official continuation of our fallen comrade's campaign.

'In you, Patrick Michael Rossi, we install and endow the authority to triumph in the name of our beloved fallen comrade Conrad Courtney. In the trenches of this holy war against crime, you will lead us over the top to victory. And may God,' he quoted Dickens, 'bless us one and all.'

Overnight, there was a great howl from the Republicans: the clear inference was that Garvey had bought the massacre. By Monday evening, the Mayor's whine of indignation had been quantitatively condensed to a few angry words.

Instead, pundits and political figures were being polled by

reporters who learned that there were no precedents for what Tammany had done. The move caught people's imagination.

A Larry King phone-in on involuntary cliterectomy as a weapon of auto-genocide found itself hijacked by viewers who wanted to sound off about Manhattan's mayoralty election.

'What the heck,' someone in Sioux Falls, South Dakota, observed, 'all the latest goofball fashions come from New York. Why not go with the flow?'

The Garvey forces should have done something equally startling. They should have kept all polling places locked on Tuesday morning. But this was a free democracy.

DEMS STEAL

CITY HALL

in 96-point type was the way a Republican-leaning newspaper reported that, votes having been counted, Rossi had out-polled Garvey two to one.

The many legal protests the Republicans had planned to invalidate the surprise Rossi nomination were overwhelmed. A two-to-one victory was virtually a textbook example of 'vox populi, vox Dei'. Anything else was perceived as sour grapes.

In any event, by Wednesday afternoon other news had crowded into the newspapers and TV channels. Albert Santamaria, father of two small children, the lieutenant commanding a New York City SWAT team mysteriously operating on an island off the Connecticut shore, had been shot to death by two of his own men who destroyed him with twenty-seven bullets, mistaking him in the dawn's early light for a heavily armed religious-sect killer.

What followed was the kind of mad-dog police riot that hadn't been seen since the 1968 Chicago convention or the Waco massacre. Sixty SWATs and state troopers rushed the sect's headquarters building. Despite great risk, they stormed the frame building weakened by two days of gunfire and covered by inflammable cedar shakes. In the process, of course, they torched it.

A search of the ashes late Wednesday disclosed two heavily charred John Does, one rich with dental work so distorted by furnace-like heat that it had yet to yield an identity, the other poor and free of dental additions. Obviously, under cover of darkness and smoke, the rest of the sect – no one could even guess how many – had made their getaway.

Jack Pierce and his mother, following the story on TV, felt a jolt: the rich Doe had to have been Paul Pierce, murdered in the gutting of his island, of the whole Athens Landing idea and ethos.

Now they would never know, from his lips, what wild schemes he had dreamed, keeping the Rossi family under such lethal surveillance. His power over Vinnie Sgroi. His hatred of Mimmo Caccia's power. Power had deformed Paul Pierce's brain. Some day, Jack promised himself, he'd make sense of his father's insanity. Now there was no time to brood.

The telephone kept ringing. Big Mimmo Caccia offered deepest condolences without in any way giving an electronic eavesdropper a clue as to what he was talking about.

Instead he spoke of his gratitude for Jack's help in reconstructing his bank along more secure lines now that Gaynor Marcus had named Jack chief executive again.

He appreciated Jack's bringing selected Pierce enterprises into the fold as bank customers. He spoke with the sureness of one who has already, perhaps, bought the enterprises at sacrifice prices. And bought Jack for a dollar more.

Finally, with great delicacy, Mimmo agreed that Eileen Rossi was ideal as the bank's new customer relations manager. It was a part-time job which left her three days a week to continue helping her hero father with his work.

Jack's hyperactive future having thus been mapped out for him, Myra busied herself mixing fat-free imitation cream cheese and herbs. She spread low-starch bagels with the mixture. Not too thickly, because she was calorie-conscious.

She brought them in on a tray with a carafe of coffee. She was wearing a different apron she had embroidered with cuddly kittens and this legend: 'A purrfect chef'.

'It's decaf, Mother Pierce.' She smiled. 'That's all I ever serve, decaf.'

Forty-Nine

January.

All lawsuits putting aside the election results had been rejected by judges. When he took office, Mayor Rossi's thigh wound had long healed. The shattered bone in his calf had grown together. The pins had been removed. He walked without a limp.

The small City Hall party he and Eileen gave was for their father. Former Detective Sergeant Michael Rossi sat in his wheelchair and stared out over Chinatown towards the Battery base of Manhattan Island.

Beyond, in the growing dusk, the Statue of Liberty's torch suddenly lit up. Everyone gasped or muttered.

'An omen, Paddy!'

'She lifts her lamp!' Dan Ludlum quoted.

'Beside the golden door,' Jack Pierce finished the quotation.

Michael Rossi grumbled on an ironic note. 'Leave it to Manhattan's Boy Banker to mention the gold.' He stared at Jack. 'Just remember, Jocko, we're letting you mix with the human beans to pick up some pointers on acting like a person.'

Enid, with the TV crew, called 'Cut'. She gave Pat a hug. 'Gotta run. Women's tennis at Madison Square Garden.'

'Pat, being Mrs Mayor doesn't attract her,' Eileen said after Enid had left. 'Being Pat Rossi's wife doesn't tremble her whiskers. Why sit in the shadow of your husband when you can catch your own mice nightly on the tube and bat them around between your paws? Pat, did you hear me, brother dear?'

'Poignantly.'

Michael Rossi eyed Jack Pierce. 'Advice to the love-lorn,' Rossi said, 'a new sideline for our little customer relations director. Why isn't Myra here?'

'Her mother's got the flu,' Jack said, opening champagne. 'Myra's at her house, helping out.'

'Which mother?' Eileen demanded.

He gave her a long, silent look, poured her glass full and said: 'I'll explain later.' His voice dropped. 'At the office.'

Jack finished refilling everyone's glass and raised his own to Pat. 'Here's to the best mayor New York will ever have.'

'Better than La Guardia?' Pat countered. He finished his drink. 'Morgenthau's due here any minute. Jack, can you and Dan wrestle Pop into the limo?'

Already mayoral in mien, he shook hands, hugged torsos, kissed Eileen and left for his silent inner office. He sat down at a long table littered with papers. 'Can we get this cleared off? With Morgenthau neatness counts.'

Maria Jenner nodded. 'But before he gets here...'

'Oh. Right.' He stared for a moment at the immense bouquet of silvery Sterling roses. 'Who did Caccia send those to, you or Eileen or Enid?'

At the computer desk Maria sat down and crossed her legs. 'All three. He should've included your Dad.' She glanced up and found him studying her knees.

'Why? Does Mimmo know he's starring in Pop's next virtual?'

'Does he? Do you? Does anybody?'

Pat shook his head slowly. 'My father doesn't exist without a vendetta. Bringing down Mimmo will keep him busy for ever.'

In the silence she recrossed her legs. 'This thing you both have about injustice. Nobody told me it was contagious. When I told Dan Ludlum I was quitting, he said: "Mary Magdalene joins the Redeemer's flock?" Now wasn't that a cute way to put it?'

She gave him one of her guilt-inducing smiles as she fed a CD-ROM disk into the machine. 'This is a first cull from the famous Rossi Injustice Lists,' she explained. 'Some cases are seven or eight years old. Totally forgotten.'

'Until now. How many?'

'Near two hundred. Sorry.'

'Don't be sorry.' He glanced out of the window at Liberty on her island. He felt a squeeze inside his chest. He had been about to sit down. Instead, he felt himself standing up straighter.

Give me your tired, your poor,
Your huddled masses, yearning to breathe free.

At last, he thought, it was time to get the old lady back in action.

Send these, the homeless, tempest-tossed, to me.

At last, he thought. Pop and a million like him will be avenged. Avenged!

I lift my lamp beside the golden door.

'No, don't be sorry,' he echoed. 'What's the old line? Just fasten your seat belt. It's going to be one helluva ride.'